"...truly a sweet and wonderful romance story that will captivate the reader from beginning to end. ...interesting plot and setting, multidimensional characters, humor and a whole lot of romance! Journeys End will definitely catapult the reader to the outer reaches of the galaxy as she pulls them in and doesn't let them off the time travel till the last page is read" ~ *Love Romances*

Four Stars "JOURNEY'S END is an excellent time travel romance with a "you-are-there" feel. The depiction of medieval England is realistic enough to make one glad that it is history. The hero and heroine are intelligent and likable and the villains provide enough suspense to keep this a page-turner without taking over the story." ~ *Romantic Times*

"Imagine this...You're minding your own business, walking the dog when you bump into Mr. Tall, Dark and Mysterious. The next thing you know, you open your eyes and you and your dog are 400 years in the past. What happened? Are you simply a raving lunatic as the people around you seem to believe? That is what Dr. Kari Lunne would like to know, because it has happened to her. A JOURNEY'S END is both historical and futuristic romance in one delightful package. If you like reading time travel romances then this is a book for you." ~ *The Best Reviews.*

"Journey's End offers the reader great characters and wonderful settings. The author does a good job of handling both past, present and future settings with skill. ...the characters are so vivid that you will turn the page to see what happens next. Journey's End a book that says, despite all the horrors we may encounter and survive, sometimes the most frightening thing of all can be discovering the desires of your heart" ~ *Futures Magazine*

Four Stars! "The time-travel premise in this story was believable and the futuristic world Aidan lived in was drawn just enough to be interesting without interfering with the story. The historical detail was very interesting and the attitudes toward women and the paupers of this period were clearly defined. There is action from the first paragraph and the love story between Aidan and Karina is developed throughout the whole. The story is fun and entertaining from start to finish." ~ *SimeGen Reviews*

"...a convincing time-travel romance, blending past and future seamlessly. With a talent for realism and attention to detail, Patricia Crossley presents a fascinating and original plot that the draws the reader into a remarkable world. Her account of the sixteenth century when women are property, not allowed to read, or even think for them selves, becomes quite pointed when encountered by the female doctor from the future. Impossible to put down, JOURNEY'S END is highly recommended." ~ *WordWeaving*

"Patricia Crossley has created a very realistic and sometimes frightening look at our future and past in her time travel romance "Journey's End". Both the hero and heroine immediately grabbed my attention and I found myself extremely captivated as to if Kari and Aidan can defeat the odds to be together. Journey's End has a sparkling romance, exceptional characters - both main and secondary, and a great story line and a joy to read. I'm now hooked on the genre and I look forward to reading more fine works from this talented author." ~ *Road to Romance*

Patricia Crossley

Journey's End

Cerridwen Press

A Cerridwen Press Publication

www.cerridwenpress.com

Journey's End

ISBN #1419954369
ALL RIGHTS RESERVED.
Journey's End Copyright© 2005 Patricia Crossley
Edited by Ann Leveille.
Cover art by Syneca.

Electronic book Publication September 2005
Trade Paperback Publication March 2006

Cerridwen Press is an imprint of Ellora's Cave Publishing, Inc.®

JOURNEY'S END

෨

Trademarks Acknowledgment

~

About the Author

🙰

Patricia is married to her own romance hero, Rod. She just celebrated the joyful weddings of both her sons, Matthew and Paul, during the summer of 2005. Daughter Alison has been married for a number of years, so Patricia and Rod are hoping for grandchildren at last. Patricia has spent over 6 months each year since 2001 volunteering in rural Kenya where she works with teachers and administrators. A Rotarian, she is also involved with bringing clean water to isolated villages through Rotary grants and helping a women's cooperative to raise goats. A native of London, England, she has lived and worked in six countries and is now settled in Victoria, Canada, where her office window overlooks the busy harbor.

Patricia welcomes mail from readers. You can write to her c/o Ellora's Cave Publishing at 1056 Home Avenue, Akron, OH 44310-3502.

O mistress mine, where are you roaming?
O, stay and hear; your true love's coming,
That can sing both high and low:
Trip no further, pretty sweeting;
Journeys end in lovers meeting,
Every wise man's son doth know.

W. Shakespeare: Twelfth Night
Act ii Sc. 3

Prologue
July 11, 2000

෨

Page 5 of THE LONDON ENQUIRER
Police Continue Search for Missing Doctor

LONDON. The Metropolitan Police are still following every lead in the case of a thirty-two-year-old medical doctor missing since July 8, but so far haven't been able to locate Karina Lunne, a police representative said yesterday. "There's nothing new — she's still missing," he said. "The one other hope now is that perhaps she went to visit a friend."

Although police have checked the businesses and shops in Camden that she used to frequent, as well as followed up on numerous leads from the public, they have yet to find a clue as to her whereabouts.

Dr. Lunne had resigned from her position at St. Mark's Hospital and was last seen on the evening of July 8 with her dog, an Irish wolfhound, in the vicinity of Hampstead Heath. The spokesperson confirmed today that the Metropolitan Police have been unable to trace any of Dr. Lunne's movements after she was seen in a street leading to the Heath.

She is five feet, six inches tall (one hundred sixty-five centimeters) and weighs about eight stone (fifty kilograms). She has shoulder-length, curly auburn hair and normally wears glasses. When last seen, she was wearing red shorts, a pale shirt and a dark jacket.

The family of Dr. Lunne has offered a substantial reward for any information leading to the solution of the mystery still surrounding her disappearance.

"They both vanished off the face of the earth," said Dr. Lunne's brother, Michael, announcing the reward. "Kari had no reason to disappear. She was planning to take up a position with *Doctors Without Borders*. She was happy and excited. We pray that she is alive somewhere. Her family will never lose hope." Dr. Lunne's parents, opera singer Elena Rizzardo, and the eminent medieval scholar, Dr. Eamon Lunne, are planning to return from Rome to assist in the search for their daughter. So far, there has been no trace of her. Her mother is said to be suffering from nervous exhaustion. The authorities are asking anyone with information to contact any police station.

Chapter One
June 26, 2400

☙

"Aidan! There's a picture due to go missing."

Monika scooted breathlessly up to his station and Aidan reluctantly turned his eyes from the rows of data on the wall screen. The familiar prickle of excitement started at the back of his neck, but he made himself remain motionless.

"Thought you might be interested," said Monika, with an airy wave of her hand. "It's a good one."

God, how he wished sometimes that he'd never confided in her about the "lost" works. She had a lot to learn about discretion. He turned to her slowly and glanced around the lab. No one was looking their way. He took a deep breath. "So, tell. But keep it down, for God's sake." He smiled in encouragement.

Monika grinned and leant forward, pressing buttons on his console. "Can do better than that. I set it up already. Look." At least she lowered her voice when she spoke her instructions to the computer.

Then he saw which screen she had activated. "Not that one!" he said sharply and hit the cut-off pad.

He lowered his voice again. "Not the big screen, Monika. Do you want the whole lab to see? Put it on the monitor."

She shrugged. "No big deal. They think you're researching for me."

For a moment, he thought she would defy him and flash the picture on the wall over their heads, but she gave the instruction to feed to the small inset on the countertop. The screen filled with a swirl of blues and greens that resolved into the image of a quiet pond, surrounded by flowers and greenery.

Aidan caught his breath. An Impressionist. Exquisite. This could be just what he needed.

Monika was still talking. "Only a repro of a primitive twentieth-century photograph," she said. "Poor color definition, of course. But it gives an idea."

"What happened?" he whispered.

"Usual. Fire in London, late 1990s," she answered in her matter-of-fact tone. "Could have covered a robbery or could be legit. You know how it was back then. They never recovered the painting."

Aidan feasted his eyes. The longing surged through him.

"So?" she said. "Want to add this to your secret hoard, good friend?"

"When is it due to go?"

"In five days."

He moistened his lips. The timing had to be just right, and that added an extra bonus of excitement. He was beginning to suspect he was as much hooked on the adrenaline rush of snatching these priceless treasures from oblivion as he was on his historical research.

"Can I get it?" He ran his hand over his jaw to hide the clench of his muscles that threatened to spoil the mask of composure.

"Thirty seconds," Monika said in triumph.

"What?"

She grinned, irrepressible. "Last time it took you nearly a minute to decide." She bent closer. "Well, Howard says no more FLIPs." Monika ran her hand teasingly down his back. He moved away gently but firmly. She must be coming up to an R&R. For once he was thankful that he was on a different cycle.

He was still drinking in every glorious detail. "I know what Howard said." The Forcefield Line Intercept Program, or FLIP as it was usually known around the lab, was Howard's baby and he guarded it with fierce jealousy. He was wary of Aidan's enthusiasm, thought it might make trouble. Too bad. Howard was paid to worry, Aidan wasn't. He tore his eyes away to glance at Monika again. "Can you do it?"

Monika smiled mischievously. "I can do it, if you can convince Tanice. It's not a hard one. Bring me back some good data for the project."

"So that's it. You need something."

Monika shrugged. "Just a few details you could check out," she said. "Nothing much. A couple of images, some speech patterns… I'd like some football fans for the sport hologram. Not mega-big."

He chuckled. "You serious about me mixing with soccer hooligans?"

She punched him lightly on the shoulder. "You can take care of yourself. You know how the Outers like the exciting stuff when they're on vacation. Your dry old palaces and churches bore the kids out of their tiny skulls after two days."

Monika and her opinions. He sometimes wondered what stopped her applying for the Outworld circuit, but he'd never wanted to ask. Best to keep his own counsel and allow others to keep theirs. All of them in this lab had some reason that kept them Earth-bound rather than facing the challenges of the space colonies.

But they were a good team, he with his careful research and she with her creative interpretations. The Twenty C Hologram project could maybe use a few more authentic details. It was tempting.

If he went, he would be doing the department a favor.

"Wouldn't mind giving the research a rest. It would be good to go back on another trip, get some real stuff again." He could use the time to check some information on the secret services in different countries after the end of the Cold War. And pick up another painting. The department wouldn't lose, and if things went well, as usual, no one would inquire too closely as to how the data was acquired.

He thrust back his chair and stood. "Do it. I can handle Tanice. Let me know what you want."

* * * * *

Two days later Tanice fussed around him in the departure module.

"Here's your medical kit and your responder," she said. "Don't lose it, and keep it activated. Look at the countdown screen. Watch out. It's different from what you used before." She pointed to a display on the rectangular black box. "A bit primitive, but it's a prototype. With this one, we need a warning of your return to calibrate the field. A bit more prep for you, but more accurate. You have to beam in your coordinates, wait for us to signal back that we can receive you. So don't get into any trouble that needs a fast getaway. After ten o'clock at night in ten days' time, be on Hampstead Heath. No second chances. Understand?"

"Check, Tanice," he responded. No point in getting her more agitated. She always acted nervous before he traveled.

He checked the time. Only ten minutes since the director's personal transporter had left. Back on the ground, they'd all watched on the line feed as Howard pulled away from the vehicle deck, and then Tanice and Monika had moved purposefully to set up the FLIP. Aidan had slipped into position behind the protective screen. What Howard didn't know wouldn't hurt him. This was the FLIP that they'd been waiting for, according to Monika, the one that would provide the insights and final authentic details they needed for the project, with or without permission. It was as good a reason as any.

Aidan shifted his weight and hitched the leather belt around his hips. He took a deep breath and slipped into waiting mode. Best to conserve energy by limiting movement and words.

The machinery gave out a faint hum, ready for the impulse that would trigger the Forcefield Line Intercept Program. Even this morning Tanice was still insisting that the director might have authorized this fourth FLIP, had he received the request in time. But Howard had said only three FLIPs this summer and, all things considered, Aidan had preferred not to ask.

They were targeting London, England, at the end of the twentieth century. Aidan had his moves all planned out.

He shifted uncomfortably once more in the strange clothes, working his shoulders and loosening the muscles. Although this would be his fourth FLIP, the adrenaline still pumped before each trip. He loved the rush of energy and tension. Why else would he be doing this? That and the works of art, of course.

They had fitted him with stiff, scratchy, black jeans. The denim clung irritatingly when he moved. Some bureaucrat must have decided on a standard color, because even the changes of clothes in the canvas bag were black. Monika had packed pleated pants in a softer material with a clumsy front fastening and cuffs on the bottom.

"Are you sure these things are right?" he called to her.

She glanced up from stuffing colored paper into a flat leather pouch. Monika, the expert on costume and artifacts, would have been insulted by the question from anyone else. She pulled a face at him and then gave her usual sunny smile. "I choose to ignore that and put it down to pre-FLIP nerves. Besides, you should know," she retorted. "You've read nearly as much as I have about it."

That was true. He always did his homework.

Tanice turned from the bank of machines where she was checking readouts and examined him critically. "Looks good on you," she said. "What was the word back then? Sexy."

Monika strolled toward him and stood, hands on hips, cheeky grin in place under the smooth cap of black hair. Nonchalantly, she ran her hand along his shoulder and down the muscles of his arm.

"Mmm. They liked to show what was underneath without revealing too much. Clothes were a statement—tight jeans, molded shirts." Her hand continued down over his chest.

"Monika, enough," Tanice interrupted. "Save it for someone on your Relaxation month. Time to start up."

With a last lingering look at his lean frame, Monika sighed and turned obediently back to her list.

Tanice checked Aidan's position on the platform. A timer had begun the countdown. Synthesized speech intoned the seconds.

Monika's voice intruded. She never could resist giving last minute instructions. "The money is in your pack," she said. Aidan nodded and lifted his hand to show he had heard.

Tanice slid behind the console and began the log for the trip. Aidan could hear her clear voice starting the tape, checking his vital signs. Finally, "June 28, 2400," she intoned. "Preparations complete. Ready to transport."

* * * * *

The FLIP went without a hitch. Aidan materialized on Hampstead Heath at the end of June 2000, just before dawn, as planned. His black jeans and shirt blended well into the shadows. In the distance a few cars swept by, headlights briefly revealing their presence before they disappeared. His pack had come through unscathed and lay by his feet. He shivered in the cool air and dug into the side pocket for a jacket. It, too, was black. No one seemed to catch even a glimpse of his tall shadow as he left the Heath.

* * * * *

July 8, 2000

Kari heard the church clock down the street strike eleven. Damn! She hadn't meant to spend so long on the letter to her parents. She was bone-weary after all the last minute packing, not to mention the full day in Casualty at St. Mark's and the farewell party, but she was too strung up to sleep. She had to walk Ben and it would be the last walk here for a long while. One last time. She wouldn't shortchange him. The long summer dusk had melted into darkness, but no matter. They would be back in an hour.

She'd made a cup of tea at six when she'd arrived home and then forgotten it. It had acquired an unpleasant, grayish film. She pulled a face and left it on the counter with a half-eaten biscuit. Tomorrow would do for cleanup. She rubbed her eyes. They stung, gritty with fatigue, and she popped out her contacts, blinking hard with relief. She could do without corrected vision for this activity as long as she could see not to fall over anything. One of these days she'd probably take laser surgery to correct her nearsightedness. She grinned at her slightly fuzzy reflection in the bathroom mirror.

"You're really going," she said. Mere words were too simple. She tried them as a song, like one of her mother's operatic warm-up exercises. Her voice echoed in the half-empty flat, and she giggled as the little bubble of excitement popped to the surface again. It was true. Two weeks' vacation and she would be flying out. Farewell to road accidents, drunken brawls, domestic disputes. Now she would find out what kind of doctor she really was. She would face real issues of nutrition, child care and disease control with people who desperately needed her help through no fault of their own. She shook back her hair and pulled on a thin jacket.

Ben sat waiting at the door, quivering with anticipation. He was a big dog, an Irish wolfhound, and walking him twice a day gave her more than enough exercise. An hour before she went to work and an hour when she came home, no matter the time. When she was unavoidably delayed by some emergency, there was the fourteen-year-old boy next door who was always glad of the excuse to put aside his homework and earn a pound or two. She only had to call.

She loved to see Ben run on Hampstead Heath, stretching the long legs and sturdy muscles bred centuries before for hunting animals nearly as big as he. The breed could be protective to a fault and his gray, shaggy head came easily to her waist. She had never worried about being out alone at night with Ben close by her side.

She grabbed the leash from the rack by the door and struck up another tune, trying the Toreador chorus from *Carmen*, using silly words like she and her brother had done to irritate their mother, Elena.

"Toreador…can't stand any more…don't care a bit…mind you close the door." Their mother had never shown much of a sense of humor.

Out on the narrow landing, Kari fixed Ben's leash and started down the stairs, finishing them with a skip and a jump. It was almost too good to be true.

She and Ben had a favorite route from Camden across Rosslyn Hill, down Pond Street, over the intersection by the tube station, and onto Heath Road. They usually came back by Keats Grove, so she could admire the poet's house. Tonight it would be too dark.

The shaggy wolfhound pulled impatiently at the leash, forcing her into a half-jog. She had been right to come out; the air was doing her good. She felt clearheaded, ready for anything. A few drops of rain struck cold on her face and hands. Hopefully it would hold off for a half hour or so. They needed the rain, the London parks, usually so green, were parched and yellow. She zipped up her jacket.

The road was quiet at this time in the evening. She caught the smells of cooking and the sounds of conversation that drifted from open windows of the old houses, now converted to flats. The full-blown roses sent a heady perfume through the gardens. The careful merchants who had built the solid terraces had planted most of them long ago. Neglected and forgotten, besieged now by tricycles, motorbikes, and baby prams, a few hardy bushes continued to flourish and bloom against all odds.

The brief summer shower had brought out their scent in the night air. An aroma of spices floated from the Indian takeaway on the corner.

The wolfhound took the lead on the familiar way into Hampstead, where the houses grew more spacious, sitting serenely in carefully tended gardens.

Once on the Heath, they slipped into the cool, dusky areas under the trees. The thick foliage screened the buildings, and the rumble of traffic on Willow Road grew fainter as Ben plunged on 'round massive and ancient rhododendron bushes. The rain fell harder now, and Kari inhaled the damp, earthy smell of the leaves.

At last, she stooped to unhook the clasp of the leash, and Ben bounded away eagerly to the open grass, seeking his own delights and smells. The gray shape blended into the shadows, and Kari followed slowly on the gravel path. Her one regret at leaving London was deserting Ben. They'd been together a long time. He'd been an adorable puppy, all feet and legs topped by a lolling tongue and a big grin. He was a good dog, he wouldn't cause Mike any problems and her brother had better take special care of him. She caught the blur of movement in the distance—it had to be Ben again, covering the space between them with long, determined strides and she smiled in anticipation. He would come back, check in briefly with her and be off again in a flash. She braced herself for his size and weight as he made straight for her.

Suddenly there was movement between her and the dog. A crouched figure rose up, ghostlike, from the grass, giving the bounding animal no chance to veer away. Kari heard the soft thud of the impact as the animal and the stranger met, and both went flying back on the turf. The dog recovered his footing first and barked a warning, the hair on his neck bristled. Kari hurried nearer. The shape rose more slowly and she distinguished the outline of a man, a large man, dressed in black. Beside him lay a bag and a package. Was he a burglar? A drunk? A drug addict maybe, looking for any source of ready cash? Or preparing to shoot up?

She stood close to the dog, laying a hand on his collar. The man had risen to his knees, shaking his head. She could make out broad shoulders and dark hair that shone with the misting of raindrops. She pushed back her own damp mane. Ben had quieted, and she stepped closer to the stranger. She peered at him, trying to see him better.

"Look, I'm sorry. Are you hurt? Can you stand?" Kari thought of all the warnings she had disregarded about walking alone at night on the Heath. Prudently, she decided not to go too near in case he made a grab. "I'm a doctor. Can I help you?"

With a grunt, he pushed himself up on his feet and brushed the grass from his side. He was not merely wide in the shoulders, but tall and well-shaped in the black T-shirt tucked into black jeans that hugged slim hips. His silence added to her wariness until another thought struck her. "Do you speak English?"

Without her glasses and in the dim light, his features were still a blur. She tried narrowing her eyes to bring him into focus. For once she should have left her contacts in. This time he seemed to have heard her question and stopped the movement of his hands to glance at her. She had a flash of strong features and luminous gray eyes, and then the brief impression was gone. The muscles in the pit of her abdomen tightened. She put it down to the apprehension caused by stopping to talk to a stranger in a lonely, dark place.

They both stood, frozen in time, caught in a cocoon of darkness and misty rain. The distant sounds of the city faded, drowned by the pounding of her blood in her ears. Her quick breath sighed in the still air. Ben pressed against her side, his damp fur rubbing her bare leg. She felt the wiry hair against her palm as she laid her hand on his head. She could smell the wet grass where the collision had released spores from the bruised stalks.

She was no longer afraid. Her senses were sharp, taking in every detail that she could see, every scent, every touch on her skin. *I shall remember this moment,* she thought.

The stranger broke the spell as he spoke at last. "I do indeed speak English." He bent to pick up a black jacket. "I apologize if I spooked your dog." He turned away so she could no longer see even the pale oval of his face.

"No problem, he'll live. Ben doesn't frighten easily." She dragged her mind back from its reverie. She was still in a lonely place with a strange man doing God knows what. *But you seem pretty suspect to me,* she said to herself. *There doesn't seem much the matter with you. Maybe you don't need any help.*

He ignored the ironic emphasis on the dog's name. Didn't he have any manners? He stood still again. She felt his scrutiny, but his back was turned to the distant light. Damn, if only she could see his face properly. The memory of her mother's cat, a sleek, black creature, came unbidden to her mind. The animal would watch patiently for hours, willing to outwait wary birds and mice. She cleared her throat.

"I hope there's no damage." She wanted to add, "*Although it was your fault for rearing up like that right in front of poor Ben.*"

Instead, she stepped forward and picked up the bag. "Don't forget your shopping." She held it out, although it felt empty.

He gestured impatiently. He was holding something in the waving hand. "Please," he said curtly. "Go away! You shouldn't be here. Take the dog and go."

Her eyebrows rose in reaction to his churlishness.

"I most certainly will." She dropped the bag. Let him pick it up himself. She turned her back on the rude stranger, Ben at her side. The dog sat for her to attach his leash.

Behind her, the man cried out. "Go, go, get back! Why are you waiting? No, Tanice, no, not yet!" His voice rang with despair.

It was the last thing Kari heard as something hit her full force between her shoulder blades, and she fell, spinning endlessly through a deep, black tunnel.

Chapter Two

ॐ

Kari blinked, shook her head, then cautiously extended one hand. Her exploring fingers encountered rough, wooden planks. She was half-sitting, half-lying against a wall whose stones jutted uncomfortably into her back. The air was still, and it was very dark. How long had she been laying here? Had she been mugged? She struggled to sit more upright, trying to remember. There had been a man. What had happened to the stranger on the Heath? The park was quieter than she had ever known it. The lack of traffic noise made it eerie, and deep shadows concealed everything more than an arm's length away.

Her head throbbed, and she put up a wary hand to the source of the pain, only to encounter a swelling bruise above her eye. The touch made her wince, but her fingers stayed dry. No blood. She sniffed the air. The odor of straw and animal sweat and dung brought back childhood memories of days on her grandfather's farm. Maybe the blow on the head had sent her sense of smell haywire?

As her eyes adjusted to the darkness she could make out the shape of the stranger's empty shopping bag, still lying on its side on the ground. So her memory of the moments before her blackout was correct. As she peered into the gloom, a faint snuffle came from beside her, and a wet nose pushed against her arm. Kari put out a hand.

"Hallo there, Ben," she whispered. "Are you okay, boy? What do you think happened?"

The dog licked the back of her hand. She could feel him shivering and rubbed his ears with a reassurance she was far from feeling. What were her senses trying to tell her? She pushed herself up a little more, looking around. Surely, it was darker than she remembered? She felt for her watch and found it still on her wrist. So the man in black was not a mugger—or he was an inefficient one.

The luminescent hands on the watch glowed faintly. She held it closer and squinted at it to make out the time. The hands showed twenty minutes after eleven, and the sweep hand was still faithfully marking the passing seconds. She frowned. It could not have been more than ten minutes ago that the man on the Heath had collided with Ben. There had been distant streetlights, traffic, all the background noises of the city. Now it was as if a curtain had come down between her and the pulsating life of the great, busy metropolis.

Suddenly, her straining ears picked up a footfall, and a gleam of light appeared. Someone at last! She gathered her feet under her and prepared to stand up, hooking her arm through the handle of the shopping bag as if it provided a link with reality. She tucked her fingers under Ben's collar.

She concentrated on discerning any movement behind the swinging light and at last made out two formless shapes, deeper black against the shadows of the trees. They advanced rapidly, one larger than the other, the smaller one leading and bearing a flickering lantern. Kari could still make out little more than the outline as they drew abreast, but she took a breath and put out her hand to draw their attention.

"Please—" she said.

The stunning blow to her extended arm made her cry out. Needles of pain shot from her wrist to her elbow, forcing her to clutch the injured arm to her as she doubled over, dropping the shopping bag. Beside her, Ben growled deep in his throat.

She squeezed her eyes shut, coping with the hurt, then forced herself to look at her attacker. A face swam into view through the tears that sprang to her eyes. The features looked vaguely male and young, but long, fair hair and a shapeless garment made it impossible to be sure of anything. The creature poked at Kari with the stick that had struck her arm. Ben rumbled again softly. My God, what had she gotten into?

"Get back wi' thee and thy hellhound. No pickins 'ere fer the likes o' thee, be thou hoor or beggar."

As the light swung, it revealed the other shape as a woman in a dark gown with voluminous skirts, her hair covered with the hood of a yet darker cape. She stood behind the boy. She put a pale hand on her companion's shoulder, and spoke in a gentler voice.

"Malcolm, be sure to cause no hurt if none is given." The restraining hand remained on the lad's shoulder. The boy stood alert, ready to pounce like a leashed dog.

One night when she was on duty, Kari had dealt with some revelers from a masquerade ball who had imbibed too well. An elaborately costumed Marie-Antoinette had fallen down some stairs and her bizarre companions had insisted on helping her to her feet. Kari had no patience with such nonsense that interfered with her job. Once had been enough.

"I'm sorry if I startled you," she began, moving into the beam of light cast by the attendant's lantern. She rubbed her arm. The pain was fading a little. "Look, I assure you I meant—"

A gasp escaped the woman, whose eyes were now riveted on Kari's legs beneath her shorts. The boy crossed himself, muttering. Kari glanced down. Everything seemed to be in place. No dirt or blood. She looked up, ready to begin her explanation again. Before she could continue, the woman spoke, "Where—where are your garments?"

"Look, if you could just—"

"Who has done this terrible thing, to leave a poor soul half-naked at my gate?" The woman's voice rang with pity.

Kari pushed back her hair. Half-naked indeed! These people were going a little too far. "Look, I'm sorry to interrupt whatever it is you're doing, but I think I must have blacked out for a few minutes. I've never done anything like that before. I'll just walk with you back to the main road and I'll get a taxi straightaway..." She picked up the shopping bag.

The boy sprang in front of the strange woman and lifted his sturdy stick in protection again. "Take no heed, mistress. This one's in league with footpads, you can be sure."

"Malcolm, is it not evident the poor creature is deranged? She babbles, and her words are not to be comprehended. No footpad's lure would dress so. Someone has turned this poor half-mad creature into the woods to fend for herself like some unwanted beast. Charity dictates that we try to help. Come, my dear," she said, stepping forward and unhooking her cloak at the throat. "My house is nearby. Come home with me, and my husband shall decide what to do when he returns. I shall put a salve on your arm. Do you know your name?"

To Kari's astonishment, the woman folded the cape around her shoulders, covering her from head to toe, and firmly took her arm to lead her away into the darkness.

Malcolm stood guard, silencing any protest or refusal to follow by eagerly brandishing his stick. Kari sensed he longed for an opportunity to use it, and she had no desire to taste the end of it again.

Still dazed, she allowed the woman to lead her along a path. If they were really going to a house, there would at least be a telephone, and a bathroom to clean up in. An ice cube on her arm would help. The idiot could have broken it.

Ben trotted behind. In a very few minutes the bulk of a building loomed out of the gloom. The puzzlement was that it stood in the middle of the open green space that she and Ben knew so well. The small voice of common sense whispered that a house could not have been constructed on this protected space since her last walk in the park.

The woman opened a wooden door and motioned Kari to follow. The lintel of the low doorway brushed her hair as they entered. The boy, Malcolm, scampered ahead, eagerly calling the household together to marvel at the creature Mistress Godwin was bringing into a God-fearing home.

Ben pressed close to Kari's side. He was tense, all his senses alert, as if he too knew that something beyond all reason was taking place. Kari kept her hand on his neck, as much to reassure herself of a link to rationality as to restrain him.

The woman kept her arm around Kari, gently urging her across the threshold. "Come, my dear," she repeated. "Are you hungry?"

Deft fingers drew the hood from Kari's head, smoothing her hair with a motherly touch.

"Such a color," the woman whispered. She made a small sound of alarm as the movement of the cape again revealed Kari's skimpy clothing, and she hastily pulled together the folds of the cloak. Kari shook her head, her incredulous eyes taking in the scene in the room.

The space was longer than it was wide, faintly lit by a few guttering candles. Stone slabs, worn by use and covered with a scattering of rushes, formed the floor. At the far end, close to a small, dark window, Kari could make out a large shape that turned out to be a table.

The woman urged her closer, and she saw a setting of pewter dishes, a carafe and a goblet. A hunk of bread, torn from a loaf, lay by the plate. A bowl of apples completed the setting for a late supper.

No fire burned in the massive fireplace, although sticks and logs lay ready for lighting. Ashes from many previous burnings lay beneath the fresh kindling.

Thick beams supported the low ceiling, throwing more shadows into the corners of the room. A rich aroma of roasted meat, smoke, and the odors from the barnyard mingled with the fresh scent from the floor rushes. Kari allowed herself to be led unresisting to the table and sank down on a hard, high-backed chair.

The woman settled beside her, smoothing her wide skirts, which swung bell-like around her, and adjusting the long sleeves of her gown where they gripped tight about her wrists.

Smiling, she lifted the cover from a dish, revealing a slab of hard, yellow cheese. Creamy butter stood nearby in a crock.

As her busy fingers buttered the bread and cut the cheese, she talked gently in a soft flow of inconsequential words, darting the occasional sharp glance at Kari's face. She spoke slowly, picking her words as if unsure of the stranger's ability to comprehend. Kari recognized the technique of using the reassurance of the human voice talking of everyday things. She had used it herself with people overcome with horror and shock.

"We supped earlier, of course," the woman said softly, "but the walk to the village always makes me hungry. Joan knows that I am ready for a bite extra when I return. Tonight, I went to see Agnes Miller. She sent word for me just before dark. Poor woman, so sick and weak."

She shook her head in sorrow. "If that husband of hers thought more of his work and less of his ale, he would have less need of me to provide the dear soul with nourishing broth." She sighed. "But their misfortune is not entirely of their own doing, and it allows me to gain grace in an act of charity. We have so much when so many have so little."

Kari's eyes took in the sparse, heavy furniture, the weighty plates and cutlery. Her wide gaze returned to the woman before her. The goodwife's round face still bore traces of a faded beauty. Her pale blue eyes crinkled at the corners when her mouth curved in a ready smile. A lace cap almost totally covered her hair, but a few wisps showed gray mixed with the gold. The woman's complexion was clear, the expression kindly. Kari sought in her memory for the names of the few actresses she knew of. This was no amateur production with such an elaborate set. But why should she be included in the scene against her will?

Kari licked her lips. "Who are you?" she whispered.

Without pausing in her task of setting food on the plate, the woman answered in the same amiable voice, "God be praised that you can speak like a Christian. Thomas cannot abide a babbling woman, with or without her senses. I am Martha

Godwin, as you must surely know, if you dwell nearby. My husband," a note of pride came into her voice, "is Thomas Godwin, the wool merchant. He is away from home now, since there is possible trade that takes him to the Low Countries. He and our son-in-law Jonathan Howard should return, God willing, within the week—we hope sooner." She smiled again and set a plate of bread and cheese before Kari.

She ignored Kari's silence and continued her story, her voice warm and comforting. "Our daughter, Anne, is great with her first child. She would dearly love her husband to be here for the birth, though I tell her 'tis woman's business and not something with which to bother our menfolk. Here, eat. It will build your strength." She gave the plate a little push.

The bread was coarse, but freshly baked. The scent of it reminded Kari of her missed supper and the cold cup of tea. She was hungry. Carefully, she brought a piece of the loaf to her mouth. It was studded with gritty, unmilled grain and the crust had hardened like armor. She tried in vain to swallow the lump past her constricted throat. Martha continued talking as she poured a liquid into the goblet.

"All we have is cider, but 'tis brewed from our own apples. Thomas will not leave the household free use of his wine when he is away. He is very wise." She looked up, as if expecting a contradiction. "He will know what best to do with you."

"I must go home." Kari sat up straighter and took a drink to rid her mouth of the glutinous lump of bread. She pushed back the chair.

"Look," she continued. "I have no idea what is being played out here, but I've had enough. My head is quite all right." She touched the sore spot on her forehead. "It's not even bleeding. My arm is fine, no thanks to that boy. I'll use some ice when I get home, and we can forget the whole thing. If you believe you are helping me, then I am grateful, but you must find someone else for your silly game."

Ben scrambled to his feet as she stood and took up his position at her side. She flung the cape from her. "Put this back in with your props. You are a good actress, but your humor is misplaced. Goodbye, Mistress Martha Godwin—or whatever your real name is!"

Unheard and unnoticed, the boy Malcolm had crept back to the room, bringing with him a girl of about his own age, a buxom woman in late middle age, and a bent old man. All were in costume, and all stared with well-simulated horror at the glory of Kari's tanned legs and bare throat. They were well-rehearsed. It would have been nice if they had let her in on the game.

Malcolm's gaze traveled down from her face—she remembered she was not wearing a bra under the thin shirt. Uneasy, she pulled her light jacket more closely round her. The youth breathed more rapidly, and his tongue flickered over his lips. He shifted his position slightly.

The old man broke the silence first with a peal of cruel laughter. "Look at 'er," he cackled. "From Bedlam she be. Escaped she 'as. I saw one like 'er when the master took I to see the show." He waved a gnarled stick in glee.

"Be quiet, Dick." Martha's voice grew suddenly stern. "Joan, prepare a bed for this poor creature. We will show Christian love to one of God's unfortunate ones."

The serving woman sniffed in disapproval, but turned to do her mistress's bidding.

"Bedlam?" Kari turned back to Martha. "That place doesn't exist anymore, and the public visits stopped in—" She broke off. She remembered the silence and the darkness outside. She recalled the lack of streetlights, the absence of traffic noise, the situation of this house. Fear gripped her as her heart began to beat faster.

"Where am I?" she whispered in horror. She blurted out the question she dared hardly think, "And what year is this?"

Chapter Three
July 8, 2400

ಐ

Getting back was harder and longer than usual. Aidan hovered frustratingly in ultraspace at the threshold of the research station as the energy field pulsed and faded, refusing to materialize him completely.

He could see Tanice staring intently at the platform that took up most of the center of the room, but could not communicate with her. He floated free, like someone in a health reconstruction station, lingering between life and death, waiting for the surgeon's decision. The console screen showed a flickering, green line of light.

The stark room gleamed. He could feel the faint vibration of the machinery around the walls. Tanice shifted position in the upholstered chair, and the mechanisms adjusted smoothly to the movement. Her eyes flicked constantly from the screen to the platform, her hands poised over a series of keys protruding from the desktop.

As he watched, she caught her lower lip in her teeth. He could even hear her mutter under her breath.

"Yes," she whispered. "Yes, come through, come on."

The line fluttered, disappeared from the screen for a second, and then pulsed stronger, forming a bright green bar.

The large, square package wrapped in brown paper, tied with tape and string, vanished from his side and appeared on the platform. Damn, if he had held it, maybe he would have gone through, too.

"Come on, come on, Aidan," Tanice muttered between her teeth. "Where in perdition are you?"

He waved, but of course she couldn't see him. He wondered dispassionately how long someone could exist in this disembodied state. The package sat for a long moment, incongruous and clumsy on the wide, empty expanse while the line returned to the intermittent flicker.

Tanice pressed two pads, one after the other.

"Don't do this to me, goodfriend. What did you do out there?" She pushed back a wisp of gray hair.

The line strengthened again, fluttered and held. The pulsing grew stronger, the bar formed, and suddenly he felt the familiar tug and tingle of the force field, and he was there, calm, smiling, flicking imaginary dust from his sleeve. He had known he would make it. He lifted a hand in salute.

"'Lo, Tanice."

She let out a long breath and leaned back in her chair, running her hand through her hair.

"Welcome back, Aidan." She smiled, but her eyes were still worried.

He stood patiently while the cleaner robots scuttled over him, removing all traces of dust, dirt and fibers from his clothing. When they dropped off, satisfied, he began to undress.

"Aidan!" Tanice hurried to him, her hands outstretched as if to touch him, but her training was strong and she held back, waiting for his cleansing routine to finish. "Are you all right? The force field was intermittent… Thought I'd lost you."

He shrugged in the black jacket. "Can't wait to get out of these ridiculous clothes." He unclipped the leather belt. "How long did men wear these instruments of torture anyway?"

"A couple of hundred years," Tanice replied distractedly. "Don't change the subject. Something drained the field, Aidan. What was going on? Nearly didn't get you back." She swallowed. "Scared me."

"Not that easy to get rid of me. Give me a nanosec." The faint buzz persisted in his ears. He put his head back, closed his eyes and shook his head. "Whew. Let my head clear. Was a weird go."

"Knew it! Too dangerous! How do you feel?"

"Mean, am I all in one piece?" He was naked now, the clothes sucked aside by a probing robot. He grinned at her and patted himself down. "Think so. See anything missing? Haven't come back without the back of my head or with a dog's ears?" He stood, pretending to check around with his hands.

"Don't play the fool, Aidan. Do you feel different?"

"Come on, Tan. Where's all that training in keeping it all in?"

"No joke."

He saw tears gleam in her eyes. She swallowed hard.

"And wouldn't that have been difficult to explain to our leader? Try telling him that his favorite operative went scattering on an unsanctioned mission." He grinned.

"Stop it, Aidan. We know what would happen if Howard found out how far you've gone." She shook her head. "You could lose everything."

The hiss of the parahydra shower provided the excuse not to answer. Invisible beams probed every crevice of Aidan's body, sanitizing his skin, reaching into orifices. He opened his mouth and spread his arms and legs, heedless of his nakedness. Of course, both he and Tanice were dosed with anti-pheromones. Those were the rules. Spontaneous sexual arousal was considered a risk, despite Tanice being twice his age. That would interfere with the planned course of things, just as much as his unauthorized trips into time.

Aidan Torrance knew he was a handsome man even by the high standards of the twenty-fourth century. Regulated genetic engineering removed all likelihood of birth defects when a couple received a procreation permit. His parents had selected the dark hair and gray eyes of the western borders, in keeping with their Celtic and Old English heritage. For the same reason, he was only of average height for his time, but well-muscled and pleasingly proportioned. They hadn't expected a rebellious mind in the well-shaped body. They would have been distressed to know how their son grew up to flout the values of the society in which he lived.

"Calm, calm, lieutenant," Aidan continued when the green light blinked, and the shower stopped. "Let me dress while you order us up something to eat and drink. Then I'll tell you what happened."

He would give her a few minutes to calm down. She had been scared, and so had he, if the truth were known. He didn't relish the thought of becoming a twenty-fourth century Flying Dutchman, caught forever between centuries. He moved swiftly to a side door and pushed the control to pass through. The panel slid back and he stepped into the opening.

He took five minutes to pick up a one-piece suit in a shade of reddish brown, almost indistinguishable in design from Tanice's pale blue clothing. The light fabric allowed easy movement as he strode back to a table that Tanice had pulled from the wall.

"Enjoyed that shower." He rubbed his hands through his dry hair. "Still have trouble using water to clean up. Until you see it, it's hard to imagine how much they used back then. Fountains and rivers of fresh water every few minutes for showers, washing machines, and toilet facilities—" He rolled his eyes expressively.

"Don't talk about it," Tanice shuddered in distaste. "Don't scunner me, not now, not while we eat. Don't want to lose my appetite."

As she spoke, a panel opened in the wall, revealing two plates of food, drinking vessels and a jug of yellow liquid.

Aidan sniffed. "My favorite, by the smell of it."

"Abyrtaca salad with cassareep dressing." Tanice lifted the plates from the shelf with a small, self-satisfied smile, arranging them with the drinks on the table. The panel slid shut as the sensors registered the reduction in weight.

Aidan poured a glass of the amber wine and drank deeply. "Ah," he sighed, "that's better."

He tackled the plate of food with enthusiasm. "Time travel must give an appetite, have you noted that in the log?" Without waiting for a reply, he continued, "Haven't had a decent meal since I left. Everything is centered 'round meat. Boiled, broiled, grilled, baked and the conditions..." He shuddered, overacting. Must try to distract her from any thought of pulling the plug on the operation.

Tanice was still preoccupied, only half-listening. She put down her fork. "Aidan, listen to me."

"Listening."

"I meant it when I said we nearly didn't get you back. Something drained the field."

Aidan took another mouthful, waiting.

Tanice took hold of her glass, turning it on the table. "At first, I thought it might be Flynn..."

He frowned, alert. "Flynn? Is he back?"

Reed Flynn and he had been in the Space Academy together. Reed had continued when Aidan dropped out to become an academic, but the old rivalry still persisted. Flynn had acquired a reputation as a ruthless adventurer — some would say a pirate. There were unsubstantiated stories of stolen ships and cargoes, of bribery and outright intimidation. Nothing proven, of course.

Tanice nodded. "Apparently so. He was sniffing around the lab while you were gone. He makes me nervous, Aidan. What does he want?"

"My pictures, of course." Aidan's lips tightened. "But he won't get them. He'll have to get rid of me first."

"Howard sent him packing, double-quick. I don't think he was around long enough to learn much..." her voice trailed off as she frowned in thought.

"So?"

"Then I thought it might be buran interference."

He looked up at her, caught by the intensity in her voice. "Electronic windstorm?" He frowned. "I thought that was just a theory. More likely to be the pictures." He gestured to the package still sitting in the center of the room.

"Maybe," she frowned. "But I don't think so. Were they right next to you?"

"Sure, just like you told me."

"Don't understand…"

"Maybe I should hold them next time, bring them back with me."

"Next time? Won't be a next time until Howard says that the program is funded!" She took a drink. "Tell me what happened."

He thought back. Tan really was worried. "At the very last minute, just before I was due to come back, I ran into a woman and her dog. Or rather, they ran into me…"

"Tell me about her."

He deliberately misunderstood. "She was slight, about your height. I remember a lot of red hair. But the dog bowled me over." He grinned.

Tanice sighed. "You're not making sense, Aidan. Tell me what happened from the beginning."

Aidan poured the last of the drink into their glasses and recounted the unexpected collision. "Nothing much more to tell. It was my fault." He sipped. "Careless. Had set the coordinates on the responder. I carried it in a shopping bag, did I tell you? No one noticed. At the right time, I was putting the box away and tried to stand up. Great, shaggy dog came out of nowhere and ran straight into me. I still forget about animals running loose. It caught me off balance. There was a woman with it. Long, red hair foaming around her face. A face that was all huge, dark eyes." He hesitated.

"What else?" Tanice prompted.

He shrugged. "Nothing. Told her to get back, and she was turning away from me when poof! You zapped me back."

Tanice sat up straighter. "How close was she?"

"Don't know." He shrugged again. "Maybe a little more than arm's length."

Tanice had already left the table. She punched in numbers on the console, frowning in concentration.

"What year were you in? 2000?"

"Yes."

Tanice sat back, staring at her calculations. "Aphelic theory. So there is a repulsion effect." She breathed the words to herself.

"Aphelic? That's a new one. What does it mean?"

"Means, goodfriend traveler, that we have probably zapped your unknown woman, and undoubtedly her dog, as far back in time as we brought you forward."

Aidan had no need to calculate. "Four hundred years," he whispered. "You mean...?"

"Yes," Tanice nodded. "Whoever she is, if she survived, she is on Hampstead Heath in the year 1600."

Aidan had a sudden vision of those blue eyes terrified, bewildered by what had happened. If she'd made it. But there could be a worse outcome than the woman's distress. He thrust back his chair and stood up. "Set up the coordinates."

"What coordinates? What for?"

"Have to go back. Tell Monika to costume me."

"Aidan, this is ridiculous." Tanice came fast 'round the counter to grab his arm. "You can't go back. You know the rules for recovery between trips—"

"To hell with recovery!" Aidan spun to face her. "Dammit woman, if she's back there in Tudor London, God only knows what damage she's doing!"

"Damage?" Slowly, comprehension dawned in Tanice's eyes.

He thrust his head out, gray eyes blazing, jaw set. "We will have allowed the worst crime in a time traveler's book. Dammit, Tan, I'm an historian. I have some responsibility. You know I've cleaned up after myself every time I've flipped back. Never done anything to influence anyone's behavior. And now this. The woman told me she's a doctor. She and her hound will be setting off the worst cultural contamination we could imagine. Don't tell me I can't go. Got to get her out of there. Be ready in thirty minutes."

Chapter Four
July 1600

∞

Kari was not surprised to toss and turn all night, unable to sleep or rid her mind of her racing thoughts. Martha's concern, her honest face and puzzled answers had succeeded at last in convincing her of the truth. As preposterous as it seemed, somehow, someway, she had been hurled back into the past. She was thankful at least for her own room and bed, vaguely recalling that medieval people often slept huddled together.

The next twelve hours brought a roller coaster of emotions. Blind panic gave way to bewilderment, then denial, which in turn yielded to anger. That too passed. She was left at last anxious and confused, battling to beat back a deep-seated fear that threatened to boil out of control at any moment.

She called on the memories from her mother's singing roles and her father's books. At a guess, the costumes could be from the late sixteenth century. The Elizabethan English that these people spoke confirmed this. And she'd seen the movies about Shakespeare and Elizabeth, delighting in the settings, the clothes and the intrigues, all safely recreated on the screen. The reality was more daunting.

The daylight hours slid by after the near-sleepless night, and still she struggled to accept what had happened. She must be in some kind of time warp, but her mind insisted desperately on trying to contradict the evidence of her senses. It was impossible. All her scientific training told her so. She'd had enough of the mystical and the mythological growing up with her turbulent family at home. For that very reason, she'd turned to science and medicine — to get away from the irrational.

Reluctantly, she conceded that the people who had found her were no practical jokers. Gradually, she succeeded in asking enough questions to fix herself more accurately in time.

Although she managed to convince everyone of her madness by the stupidity of her remarks, she did ferret out some information. As near as she could judge, she was still on Hampstead Heath, near the village of Keystone toward the end of the reign of Good Queen Bess. She searched her scanty memory files for information, wondering if the end of Elizabeth's reign was as stormy and dangerous as the beginning. There was no royal heir of course, so there were likely all kinds of plots brewing.

Moorland stretched in front of the farm, while thick woods clothed the horizon. Kari heard talk of the criminals who haunted the desolate moor and understood Malcolm's violent reaction to the sight of her. The gossip talked of the drovers bringing cattle and sheep to pasture at Islington, the last stopover before London. Kari struggled to make sense of the names she knew so well as central areas of a teeming city; Camden was a cattle pasture, Islington offered a corn mill.

The time passed in a blur of emotions, but at last darkness came again and she sank exhausted into the bed, worn out from the surges of fear and bewilderment that beset her at each new revelation.

Did her family know she was missing? Had she left a trace? Was anyone looking for her? And who would think of looking for her four hundred years in the past, or be able to do anything about it if they did?

She searched her memory for her last conversation with her brother just before her final day at St. Mark's. At six in the evening Kari had at last had time to return Mike's phone messages.

"As of tomorrow I'm officially on leave," she'd announced. "God, Mike, I can't believe it."

"Your family has the same problem," came the rejoinder. "No second thoughts."

"None at all."

She heard his long-suffering sigh. "What now?" he asked.

"A couple of weeks to rest up and prepare and then the launch into the great unknown."

"Haven't they told you where?"

"Mike, you know they can't. *Médecins Sans Frontières* — "

"Doctors Without Borders must remain flexible," Mike had broken in, quoting. "Staff must be prepared for assignment where needs are the greatest at the time — I know all that." He'd recited the litany by heart, bitterness in his voice.

Kari understood how much her brother dreaded this posting for her. He was genuinely concerned for her safety, but she also suspected that somehow he perceived his sister's altruism as a reflection on his own comfortable lifestyle. They had rarely quarreled before. Kari wanted to part on good terms.

She'd ignored the underlying hostility. "They'll give me time to get the shots for the area they choose. I just wish I'd been able to save a little more for some equipment." She shook off the thought. "Then the opportunity to practice medicine as I've always wanted."

"In mud and filth — "

"More likely sand and drought." Kari had kept her tone light. She'd had enough negative reactions to her decisions, heard how she'd lost all her sparkle, wasn't fun to be around anymore, was too intense, too single-minded...

Before Mike could dredge up any more of the arguments as to why she should settle down in a nice general practice in England, rather than seek a tour of duty in one of the trouble spots of the world, she'd continued, "I want to take a few days off first. Would you take Ben for me now?"

"I suppose. How long?"

"Just a week—I can't afford longer." She had to smooth things over with this prickly brother. "What are you doing tonight? Care for a flick?"

Mike didn't want to quarrel either. "I can do better than that," he'd said. "Come with me to a party."

And so she'd gone to a boring vernissage, stared uncomprehendingly at bright canvases bearing outlandish prices, eaten dried-up sandwiches and sipped bad wine. It had been in a different world.

* * * * *

The second night in the house brought Kari more rest than had the first. Years of being on call in the hospital had developed her ability to shut out distractions and worries, and she had long ago acquired the knack of falling asleep almost anywhere. She was dead on her feet, and it took little effort to sink into bed and clear her mind at last.

The bed linen was scratchy and stiff, and smelled faintly of lavender; the wall rustled with the sounds of small creatures that she preferred not to think about, and the smoke from the candle drifted slowly in the drafts from the unglazed opening that served as a window.

On the plus side, they had allowed her to keep Ben in the room, and she could hear him breathing down by the side of the high four-poster bed. After some resistance, they had even allowed her to feed him with kitchen scraps.

She woke at dawn to the chorus of birds under the thatched eaves and the tramp of feet in the yard. Men's voices called out, their cries interspersed with the chink of harness. The sweet smell of hay and country flowers drifted in. The short tallow candle had burnt down to a stump, but the sun was now sending dusty rays into the shadowy corners of the room.

Kari lay in the poster bed and contemplated her surroundings. The ceiling was low, but the beams were less massive than on the floor below. Wooden slats, hooked together with a thick, black latch, shuttered the windows.

The walls curved, not one of them straight, not one of the angles square. It reminded Kari of the "crazy kitchen" she had visited in a museum when she was ten. She had the same off-balance and giddy sensation as her brain fought to make sense of the information sent by her eyes.

The walls were plastered and whitewashed; an oak chest stood under the window. It contained a clean linen petticoat and a plain gray worsted gown, a head covering and hand-knitted woolen stockings. She was expected to wear these or their twins. There was no lack of good cloth in Thomas Godwin's house and the household had assembled an assortment of garments to decently clothe "the poor, mad girl".

A good night's sleep had set her brain in order, and she must now begin to use it. Her predicament had to be connected to the incident in the park. She struggled to recall everything that had happened, beginning with her walk with Ben. Maybe she could track down the start of the nightmare. She forced herself to go over every detail, starting with her return from work, so as not to miss any clue.

She'd found two eggs and the heel of a stale loaf sitting in lonely splendor in the refrigerator. She'd boiled the eggs and toasted the bread, fed Ben the last can of dog food and made some tea.

She recalled flicking on the TV to a news broadcast as she ate. The usual harrowing scenes of senseless war and human suffering had rolled pitilessly across the screen. An exhausted doctor had given an interview against a background of tanks and armored trucks. Everything had looked dry and dead.

She'd wondered if she would meet that doctor or if he would burn out and be recalled before she arrived. Always assuming that was the godforsaken corner of the world chosen for her to spend the next two years. The frantic commentary of a sports reporter had intruded, and she'd switched off.

After finishing the letter for her parents, she'd been glad to leave the empty flat with its piles of boxes and rolled-up rugs. So she'd taken Ben to the Heath and there met a man in black...

There was no other possible cause of what had happened to her. It had to be connected with that stranger and his shouted warning to get back. What had he known? What had he done?

A tap at the door broke into her reverie.

"Who is it?" she called.

There was no answer, but slowly the gap widened to allow Anne Howard to duck through the low opening. A younger version of her mother, she had the same fair hair and blue eyes. Her gown hung loose in deference to her advanced pregnancy, and she panted slightly from the exertion of the stairs.

Kari sat up in the bed, pulling up the sheet to cover her breasts. She had never realized that nightclothes did not always form part of one's wardrobe in the past. She balked at wearing the same shift day and night, not being at all sure that it would ever be washed.

"Good morning, Kari." Anne smiled and offered a cup of fresh, foaming milk. "Look what I have brought for you."

Kari accepted the wooden goblet and put it to her lips, resolutely pushing aside all newfangled notions about pasteurization. The creamy liquid slipped deliciously down her parched throat. She had taken very little of the proffered food and drink yesterday.

"Thank you, Anne." She licked away the white mustache and patted the side of the bed. "Sit down here."

Anne sank onto the bed with an unconscious sigh. "Did you sleep well?" she asked.

"I did, indeed. I'm not quite so afraid. And you?"

The young woman nodded, patting her distended stomach. "As well as the babe would allow." She looked shyly at Kari. "'Tis hard indeed to think of you as being afraid. You seem so strong."

Kari would have thought she seemed anything but strong at the moment. She caught the expression on the girl's face. "Are you frightened, Anne?" she asked.

Anne nodded. "A little."

Kari took her hand, sliding her fingers unobtrusively up to her wrist to where she could feel the strong pulse beat. She watched the movement of Anne's chest as she counted in silence.

"Are your legs swollen?"

Kari tried for as accurate a picture as possible without a physical examination. Anne answered innocently, until something about Kari's tone and manner gave her pause. She stood up.

"Why do you ask these things of me?" A cloud of concern passed across her face. "Why should I tell you such details of my body, my—" She frowned, fumbling for words, a flush of embarrassment high on her cheeks.

"Please, I don't want to frighten you," Kari soothed. "Look, I have some knowledge of medicine. I—"

Anne interrupted with a sigh and a gesture of her hand. "Poor Kari. We forget your brain fever when you speak low and quiet. How can you know medicine, poor soul? Perchance you have seen a midwife working and have some memory…"

The past day had repeated the same pattern. Kari would gradually begin to speak naturally and freely, only to be jerked back to the attitudes and customs of Tudor England by the startled response of her audience. She must go slowly.

Anne adopted the same strategy as her mother and covered the silence with chatter. "I almost forgot our news! Father is home!"

That explained the sound of horses and the shouts outside the window.

"And your husband?"

The expressive face fell. "Not yet. He must bide in London two more days, Father says. There is important business." She shook off her sadness and touched the bodice of her gown. "Jonathan is well, he has written. I have the letter here, next to my heart. Father says he will read it to me when he has time. He has much to attend to."

"Can you not read, Anne?"

The young woman shook her head. "A little. Some prayers. I can write my name. And I can form my numbers," she said proudly. "Father said that would suffice for a gentlewoman. Too much learning serves to distract a woman's thoughts from her household duties, and my husband will read to me if I have need. Father does not approve of much learning for girls, although he does admire the Queen. She knows languages and philosophy, but what use would that be to me? I have only once in my life been to London, and there they still speak English." She laughed prettily.

Kari's London extended so much farther than this present town, barely out of its medieval state.

"I see," she said, watching Anne's fingers stroke the corner of the paper that edged out of her bodice. "Would you like me to read your letter to you?"

"You? You have the knowledge?" Anne's eyes grew round with disbelief.

Kari nodded. "My father allowed me to learn."

Well, that was more or less true. The man had sat her down with a book as soon as she could hold it in two podgy hands. Her earliest memory was of sounding out the letters on a page. Graduating to deciphering the cramped medieval writing on her father's research documents had been a natural progression. This letter was later than the ones Dad had been interested in, and should be easier.

Anne took out the thick paper and unfolded it. She ran her hand gently over the crackling surface. "Just look," she said longingly. "If you cannot read, no matter. I shall wait."

Kari took the pages and hunched over. The writing was not as bad as some she had seen.

"Dearest wife," she began. Anne gasped in astonishment and came closer on the bed. Kari took back the girl's hand and began to read aloud the sweet love letter of a young Elizabethan wool merchant to his pregnant wife.

Chapter Five

✍

Aidan Torrance strode calmly down the road, but inwardly the anger churned. In fact, it would be fair to say he was as mad as hell. Monika had outfitted him from the museum in double-quick time, and Tanice had at last agreed to transport him. But she had set conditions. She would bring him back in ten days, whether he had the girl or not. She expected regular reports on his location and progress, in case they needed to recalibrate the monitors, and she forbade him to reveal his identity to anyone—least of all, the girl. Tanice had been even more tense when she heard that Reed Flynn had been sniffing around the lab. Again.

"I don't trust him," she'd said. "Why does he need to be around here? What does he think he'll find that he can sell to some gullible Outer?"

"Watch out for him, Tan," Aidan had muttered. "Keep him away from my collection."

Aidan suspected that he knew what drew Flynn—the trader had probably caught wind of the latest of Aidan's pictures. It was too hard to keep everything off the networks. Tanice was right. Reed Flynn was unscrupulous and dangerous—not to mention greedy.

He pulled his thoughts back to the present problem. Of course, he had no idea what emotional state the woman he sought might be in. Tanice was nervous about records and archives and wanted complete secrecy. It stood to reason, he would aim to deposit the woman back just before the moment when Ben crashed into him on the Heath.

She would remember nothing if they coordinated it correctly. He could take her fast and smooth—he thought there would be time enough for explanations after. But Tanice always wanted a fail-safe plan. He needed her, so he'd agreed. And there had been no time for his booster shots. God knew what pestilence he would be exposed to! Things had to be quick.

Tanice's demands were logical, and they were not the real cause of his anger. The thought of what some unsuspecting woman and her dog might be doing to the flow of historical events infuriated him. He was angry with her for walking her dog at that particular moment two days ago and four centuries away. He was angry with the dog for running loose and uncontrolled. Most of all, if the truth were told, he was angry with himself for the lapse of concentration and attention that had allowed the meeting to happen.

He thought he would recognize her if she'd survived. He could remember a woman, probably in her early thirties, with long legs and slim hips. Her shape had been well revealed in the skimpy shorts and jacket.

Despite himself, he felt a stirring as he recalled the thrust of her breasts under the thin material when she'd pushed back her hair. It flowed long and dark, and glinted with a copper sheen in the reflected light. He pushed the images from his mind. He'd neglected his thought control exercises in the flurry of departure. He needed to concentrate on the problem at hand.

He moved under the overhanging branches of an oak tree. What a mission! Find this woman—with or without the dog, for God's sake—get her somehow to some place that remained open enough in the late twentieth century so that she did not rematerialize in someone's bedroom or a locked warehouse. Get himself back to his own time, and all without revealing his own identity. No problem, goodfriend!

Although it was early in the day, the sun beat down already, and he sweated in the woolen hose and leather jerkin. Maybe he could afford to rest for a moment and think through his plan again.

He settled on the grass with his back to a tree trunk where the branches hung low, giving welcome shade, pulled off the soft hat and let the faint breeze cool his forehead. If he'd thought twentieth-century clothing was confining and restrictive, this was worse. The coarse material had already acquired a faint scent he didn't recognize. Could be from vegetation, or animals, or, he supposed, his own body. The thought didn't please him. The sooner he was out of this, the better.

He fumbled for the responder in his pack and punched in the coordinates to let Tanice know where he was.

First Report: DAY 1

Operative: Aidan Torrance

Location: Hampstead Heath

Date: July 10, 1600

Report: Located outside hamlet identified as most likely landing spot for subject. No sign of disturbance. Local innkeeper has heard of a poor madwoman taken in at Thomas Godwin's house. Could be a witch, so the good man says, but Martha Godwin is well known for her good deeds and would take in a mad dog — and may have done so this time, according to the gossip. Am on my way to infiltrate the Godwin household. Out.

* * * * *

"So, Mistress Kari Lunne, if that be your heathenish name, you judge yourself better able to read than I?"

Thomas Godwin's voice thundered in the small room. He clasped his hands behind his back and frowned, fixing Kari with an imperious stare. He was a formidable man and gloried in his power. Even without the additional bulk of the layers of clothing, he would be large. A hip-length, green velvet jacket swung above a pale doublet with small buttons down the front. The skirt of the doublet was no more than a frill, while the patterned trunk hose molded a strong, shapely leg. A high-crowned, elegantly plumed hat lay on the table with his cane. His hair sprung low on his forehead, still thick and mostly dark brown. The mustache and pointed beard had been recently shaped. He was a wealthy man and a powerful one in the domain of his house and his business.

Kari had quickly learned he was accustomed to directing his household in the same way he directed his apprentices and workmen. A change in what he had preordained was unusual to say the least, and merited his attention.

She watched his eyes scan over her appreciatively. Martha sat in the corner, her eyes cast down on some stitching with which she busied her hands.

"My goodwife's strays are not usually so interesting. I am happy to see a gown from my household now decently covers your limbs." He paused.

Kari knew he would have absorbed Malcolm's excited recital that had made the rounds of the house about the charms now hidden from view.

Thomas stepped closer, taking in every detail of her face. "The skin is good," he said, "and the brow and nose well-shaped. The lips delicately formed and the hair—" He stretched out his hand and took hold of one long strand, rubbing it between his fingers like a piece of his wool cloth.

Kari felt herself redden under his scrutiny, but she would not cast down her eyes.

He chuckled. "I warrant this would be a fiery one, like her hair," he muttered. He dropped his voice to a mere whisper. "I have no need to add that I could pass a pleasant hour reflecting on what it would take to tame you."

"Sir?" she said, drawing back.

He removed his hand from near her face and spoke more loudly, "My daughter tells me you have wit enough to read."

"Indeed I have. I have merely been allowed to use the wits we are all born with, male and female," she added.

He narrowed his eyes at the impudence and rocked on his heels. "Some would say you have not your wits, so I shall pay no heed to your insolence. I know not if you come by your skill honestly, girl, but we have no need of more readers in this house. It seems that my wife has taken you under her wing."

Martha smiled obediently as he glanced her way.

"If you can refrain from interfering with my family," he continued, "and if you can be of use, I see no reason why you should not stay for a while. The devil makes work for idle hands, so put her to work, madam."

Martha bobbed an obedient curtsey.

With a last look that swept Kari from top to toe, he turned away in dismissal. "She shall earn her keep, in one fashion or another."

Kari fumed. How dare he assess her like a prize cow! Her nerve endings reacted to the blatant caress of his eyes, and she opened her mouth for the retort that sprang readily to her lips. Before she could tell Thomas Godwin what she thought, Martha stepped quickly to her side, laying a restraining hand on her arm. The shake of her head carried a mute warning, and Kari bit back her response.

"Thank you, husband. May God bless you for your charity," Martha said. "Come, Kari, I shall show you the sheds and the butter churns."

* * * * *

The handle of the churn chafed Kari's sore hands, and the milk sloshed loudly as she strained to raise the shaft one more time. She was beginning to hate that sound, which meant she was getting nowhere despite her efforts. She would never get the hang of this, the smooth rhythm that ensured perfect butter, the creamy yellow separating quickly from the whey as it did for Martha. Her shoulders ached, the muscles of her arm protested at each move.

The cool air, maintained by the thick, stone walls of the dairy, chilled the sweat on her as it formed. Damn them all! She was not supposed to be here. This was not her time, not her place. She had only consented to continue with the charade for the sake of Martha. Something told her that Martha Godwin would also suffer if Kari proved to be a burden.

The dairy was low and dim, well sheltered from the sun. Small windows and a thick door let in only filtered light. Dust motes danced in the few beams that penetrated inside. Kari had taken off the rough, wooden shoes and the floor stones were cool against her feet. She would ask Martha for her sneakers back—those clogs would cripple her before long.

The empty churns and pails stood lined up against the wall, ready for the next milking. The giggling dairymaids had washed them and left them with the lids open, the fragrant damp permeated the air as they dried.

The scent of the cheeses hardening against the wall mingled with the smells of hay and warm animals that wafted in from the barn. Kari swallowed down a slight queasiness. Wearily, she stopped to wipe her hand on her skirt, wincing at the stab of pain. Specks of blood decorated her palm, where the blisters had broken.

"Damn," she whispered. "I'll never get this finished." She blinked back tears of frustration.

A clean cloth lay on the trestle in the corner. She wrapped it gently 'round her blistered hand and turned back to the cursed churn.

From the corner of her eye, she caught a movement, and Ben raised his head where he lay across the threshold. A shadow fell across the doorway, and the dog growled softly.

She turned, immediately alert, fearful of being trapped alone by creepy Malcolm, who had appeared to stare and grin at her at regular intervals throughout the day.

The shape at the door loomed larger than that of the underdeveloped boy, but the backlighting made it difficult to distinguish features. She had an impression of broad shoulders and a full head of dark hair. The man leaned carelessly against the frame of the door, holding a soft hat in his hands.

"Good day, mistress."

She nodded without speaking, keeping her eyes downcast.

"The new hired man, Aidan by name."

She was not interested. "Find Dick. He will tell you where to go." She turned back to her churn.

The man ignored her words and stepped into the dairy. He came close behind her.

"Is that too hard for you?" He took her injured hand in his and folded back the cloth. The warm, firm fingers closed around hers.

Away from the strong sunlight, she could see him more clearly. He stood taller than the men she had observed on the farm, more of the height she was used to in her time, but clad in the rough clothing that classed him as a peasant—gray woolen hose that clung to his legs, and a shirt of coarse linen. He'd placed the wide brimmed hat back on his head and it hid the upper part of his face. A leather jerkin covered his broad shoulders and fell to slim hips. He wore leather shoes with wooden soles, although most of the farmhands were shod more roughly in wooden clogs.

Her eye traveled the length of him as he held her bleeding hand. She could smell the warm, earthy scent of his clothing, which was strangely enticing. He certainly presented a contrast with the white-coated, antiseptic men who had surrounded her for so many years.

Surprisingly, he'd shaved not too long before, and dark stubble showed around a wide mouth above a firm jaw. Most of the other men of his class wore beards in varying states of neatness. Even she could recognize that this man differed from the other farm workers. A faint memory stirred and she frowned.

Aidan carefully replaced the cloth. "Mistress Godwin surely has remedies for such hurts," he said. "Let me help." He pushed her aside gently but firmly and began to raise and lower the spindle with smooth, sweeping movements. He grinned. "After all, we have something in common."

"Really?" Her tone was cool.

"We are both from away, or so I am led to believe." He placed a slight emphasis on the last word. "Strangers may need each other."

She knew where she came from, and she would have bet Ben's life that no one else had the slightest inkling. How did this handsome stranger come to be here? What did he know of her? What did he want from her? And what business did he have interfering in what she was supposed to do? How could she learn if she didn't practice?

The absurdity struck her as the thought came to her mind. What did she care about learning to churn butter? She would be out of here in a few days. Whatever had happened to her would reverse itself. She would find her way home. She stood back with a shrug.

"Help yourself," she said.

As she met his level gaze, a quiver flickered through her as if from the touch of a lightly charged electric wire. She was suddenly overwhelmingly conscious of the movement of the muscles of his shoulders as he worked, the strong legs braced to give force to his efforts. The blood rose to her face. What was the matter with her? Traveling through time must have disturbed her hormone balance! She had never even bought an issue of *Playgirl* and here she was, checking this fellow out like a potential stud! All she needed was to be attracted to a man dead for nearly four hundred years! Her head swam at the thought of the added complication.

She closed her eyes and listened to the swish of the liquid. When she opened them, he was still absorbed in the task, not watching her. Looking anywhere but at the dark head and the strong back, she edged softly toward the door. Aidan glanced up at once. "Don't go."

"You seem to be doing okay—very well," she corrected herself. At least she should use a standard vocabulary and make herself understood. Before he could answer, she slipped through the door. As she and Ben left the dairy, she was sure she heard him muttering. It sounded as if he was annoyed about something.

It was probably best to avoid him.

Chapter Six

ൠ

Thomas Godwin was not given to joking. He'd expected to be obeyed when he instructed his wife to put Kari to work. Now Martha had to face the problem that Kari seemed unfit or untrained for any of the tasks that befell the mistress of a well-ordered house. Martha had clucked sympathetically over Kari's blisters and treated the sores with a poultice of comfrey leaves and honey.

Since Kari was not capable of churning butter, not to be trusted with the precious stocks of spices and herbs, knew nothing of the barnyard or of spinning, Martha was hard put to find her some work to justify her keep. Kari suspected that the threat of the almshouse hung over her if she proved a burden.

"My husband is a good man," Martha told Kari as they sat in the dusk after the evening meal. "But he cannot abide waste and sloth."

Even in the fading light, Martha's fingers moved busily, mending a fine linen shirt. "I have told him that you must be gently born."

Kari looked up from the linen she was folding.

"Oh yes, I know some misfortune must have befallen you," Martha continued, "even if you cannot remember or dare not tell. Your skin is soft and untouched by the weather, your hands are unused to heavy labor—or even the pricks of the needle!" She smiled ruefully. "Your teeth are good. Someone has taken good care of you."

The two women continued their tasks in companionable silence. The scent of honeysuckle wafted from the hedge. Kari tried to imagine the reaction of this gentle, kind woman if she attempted to explain what had happened to her. But even if she could make Martha grasp anything, what would be the point? Martha could not help her return to her world.

Martha looked up shyly. "But," she said hesitantly, "Thomas says—" Again, a pause.

"Yes?" Kari prompted her. "What does Thomas say?" She was already beginning to mistrust the source of such pronouncements.

Martha would not meet her eye. "He says that there are some women who—who are well looked after from childhood to make them—I cannot say it."

"To make them inmates of a high-class brothel, or some man's mistress?" Kari filled in the words Martha was too ashamed to utter. *How is Thomas so knowledgeable?*

Martha nodded miserably.

"Do *you* think that is where I came from?"

Martha shook her head. "I cannot say," she whispered.

"It is not true." Kari left her seat and knelt by her benefactor. Martha's fingers lay still, no longer plying the needle. Kari gently touched her hand.

"I swear to you, Martha, that although you may never know the whole story, I am no such person as your husband describes. After your kindness, I would not lie to you. Do you believe me?"

"Yes, yes I do." Martha embraced her as she knelt.

Tears came to Kari's eyes, and she hid her face in Martha's comfortable lap. Had she had to travel through time to find the maternal love she had craved as a child? Her own mother had been given to dramatic outbursts of affection between operatic assignments, but her little daughter had never known the ongoing security of a steady love. Martha's comforting hand touched her hair.

"Martha," she whispered, "what is happening to me? I'm afraid, Martha, so deathly afraid. What is to become of me?"

For the first time she'd said aloud the question that filled her with dread. She had fought hard for her own identity. The variations of her very name symbolized the struggle. For her father, the teenaged Rina had patiently looked up quotations and proofread endless speeches. Her mother had insisted on her full name and so Karina had turned pages of music and been ready with sprays and silk scarves for the precious throat. At eighteen, Kari had opted for her own version of her name, chosen the real world of medicine, and shut out the make-believe of the medieval tomes and the operatic stage.

Years ago she'd thrown down her decision to be a doctor like a challenge, proving to herself and to her parents that the family flair for the dramatic had not entirely passed her by. For the next few years she'd worked like a slave and systematically reached her goals, but her genes refused to let her settle for the expected. Looking for another challenge, she'd prepared for the move from overcrowded, noisy, dirty London to an overcrowded, noisy, dirty refugee camp or war zone. She made a face. Well done, Kari, old girl. No illusions from the start. Just the gritty reality of life in the last years of the twentieth century.

Except that this wasn't the twentieth century. It was the sixteenth.

Before Mistress Godwin could say anything more in reply, footsteps crunched on the gravel path, and the man called Aidan went by, touching his forelock respectfully. She caught sight of him everywhere. He had already proved to be a tireless worker, and as the heavy days of summer dragged by, the estate was in a fever of haste to cut and stack the hay before rain.

Martha and Kari followed him with their eyes.

"Another mystery," sighed Martha. "But an honest man, I do believe. The Bible is correct, my dear. Sometimes we entertain angels unawares."

Second Report: DAY TWO
Operative: Aidan Torrance

Location: Godwin House

Date: July 11, 1600

Report: Have located target and dog. They are established in the house. The woman does not recognize me, as I hoped. She has an undefined status – not truly a guest, nor yet a servant. Difficult to get to her, since I most definitely am a servant. She eats with the family and not in the kitchen, where the gossip is certainly more entertaining. Tell Monika I'm getting some good language bites. Had high hopes of first contact when she was alone in the dairy, but she fled for some reason. Will analyze later. Am acquiring data mass, if nothing else. Martha is a fine woman, according to her servants, but Thomas is another kettle of fish, as Joan the cook says. Has an eye for the women and stays overlong in London. Have caught him leering at Kari (that is her name), when he thinks himself unobserved.

Interesting to watch her coping with problems and trying to figure out what is happening. Tempting to make it a case study. Don't worry, Tan, just joking. I know the deadline, goodfriend. Complex calcs of course for two bodies, three time slots. There is no need to take the dog from here. He'll survive on his own. Am double-checking settings. Can't risk mistakes or losing one of us en route. I don't feel like ferreting around other centuries to find misplaced persons. Shall try to talk to her tomorrow. Out.

* * * * *

Kari fell gradually into the rhythm of the household. Her watch lay hidden, pinned to the inside of her gown, and she soon forgot it was there. The predictable day followed the course of the sun, with work beginning at dawn while the weather held. She ate bread and fruit at breakfast and tried to pick up a cup of foaming milk, rather than sip the small beer or cider. A little cold meat or cheese was considered a treat.

Until her hands healed, she was given leave to be idle, and she soon knew every corner of the house and yards. She felt eyes on her wherever she wandered and had not been able to return unobserved to the spot where Martha found her. Whether the location was significant or not, she wanted to see it again, examine every detail, but not under the eye of Malcolm or Dick.

To cheer her spirits and hold on to what remnants of reality she had, she sang as she moved around the house and gardens. She gave them Bizet and Wagner and watched their eyes grow round with wonder at the complex melodies. Of course, her voice was not a patch on her mother's but she could hold a tune, and God knows she knew the words. She threw in *Greensleeves*, of course, just to reassure them. They liked that. She thought she might try Schubert next.

She soon found the door to a corner room. Thick glass filled the small panes in the mullioned windows, and the filtered light fell upon the rich colors of leather book covers. Thomas, although apparently disdaining learning for members of his family, wished to be considered a gentleman and had acquired an extensive library of a few score books.

She was glad to find a possible retreat. If she were to slip into the corner room early in the day, maybe she could remain undisturbed until dinner. It would be a refuge from the ever-present eyes of Malcolm and the new man, Aidan. He saluted her respectfully enough when she met him on the pathways and in the yard, but his presence bothered her. There was something about him. Come to that, there was something about everyone — she was clinging by her fingertips to what she knew to be true, so why worry about an Elizabethan journeyman, who happened to be handsome, personable and polite? Better to worry about the other male chauvinists all around her.

The library looked onto the knot garden where aromatic bushes perfumed the air. A carpet, rather than the usual rushes, covered the stone floor, and a heavy, dark oak desk stood in the center of the room. Books lined the walls to the ceiling and there was even a little set of steps to reach up to the higher shelves. Thomas had done himself proud.

After breakfast, she slipped through the doorway and surveyed the collection of books, running her hands over the thick leather. At her fingertips lay medical texts, herbalist remedies, accounts from explorers, translations of the classics and medieval tales. Her father would be in ecstasy. There was the trap! She must not think of her family. They would be worried sick about her. She had to keep a clear mind, not consider what might be happening in that parallel universe four hundred years in the future.

What she needed right now was information on this place. A book about the surrounding area might help her find out more of where she was and where she could go. She checked the gold lettering of the titles and at last selected a heavy, leather-bound volume. Cradling it in both arms, she carried it to the window seat and settled with her back against the sidewall and her feet on the seat.

The casement window was ajar, and she pushed it wider to let in the cool breeze, unlaced her bodice and hitched up her skirts. She looked speculatively at the woolen stockings. Probably better not to risk it. She left them on, despite the heat. Washing was accomplished more or less successfully with bowls of cold water, but she was beginning to think she would kill for a shower with warm water and scented soap.

She propped the book nicely on her lap and wriggled her shoulders against the wall to settle comfortably. It was good to see the printed page again, even in the Elizabethan script. She was starved for reading material, never having truly realized how important a part of her life were books, newspapers and magazines.

She began to browse through the parchment pages, striving to fix her attention on the cramped and blotchy print. But, like a persistent insect, the unsolved problem of where she was and why buzzed in the back of her mind, preventing her concentration.

Sighing, she put her head back against the wall. She must get back. *Think, Kari, think*. She'd done nothing, had found no clue, had no plan for escape. Escape? To where? There was no answer. She closed her eyes and let her thoughts drift. She dozed in the warmth, lulled by the hum of bees and the rustling of the leaves outside the window.

Suddenly, the heavy book slipped beneath her arm and she woke with a start to find herself staring up into a pair of gray eyes that met hers and traveled down to the swell of her breasts beneath the open laces, then back to her face. Brazenly, Aidan leaned in the window 'til his face hovered inches from hers. God, he was a handsome man. She clutched blindly at the book and, as if mesmerized, watched the face that hung above her. She could feel his faint breath, could have traced the shape of his mouth with her fingertips. They were suspended in time.

"Be careful, mistress," Aidan whispered, "or your book will fall."

He raised his hand to brush a tendril of hair from her cheek in a gentle, caressing gesture, and his fingers left a tingling trail. He had discarded his jerkin, and his shirt lay open to the waist. Leaning yet closer, he braced himself on one arm against the warm stone of the wall, revealing a smooth, brown chest and muscles glowing with moisture from the heat and his exertions in the fields. He smelled deliciously of mown grass and male muskiness.

Her professional veneer and her natural caution were gone. Her traitorous body responded to the sexual appeal of the man and instinctively moved a little toward him. An answering flicker of desire sparked in his eyes, and he bent closer still. What the hell was she doing? Abruptly, she pulled her shoulders from the wall and sat up. The movement forced him to step back, and the spell shattered. He straightened and touched his cap.

"I feared your book would fall through the window."

"Thank you, Aidan." His lips twitched at the mention of his name. She gathered the heavy tome to her breast, holding it like a shield between them.

"Is there anything you need, mistress?"

Only a trip through time, thank you, she thought, but shook her head without speaking.

He continued. "Forgive me, but I noticed that you like to walk." His voice was even and well modulated, unlike the slurred accents of the other servants. "It is not good for a lady to walk alone. If you wish, I would be happy to accompany you when my work is done."

She intended to refuse. The words were ready. She opened her mouth to say, "I think not—"

But then he smiled at her, an open smile of one caring person to another. She craved companionship, friendship. What did she have to lose? What did she care if it was proper or not to accept such an offer from a servant? Martha walked with Malcolm. Maybe away from the house she could find out something that would give her a clue how to get back home. There were TV shows where people found 'portals' that sent them to another dimension. Why not a rip in time that would help her? She smiled back at him and discreetly adjusted the top of her dress. She cast her eyes down demurely. She should try to stay in character and not frighten him away with her twentieth-century ways.

"Thank you, Aidan," she said. "You are kind. I would like that."

He touched his forelock again and was gone. Kari stared after him, wondering what his agenda was. Could she trust him? She would be careful not to go out of calling distance from the house. Shakespeare had written some pretty raunchy sonnets about young lovers in the fields, and there were other manuscripts in Dad's collection that never made the anthologies. What was the average Elizabethan peasant's expectation of a walk in the woods? Simple talk? A kiss? A tumble on the grass? Her cheeks grew hot at the thought. She could muster a pretty good scream if she had to.

Her fingers drifted to her throat where his eyes had lingered, and she hesitated a moment before finishing the lacing of her bodice and covering her legs with her skirt. Why was it so easy to imagine his hands following his eyes, and why did her nerve ends tingle as if in expectation of a caress when he was close?

Impatiently, she tucked her hair back under the cap. It must be nearly time for the main meal of the day, which the family ate in early afternoon. She bent forward to pull the window shut and froze as she met the gaze of another observer. How long had he been there? Had he stayed silent, watching her rearrange her dress?

He was a tall man and excessively thin, clad entirely in black. The coat swung to his hips, and a white stock around his neck reminded Kari of a priest's collar. His brown hair was cut to shoulder-length and he was clean-shaven. His spindly legs were not flattered by long black hose and finished in overlarge, buckled shoes. A broad-brimmed, black hat completed his attire. Despite the heat of the day, he looked dry and cold. He bowed slightly from the waist. "Good day, mistress."

"Good day, sir."

"You must be the poor waif that Mistress Godwin has set herself to help."

He took Kari's silence for agreement and extended a hand. "Josiah Small," he said with a bow. "Priest of this parish, and come to take dinner with Master and Mistress Godwin."

Kari tried to pull her hand back from his. His palm reminded her unpleasantly of reptile skin. His grip tightened, trapping her fingers.

"I have heard speak of you," he said. "If you are in need of counsel, you may call upon me." His eyes stayed on her breast. "A homeless girl might well have need of protection in this wicked world." He gave a bloodless smile.

"I am hardly a girl, sir, and the Godwins are very kind." *And unless you are a magician, you cannot give me the help I need*, she added in her mind.

"Ah, yes, indeed. But Thomas cannot keep you forever under his roof, can he? We shall have to see how we can provide for you." With another little bow, he turned on his heel and sidled away. A small cloud passed over the sun. That was surely the reason for the cold shiver that went down her spine.

Chapter Seven

෨

The family sat down for dinner soon after the church bells rang for noon prayers. Because of the guest, Kari was not invited to eat with them. Not hard to guess who would be the subject of conversation at that table. She was beginning to chafe against the assumption in this society that the male of the species would dispose the fate of the females. Somewhat out of temper, she went to the kitchen to take her meal with the servants.

To add to her discomfort, Aidan Torrance sat enthroned among the other hands. He'd fastened his shirt and put on his sleeveless jerkin. His face and hair were beaded with moisture from the water pump, where he had stopped to cool his sun-warmed skin. He stood inches taller and broader than the other men, and he glowed with strength and vitality.

Young Margaret bustled to pour his cider and then hovered at his side, anxious for his attention. Even cantankerous Joan had a greeting and a smile for him. He acknowledged the service with a nod and a word of thanks. He caught Kari's eye and gave a little shrug as if to say, "What can I do?"

Kari kept her face impassive as she took her place at the far end of the long trestle table, trying her best to keep her eyes away from him, and forced herself to pay attention to the chattering around her. The subject was not reassuring.

Malcolm sat halfway down the long table, next to the doddering Dick. The boy's greasy hair fell in unkempt hanks over his shoulders. His pale eyes peered out from beneath his knobbly forehead, darting shifty glances around him. He served himself greedily from the bowl, snatching a hunk of bread as it passed, "What you been doin' this mornin', Dick? Tell the 'oomenfolk." He gave the old man a nudge.

Dick picked up the opening on cue. "I been seein' to the master's sword," he cackled.

"Garn wi' such nonsense," responded Malcolm, playing straight man. "Such a sword will not be well-served by the likes o' you." He grinned in triumph at the peals of laughter.

"Nor by Mistress Godwin, so I hear," broke in Margaret, not to be outdone. "He be planning another trip to London soon."

"If 'e needs to leave 'ome," Malcolm said. He nudged the girl slyly. His eyes swiveled toward Kari. "There's temptin' pickin's right on 'is doorstep, yer might say."

Joan cuffed him. "Quiet, boy."

Dick cackled, unwilling to end the joke. "Aye, a fine swordsman is our squire. Many's the tale I could tell, weren't there delicate ears a-listenin'." The pious look sat ill on his gnarled face, but earned another gale of laughter with nudges and winks.

Kari understood only too well the reference to the sword as a phallic symbol. Some men seemed to relish the idea of their weapon as an extension of their maleness, whether they wielded a stone club, a rapier or a gun. She caught Aidan's eye across the table and felt the flush in her cheeks. The others were having too good a time to stop.

"The Master be a lusty man and good luck to 'im iffen the good Lord allow 'im health and strength. 'Tis that Josiah Small gives me shivers." Margaret shuddered.

"Aye, they do say that young Sarah Miller as keeps 'ouse fer 'im…"

"Hush you…" Joan glanced quickly at Kari and Aidan, both listening in intent silence. Louder, she said, "Let us be thankful for our blessings in this God-fearing house. Eat your meat, all of you, and watch your tongues."

The servants applied themselves to their food, and the meal finished without more revelations.

Kari sipped her cider. She was slowly gathering her wits together again after the shock of what had happened to her. At first, she had told herself she was in a dream, that she would wake in a hospital and find that she'd been hurt by the man in the park. Gradually, the detail and complexity of what surrounded her made dreaming an unlikely explanation. Like a character in one of her mother's operas or her father's medieval romances, she was out of phase with the world. And now she sensed the real and present dangers in this house. The bruise on her forehead was fading, as were her hopes of suddenly waking up back in the twentieth century. If she was to leave, she must find her own way.

As a start, she had to escape from the confines of the house and locate the spot where Martha and Malcolm had found her. Maybe there would be a clue to be discovered. From there, she might be able to figure out what to do to return home.

She caught Aidan's eye again as he looked at her. This time, she nodded and smiled. It would be good to have his companionship—and possibly his protection. The others could think what they liked, she would allow him to walk with her tonight. There was no need for him to know why.

Third report: DAY THREE

Operative: Aidan Torrance

Location: Same

Date: July 12, 1600

Report: Some progress. Keep watch for transportation from close to original location. Hope to be there at dusk with girl and possibly the dog. Contamination risk growing. Out.

* * * * *

The perfect summer weather still held, and the servants and farmhands toiled in the fields and gardens from dawn to dusk. Succulent berries grew abundantly in the hedgerows, and young vegetables sprouted tender and sweet. The time was passing as if in a dream. Kari's head was weary from so many hours spent trying to comprehend, to find some kind of rational explanation. She drifted through the empty rooms of the Godwin house, observant of the routines and rituals, savoring the peace and simplicity of the ordered life.

Yet underneath, she sensed the undercurrents, the dark flows and eddies hidden by the smooth surface. She knew of the pain and dirt of medieval society, had brushed against the slimy side of Elizabethan life in her encounters with Thomas and Josiah Small. She needed a chance, any kind of a clue of how to leave this world.

Aidan waited for her that evening when the church bells rang for evensong, and the sun sank lower behind the wooded slopes around the farm. She stepped through the low doorway with Ben and saw him first.

He lolled on a low stone wall, one bent leg resting on the ledge, the other foot touching the ground. His torso was backlit against the fading sun, the light shone through the sleeves of his rough shirt. The lacings were tied almost to the neck, concealing the powerful chest and shapely shoulders that Kari remembered only too well. She drew closer to him. He had washed at the pump again, and beads of water trembled on his hair and his throat. His skin would be smooth and cool to the touch. The beard had grown a little, it was soft-looking and black as his hair. It framed the curve of his mouth, drawing her eyes to the sensuous lips.

He remained in a reverie, unaware of her approach, and she stepped softly on the grass. He was a handsome man by any standards. The clothing suited him. She could see him as a pirate, a swashbuckler traveling the known world, lording it over a mutinous crew.

What did she know of pirates, or of Elizabethan men for that matter, apart from schoolgirl stories and some three days in the house of a petty tyrant? She resolutely pushed away the fantasies — she had to keep her mind on getting information, finding out how she came to be here, reversing the process.

As she stood, collecting her thoughts, Aidan became aware of her and turned suddenly.

He stood to give a small bow. "Mistress Kari." The smile lifted the corner of the mobile mouth. "May I walk a little with you?"

* * * * *

They took the paved walk, passing through the small knot garden at the side of the house, and reached the beaten path that led to the fields. Aidan's head was bare, and his dark hair shone in the light of the westering sun. He strode as vigorously as if he had taken his ease all day rather than pitching hay since sunrise. Ben trotted beside them, sniffing assiduously at all the dog-enticing smells along the way. The air was warm, and a faint breeze caressed their faces, wafting the scents of honeysuckle and night-scented stock that perfumed the air. The birds and crickets gradually fell silent, and the croak of a toad began to fill the evening.

Neither Kari nor Aidan spoke until they reached the gate.

"Shall we walk to the wood?" His voice was low.

She remembered the dark shapes and rustling sounds of trees near the spot where she had been found. Maybe she had been near the wood. "If you wish."

Ben cavorted around them as they rustled through the long grass. Seeds clung to the hem of Kari's long skirt and speckled Aidan's stockings. The air hung sweet and heavy with the scent of growing plants. The bells had fallen silent, and the only sounds were a distant voice from the house and the whisper of their own movements.

Kari stopped and turned to look at the house. She was growing used to seeing everything as if in a fine mist without her lenses. The building lay long and low, the two stories nestled into a natural hollow so that the upper windows were now at eye level as Kari and Aidan stood on the slope. The setting sun bathed the stone of the walls in a golden light, and climbing roses garlanded the doors and windows. The sleek green of ivy climbed up to the chimney pots. A thin spiral of smoke rose lazily in the still air from above the kitchen.

"A penny for your thoughts."

"It doesn't look real. It's like a—" She caught herself in time. How could she say "film set" to this Tudor peasant, however unusual he might appear? "—dream," she finished.

"Real enough to those who live and work there."

She glanced at him. That answer was more sophisticated than she had expected. "I suppose. How did you come there?"

He was close behind her and, without replying, placed both hands on her shoulders. God, he did expect to have some fun? She stiffened and the light pressure lifted at once. He moved away a step. She allowed her muscles to relax, in relief.

"Sit," he said, "the grass is dry. We can talk a while." He placed a slight emphasis on the word "talk", almost as if he had read her mind. Was he sensitive as well as handsome and strong?

They were still within hailing distance of the house. "Just for a moment," she said.

They sank down on the bed of long grass, passing into a warm, green, private world, screened from prying eyes by the gently waving stalks. The scent of baked earth and wild flowers drifted around them where their feet had crushed the grasses, perfuming the air with fresh aromas as if from clean, sun-dried linen.

The nodding heads of the wild oats brushed softly against Kari's neck, like the caress of a tender lover. Shadows from the leaves flickered across Aidan's face in the rays of the dying sun. The noises of the busy day were all subdued now. A muffled shout wafted across the fields, and a dog barked. Ben pricked his ears and then subsided, his head on his paws.

Idly, Kari began to pick a selection of the buttercups and daisies that studded the grass. She thrust her fingers down to the base of the cool stems, plucking them low down near the leaves clustered close to the ground. Mechanically, she began to make a chain, piercing the stalks with her nail and threading the next flower through.

Aidan sprawled full-length, propped on one elbow, his face close to her busy hands. One warm hand closed over hers.

"What are you doing?"

She laughed a little. "Surely you know? It's just habit—just a daisy and buttercup chain. We used to see who could make the longest."

"We?"

"My cousins and I on grandfather's farm. All kids do it."

"Kids?"

God, she'd done it again! "Children. Surely you did too?"

He hesitated, seemed disconcerted. "Of course. But that was for little girls."

She glanced at him. "Really? I suppose so."

In reality, she was paying scant attention to the meaning of her words, for his hand was still on hers, and he was moving it gently, caressing her fingers. So much for just talking! But she liked it, it felt wonderful. Her skin prickled deliciously where his fingertips lingered. She turned to him. The same tingling coursed through her again, just as on the window seat in the library.

Something warm washed over her. He gazed at her as if trying to memorize every detail. The realization both chilled and thrilled her. What thoughts were going through his mind when he stared at her?

He was so close the warmth of him seeped through her clothing and into her bones. She could feel the heat from his body, see his chest move with his regular breathing. Her pulse quickened.

His dropped his eyes to follow the line of his fingers on her arm. Her fingers trembled to touch his cheek, trace the soft, tempting line of his lips. He was one of the sexiest men she had met in her own century or this one. He raised his eyes and caught her gaze. His grin made her blush.

"Your eyes are like the sea on a summer's day. Never have I seen such a shade of blue, my lady." He picked up a strand of her hair and rubbed it between his fingers. "Hair as red and glorious as the setting sun."

She trembled at his words.

Did she have to travel through time in order to find a man who could turn her knees to water by the merest glance? What would he say if he knew she was from four hundred years in the future, and that for her he was long dead? That all the inhabitants she was learning to know were gone and forgotten? Old Dick was as dead for her as was Anne's unborn child. She pushed the thought away, refusing to let the little worm of panic take hold.

But the thought gave her a chill and killed any wild idea she might have had to confide in him.

He brushed an exploring ant from her bare arm, sending tremors through her once more.

"Tell me, Master Torrance," she said quickly, pulling her hand from his grasp, "what brings you here?"

He plucked a long stem of grass and drew it slowly up her arm to her shoulder. She quivered.

"You could say I'm a traveler."

The grass moved up to her throat.

She swallowed. "Please don't," she whispered and closed her eyes.

"You make a lovely picture against the leaves. The sun is catching your hair, turning it into a halo of fire—"

"Stop!" This was not helping. She scrambled to her feet. "I must go back."

"I can't say I'm sorry just for admiring you." He stood up swiftly beside her, reaching out to clasp her forearms.

At that second, Ben let out a bark and then a yelp as something thudded into his side. Kari and Aidan whirled to find Malcolm watching them intently from a few feet away, poised to throw another stone. He chuckled spitefully.

"Got 'im, dirty beast." His pale eyes fastened on Kari, standing half in Aidan's embrace. "She be willin', Master Aidan. We seen 'er when she come 'ere wi'out a decent clout to 'er body. Pretty sight it were too. You can 'ave 'er fer sure and tell us tomorrer. Just be sure the Master agrees, though. Maybe our turn next." With another spurt of malicious laughter, he turned away and jogged back to the house.

Kari's cheeks flamed with shame and anger. So Aidan was the same as the others! He had been conniving at an easy seduction of the halfwit, and the story would be the entertainment at the noon meal. Too bad for him that slimy Malcolm had given the game away. The anger surged, fed by the precarious state of her overburdened emotions. She flung away from Aidan's restraining arms.

"Keep away from me," she hissed. "I am sick and tired of the men here. Whatever you think, Master Torrance, I am not fair game for any of you. Forget any ideas you and the others have cooked up."

Tears blurred her eyes as she turned in a swirl of skirts and sped back down the hill to the farm.

Chapter Eight

ಐ

The small world of the Godwin household gradually grew familiar and strangely comfortable. Kari struggled to hold on to the truth, that this world was in reality long gone. She found out that Anne was sixteen, married not quite a year. The girl had been raised to anticipate marriage and motherhood and was sleekly satisfied with her fulfillment of society's expectations.

Anne followed Kari whenever she could after her reduced household tasks were done. She was restless, bored with her enforced inactivity and the wait for her husband's return. One morning she found Kari sitting in the knot garden.

"Come," she said, "Let me show you my treasures."

She grasped Kari's hand and tugged her toward a side door of the house. She pushed it open, revealing a small storeroom full of oaken chests. The smell of cedar and camphor was strong in the air.

Anne moved toward a carved chest pushed against the wall and slipped the latch. She knelt to raise the heavy lid.

"Help me, Kari," she puffed.

Together, the two young women lifted the ornate cover and swung it back on its massive hinges. Anne sat back on her heels and stretched out a hand to the folded linen inside. Gently, she took one corner and raised it high.

"See," she said.

Kari caught her breath. In the chest was a shimmering, glittering mass of green and gold, sparkling with embroidered threads and gleaming with pearls. Despite herself, she gasped.

Anne was pulling herself to her feet and digging into the rich mound. She stood, a waterfall of green silk falling around her. Kari hastened to help her free the last yards from the chest and shook out the skirts of the opulent gown. Anne held it against her, her small face incongruous against the richness. She thrust her laden arms toward Kari.

"Put it on."

"No," Kari said. "I —"

"Please, Kari, I want to see it again." Anne threw the gown to one side and rummaged again in the depths of the chest. She reappeared with horsehair bolsters and strings of pearls, which she passed to Kari, not waiting to see what became of them before diving back for more. The last to appear was a white ruff, studded with gold thread and held stiff with bone.

"Now," declared Anne, "that's everything. Put it on."

She began tugging at Kari's bodice. Laughing, caught up with Anne's enthusiasm, Kari stood still while the underpinnings of the Elizabethan costume were fastened around her. They both giggled as Anne tried unsuccessfully to put her arms 'round Kari to fit the hip pads.

"Let me," Kari said, taking the stuffed canvas pieces.

Anne stood back, massaging her abdomen. "To think," she said, "that I wore that gown not two summers ago, and now I am so large I cannot even come close to you."

Kari picked up the dress and lifted the weight over her head. "I'm going to need some help here," she gasped. "Hold it up if you can."

For a moment she was lost in the dark, heavy folds as she fought to find the openings and fresh air. Thankfully she emerged, flushed and disheveled, and the gown settled around her, tight in the waist and sleeves, loose and flowing in the skirts. The ruff sprang from her shoulders, framing her head. At last everything was on, and Kari stood in a court gown, shimmering in the dimness of the room.

"This is no good," said Anne impatiently. "I can see nothing of you here. Come outside." Once again, she grasped Kari's hand and pulled her out into the sunshine of the garden.

There she fussed around, straightening the skirts, adjusting the sleeves, twitching the ruff, piling Kari's untidy hair on her head and twisting it with ropes of pearls.

All the time, she chattered, "I wore this when I went to London. It was there that I met Jonathan. We were betrothed, of course, before then—when I was ten and he fourteen. I was so happy to meet him and to know that I could love him." She cast down her eyes demurely and blushed. "I shall wear it again, he says, when I am recovered."

She stood back and clapped her hands in childish glee. "There, you are beautiful!"

Kari stood in the sunlight in the stiff, heavy clothing, weighted down with gold thread and beads. The huge pearl drops swung from her ears as she moved her head. She could feel the other strands, holding her hair from her neck.

The bolsters clung to her hips, keeping the wide skirts away from her body. They swung like a bell when she took a step. She felt top-heavy, unbalanced. The constricting bodice enclosed her like a corset, and her arms splayed awkwardly in the tight sleeves.

"This is a joyful gown," Anne was saying. "I know!" she exclaimed, "I shall lend it to you for your wedding!"

"For my what?"

"Why, Kari, you must wed. In your state, what else can you hope for? I shall ask my father to find a husband for you!"

My God, this well-meaning child could trap her forever in this time warp!

"Show me, Kari," Anne called out, oblivious of the effect of her words. "Show me how it looks when you walk."

Not to disappoint the girl in her simple pleasure, Kari took a step forward. It was not quite as bad as she expected. Her head held high against the white ruff, she imagined she was the queen, come to visit her loyal subjects. She tossed her head proudly and strode forward with confidence—and came face-to-face with Aidan Torrance.

It was apparent that he was as taken aback as she, but he recovered fast. In an elegant gesture, he swept his cap from his head and bowed low.

"Milady," he murmured.

Kari felt like pursuing the charade. After the fiasco of the walk in the fields, she would emphasize the distance between her and this farm worker. She gave a gracious acknowledgment, nodding with a slight bend of the knee. Probably even that was too much in the rigid class system of this time.

"Sir," she said.

Anne pealed with delighted laughter. "Perfect, perfect," she said. "Is she not a perfect court lady, sir?"

"She is indeed." Aidan's gray eyes were fixed on her face, and Kari felt the warmth flood through her from more than the weight of the clothes.

Anne was enjoying the game. "Take her hand, Master Torrance," she commanded.

Obediently, Aidan reached for Kari's hand and held it high between them.

Anne looked at them critically. "'Tis a pity Master Torrance has no finery," she said, "but no matter. We can imagine the doublet and hose." She scooted with a fast, ungainly walk to the end of the path and turned to face them.

"Now," she said imperiously, "this is your wedding. Walk toward me as if you were leading the marriage procession."

Kari tried to pull her hand away, but Aidan's fingers curled tighter around hers. He looked at her with that devastating small grin. Her pulse raced and she felt the rapid beat in her neck above the lace of the ruff. Aidan fixed his eyes on the same spot. Could he see how this was affecting her?

"Come, madam," he said softly. "Let us obey our master's daughter." *He was enjoying this!*

Gently, he pulled her beside him and led her along the path.

In front of Anne, they stood like awkward children in a play. Kari was acutely conscious of the heavy clothes, the clasp of Aidan's fingers, the closeness of his body. The charade was opening her mind to possibilities that she had no wish to entertain.

She tried no to think about the way he felt next to her, the way the muscles in his arms and thighs rippled when he moved even a little, the way her heart danced a tattoo when he looked at her from the corner of his eye with that glint of male awareness, of wanting…

The heat of desire wafted through her.

If she were forced to stay in this time, could she be married off to a man like this? How much power did Thomas have in such things? Would she have any choice? Would she choose Aidan? Would he want her? The thoughts scurried through her head like scattering mice, each more disturbing than the one before.

Aidan was the first to move, releasing Kari's limp hand. He bowed to Anne. "Have I your leave, mistress?" he said.

Anne had obviously run out of ideas. "Yes," she said. "You may depart, sir."

With a final bow, he stepped back to continue on the path 'round the house.

"Hmm," said Anne. "Do you like him, Kari?"

"I do not know him."

"I think he likes you, I saw his eyes when he looked…"

"What nonsense, Anne. Now, help me out of these things before I suffocate or melt."

But she had seen the expression in his eyes too. She would have to be careful to keep her mind on what she had to do and not get enmeshed in territory that could do her no good. She had thought that he might help her in her escape. Now she suspected he represented more of a danger than a source of assistance.

* * * * *

Jonathan Howard returned to the Godwin house. Kari was glad to see that he bore out the promise of his letter and cared deeply for his young wife. Anne and he were now seldom seen out of their chamber, and the household tolerated their idleness in the last days of waiting for the child.

Kari watched Martha Godwin bustle around her house from cockcrow to sundown. Few goods came from the city over the rutted and narrow roads, and Thomas expected his household to be self-supporting. Outbuildings provided a malthouse for ale, a bakehouse and a cheese press. These and the gardens for herbs, fruits and vegetables, as well as the services for clothing and linen, were Martha's undisputed domain. She concocted medicines, perfumes and sweet waters in the still room, directed the cooks in sifting flour and preparing for baking in the bolting room, oversaw the preparation of food in the vast kitchen.

As the fruits and vegetables grew and ripened, she began an endless round of cooking, distilling, preserving and pickling to prepare for the barren months of winter. Seeds were carefully harvested and set aside for future planting, honeycombs were extracted from the hives and stored, festoons of onions and garlic hung from the rafters to dry. Amongst this activity she did not neglect her works of charity and bore practical gifts of food and drink, as well as her cheerful encouragement, to the sick and downhearted. The next morning after the wedding charade, finding Kari lurking in the kitchen, she issued an invitation to accompany her on her rounds.

Kari stood by as Martha carefully poured her salves and medicines into precious bottles and jars.

"What is that for?" she asked curiously as a strange-smelling paste was ladled into a tiny container.

"Rhubarb and senna," Martha replied and chuckled at Kari's expression. "'Tis physic for a young lad that ails. I shall leave it at his mother's door. 'Twill purify his blood and set him up strong." Martha loved to talk and she continued with no prompting, "He and his father are Morris men and will be dancing to bring in the harvest. He'll need his force."

Kari had seen pictures of the grotesquely garbed Morris dancers with their ribbons and bells, a true remnant of pagan England, as was the maypole. She brought her attention back to Martha's potions.

"Will you teach me some of your remedies?" she asked.

Martha flushed with pleasure. "To be sure I will, my dear. Let me show you…"

The lesson continued as she finished packing her basket, they collected light shawls for their shoulders and set off to make their way down the dusty lane.

Chapter Nine

ℬ

In the village, a handful of houses huddled around a piece of common land containing a smelly pond and a pillory with stocks. To Kari's relief, no miscreant occupied either of these, although rotting eggshells and a collection of small stones bore witness to fairly recent use. At one end of the green, an alehouse advertised its presence with a creaking sign and a decrepit bench outside. It hunkered down, dark and slovenly, staring sullenly at the stone church across the pond.

Kari ducked after Martha into a small wooden house whose tattered thatch hung like unkempt eyebrows over the low door. Inside, she strained to make out the details of the single room. There was not much to see. One window of polished horn hung ajar, but did a poor job of admitting light and air or of letting out the smoke from a miserable open fire. Several dirty children huddled together, crouched around a pot set on the smouldering wood, waiting without hope for something.

A movement in the rough bed in one corner drew her eye to a man stretched on his back, fully dressed and snoring drunkenly. Beside him lay a woman with tangled hair whose dull eyes lit with a spark of recognition as they entered. Kari noted the unnaturally bright color that flared high on the sunken cheeks. The stench of stale food, unwashed bodies and dirt pervaded the air. Two steps inside the door and Kari's stomach heaved. Her lungs longed for the fresh breeze outside.

She breathed shallowly through her mouth as she took in the appalling scene, but Martha sailed into the room, seeming unperturbed by the squalor, and set her basket on a rickety table.

"Good day, Agnes," she said cheerfully, "and how are you today? See, I have brought a friend to help me today. Together we shall set things to rights."

Without more ado, she bustled to set out food and drink and motioned the cringing children to draw near. With fearful glances at the sleeping man, they approached and fell upon the bread, cheese and milk as if they had not eaten for days. A fit of coughing shook the woman's frail shoulders, and she struggled to sit in the filthy bed.

Kari moved forward and began to help. Between them, she and Martha fetched water from the pump, swept the cottage and washed the children as best they could, although the ingrained grime of years could not easily be removed. Kari gently handled the scrawny limbs and checked teeth and eyes, pushing back the tousled hair to peer into ears. They all needed vitamins, shots of antibiotics, and above all a bath and good food. Anger began to build inside her at the hopeless situation.

Gentle Martha produced her herbal remedies — mint for Susannah's colic, parsley for Edward's toothache and St. John's Wort for Agnes' aching joints. A container held a licorice infusion for the cough. Kari helped Agnes to wash her face and brush her hair and then supported her as she sipped weakly at the liquid.

The sick woman sank back with a feeble smile. "Thank'ee mistress," she whispered. "'Tis better already."

The man snored on. Kari could find no words and smiled her response, then worked in helpless silence beside her benefactor. She didn't feel like singing.

As they were preparing to leave, the door opened and a girl of thirteen or fourteen paused on the threshold. The high cheekbones and mop of hair identified her as yet another child of this unfortunate family. She was poorly dressed in a tattered gown that nevertheless looked as if it had been washed not too long before. Her hands were rough and red and her feet were thrust into the usual wooden shoes.

"Sarah," greeted Martha. "'Tis well you are come before we leave."

Sarah bobbed a curtsey and produced a bundle from under her shawl. Half-chewed meat bones and cabbage stumps fell out, and another child swept them up and into the blackened pot before other little hands could seize them.

"Reverend Small ate meat last night," said Sarah tonelessly.

"So I see," rejoined Martha. "How goes it with you, my dear?"

The child's thin face flushed, and she looked aside. "I am well."

The shawl fell away. Kari's eyes were drawn to the bruises ringing the thin wrists and repeated on the upper arms. She stepped closer. Like a fearful little animal, the girl spun toward her, covering herself with the thin wrap.

"Please," Kari put out a hand. "Have you been hurt?"

Sarah's mouth turned down in a grimace. "No more than usual. Meat nights are long ones."

Horrified, Kari turned questioning eyes to Martha, but the older woman busied herself with her basket and would not meet her look. "Come, Kari, we must leave these good people." She raised her voice. "Tell that goodman of yours that I have work for him if he wishes it, Agnes." She gathered her basket and hastened from the cottage.

Kari sped after her, catching her in a few steps. "Why is this allowed?" she demanded, stopping Martha with a hand on her arm. The older woman was obliged to halt.

"How can these poor people live this way?" Kari continued. She rubbed her hands over her face. Tears were close. "What can be done?"

"You ask difficult questions. Reverend Small says it is so because the Lord wills it so. Thomas has no need of the cottage for now and is truly not aware of Edward Miller's state. I see no need to trouble him with—"

Kari interrupted. "You mean that filthy hovel belongs to you?"

Martha nodded in reply. "To the estate. It is an act of charity to—"

"Charity!" Kari spat the word. "Look, that woman is sick. She needs decent food and housing, the children—"

"Oh aye, the children." Martha turned to continue the path. "Agnes would die if the children were taken away, and who would have them? The almshouses are full. They are too young and weak to work. Sarah is fed and clothed at the manse and can bring some food."

"But at what price?" Kari whispered. She saw again the bruises on the girl's frail arms and the dead light in her young eyes. "Oh God, what is going on here?"

"Edward's family has been tied to the estate for many years. He grew to be a fine young man. So proud he spoke of his first boy." Martha smiled in reminiscence. "But after the fall, he could no longer work as a groom. He carves wooden pegs and other things to earn a little money, but he lacks tools. Then Agnes got the sweating sickness—" She shook her head sadly.

Tuberculosis, Kari thought. There was no cure, and Martha might as well continue with her folk remedies if they brought some relief. Martha had said that the man had fallen.

"What happened to Edward?" Kari asked.

"He fell from the big oak near the house. Thomas says he was drunk and it was his own fault, but Edward did not love the ale then. Thomas insisted he climb to clear the rooks' nests. Young Edward was so fearful of the great height, and Dick gave him a draft of ale for courage." Martha sighed and shook her head. "Poor Ned Miller broke both his legs and now scarce can drag himself with two sticks. He has much pain and seeks to quell it with the ale. I do what I can," she finished in a low voice.

"I know you do, Martha." Kari marched on with new determination, a plan of action fermenting in her mind.

A few minutes later, they met Aidan Torrance, sauntering along the path a short way from the house. He saluted them politely as they passed and fell in step behind. Kari sensed his presence at her back, knew that his eyes were on her. It seemed that scarce an hour passed but that he hovered somewhere near. He always had a good reason to be there, was always polite, fading away as soon as the greeting was given, only to reappear a short while later. Well, she had other things to think of than a hired man, whatever he looked like and whatever effect he had on her. She needed to decide how and when to confront Thomas Godwin.

"Martha," she said, "may I take bread and cheese with me? I need to walk." The idea of a picnic, of eating outside for pleasure, would be totally incomprehensible to Martha, so she did not offer any further explanation.

Martha looked relieved to be spared any more discussion of the Miller family and nodded her agreement.

* * * * *

Aidan watched Kari and Martha enter the house. Would he never get her alone for long enough to set up the FLIP? If he could do it right, her memories of the Godwins and the entire household would seem like a dream and she would pick up her life back in the twentieth century as if nothing had happened. At worst, she would have a slight headache, a buzz behind her eyes that would soon fade.

Of course, she would have no memory of him, either. The walk in the fields, the scene in the library and the mock wedding might never have taken place. Why did that bother him, fill him with a sense of loss? He would not forget her. How could he lose the memory of her flaming hair outlined against the setting sun, or of the swell of her breasts above the bodice of that sumptuous, ridiculous gown?

Around the farm and in the servants' hall he had too often made the mistake of allowing her to capture his gaze. Every time the impact seized him by the throat and held him prisoner. He couldn't breathe. He couldn't move, he couldn't think.

While Anne tormented him with her playacting, Kari had laid her hand on his arm and he'd flinched as if burned, but couldn't pull away. She'd drawn a deep breath, taunting him with her magnificent beasts. He'd tried to hide his reactions, swallowing hard, forcing his gaze back to her flushed cheeks and her deep blue eyes.

He knew he had to send her away, but he was so drawn, so imprisoned by this woman that the necessity cut him to the heart.

What would happen if he were to defy all reason and take her back to his time?

Impossible.

His lips twisted wryly. He could hear Howard and Tanice now, could hear his own lame explanations to the Identity Office.

What about staying here? Or could they both live in her world?

Equally unthinkable.

Impatiently, he brought his mind back to the present problem. His thoughts were out of character. He well knew that the chaos theory made outcomes impossible to predict. As with water pouring from a spout, or air flowing over a flying wing, tiny differences become amplified. Straight linearity is artificial.

Every moment here in the past was fraught with risk. He had to think himself back into the urgency he had felt when he first discovered what had happened to Kari and Ben. Enough of these impractical ideas that were filling his head with disturbing frequency. They were just one more result of neglecting all his mental routines.

As he stood, lost in thought, the door to the house opened again. A tall man appeared, his flaming beard and flowing hair vivid against his drab clothing. Aidan tensed and quickly stepped behind a thick bush. How likely would it be that Reed

Flynn would have a sixteenth-century double who frequented the Godwin family? There was no need to ask the computer to calculate the probability. If Aidan Torrance could time travel, even if illegally, so could Reed Flynn. Tanice's installation wasn't the only one in the universe.

He had to move, the situation was growing more and more dangerous. Reed was ruthless, a pirate of the first order. Aidan knew if worst came to worst, he would have to tell Kari the truth. But all his training told him this was a last resort. He must do his best to complete his mission as planned.

His mind busy with the implications of this sighting, he watched the burly man leave the farm and take the road to the village. Kari had not reappeared on this side of the farm, and his immediate task was to locate her. He had to know where she was at any given moment.

Anne appeared on the path, bearing a basket of vegetables. She smiled at Aidan and made to pass by.

"Pardon, mistress." Aidan removed his cap. "Do you know where Mistress Kari went?"

Anne smiled knowingly. "Why, Master Torrance, I do believe I am right," she said enigmatically. "Of course I know. She has gone with her dog to the pool in the woods. She left not a quarter hour since."

* * * * *

In the early afternoon, Kari and Ben strode freely up the hill behind the house. Kari carried a linen cloth in which she had wrapped bread and cheese and apples. She would find an abundance of water where she was headed. Two pairs of eyes watched her departure.

The grove of oaks grew where the stream widened into a pool. Their massive branches cast a cool shade over the thick grass, but left the water in sunlight.

As far as Kari could tell, no one came to this place, and the chances of anyone finding her here were slim. This was largely unproductive moorland, surrounded by the vast forest of Middlesex. She would need to keep an eye for the homeless, shiftless men who were said to roam the area, but Ben would be even more alert than she. The cattle grazed far away and the path to the village wound in the opposite direction.

When they arrived at the pond, she and Ben lay for a moment in the shade to recover from their hike. The air hung still and hot, although a faint line of clouds was forming on the horizon. Ben nuzzled close. She stroked his bony head and ran her hand down his flanks. He had lost weight, and his ribs stood out under his matted coat. In this century where they both now lived, dogs in the countryside were not regarded as pets. Ben did not earn his keep by hunting or guarding the flocks and so was rarely remembered. Kari gave him most of the cheese and bit into an apple.

She thought of how she could sweep away the dirt and poverty that she had only glimpsed, and use her twentieth-century medical knowledge and skills. The lack of simple care for those in need revolted her. She still desperately wanted to find her way back home and return to the world she knew, but the thought was growing in her mind that she could perhaps leave things better than she had found them.

She wanted to shake Thomas Godwin from his complacency and make him responsible for looking after his people properly.

She wanted to expose the rottenness in Josiah Small's heart and make him regret exploiting and abusing that poor half-starved waif in his house.

This was more clear-cut than other cases she had seen. She recalled poor, cringing little Tommy from the East End of her modern London—a little boy who clung to his neglectful parents because they were all he had. But even that had turned out well. Although she'd had to use all her powers of persuasion and coercion to make the parents listen to reason, she had been persistent. At last, the mother had taken Kari's advice and attended some classes. Even the husband had eventually gone along. They were proud of their success in becoming better parents, and Tommy was blooming. She had never backed down from protecting the weak and innocent and wouldn't start now.

That settled, she returned to compiling her wish list. She could add that she wanted to run her hands over the smooth, broad shoulders of Aidan Torrance. She frowned. The man continued to intrude, contributing yet another disturbing factor to the fantasy she was living. There was no basis for a relationship, they had nothing in common, and they were centuries apart. Why, then, did she persist in imagining him slipping her clothes from her body and holding her close, kissing and caressing her eager flesh? Yet she had too much to contend with to deal with the sensual pull of such a man.

The memory of his touch on her arm the evening before was enough to make her quiver again. She recalled the look in his eyes as he gazed at her in the court gown and the warmth that had spread through her from a burning core within her body. In her heart she knew that she had misjudged him, accusing him of complicity with Malcolm. She had been overwrought. Never had he given any hint of descending to the level of humor of Malcolm and Dick. Nor did she want to believe that he was other than what he appeared — honest, courteous and true. She closed her eyes, resisting the fantasy.

She also wanted to feel clean again. She wanted to wash the grime of that cottage from her, wanted to submerge her limbs in cool, clear water. She stood and threw the apple core from her. Ben cocked one eye and ear. She stretched her arms above her head.

"A swim," she said to the dog, and started to undress. "That's what I came for."

Chapter Ten

శ

Aidan Torrance tensed in his hiding place deeper in the oak grove. He'd told himself he should follow her, hoping for an opportune moment to sweep Kari back to her time. But first he had to win back her confidence after the fiasco with Malcolm. She had to stand still with him while he operated the responder. It was not hard to understand her reaction as taut nerves were strained to their limit. He was finding it difficult enough to adapt to this time and he had come prepared, knew why he was there and how to get back. How much more difficult it must be for her.

At the start she had been an irritant in his program, a bug to be removed as Tanice would eliminate an annoying anomaly in her database. He hadn't expected to sympathize with her in her plight. She had become real to him, he found himself worrying about her welfare, calculating her chances. Worse was the treacherous thought tugging at the back of his mind, whispering that when he beamed her back he would not see her again — ever.

Suddenly, the gulf of the centuries yawned before him, cold and empty. He shuddered. He could not allow these strange feelings for her to grow. He set his mind to the exercise of visualizing the circumstances of their return through time and their ultimate, inevitable separation. Only by living it through many times in his head, imprinting the patterning, would he be able to act coolly and decisively when the time came. At that moment, Kari began to prepare for her swim.

With a tightening in his groin, he watched her joyfully peel off the dress and stockings. She moved down to the water's edge, barefoot, but still wearing her petticoat. The linen swung from her shoulders, allowing the light to outline the slender shape of her body. He feasted his eyes on the contour of firm breasts, the fluid line of hip and leg. Her loose hair hung thick and red to her shoulders. She held it away from her face and tentatively dipped one toe into the stream.

Aidan caught his breath. The scene was frozen in time. Like painters through the ages, he watched the scene, enthralled, waiting for the girl to disrobe, to reveal all the sweet curves and shadowy hollows before slipping into the welcoming water as into the arms of a lover. The graceful pale shape of her, leaning toward the water with one foot poised, shone against the dark green shadows of the trees. The whole of nature held its breath with him.

Delicately, she advanced the other foot, breaking the spell. Birds twittered again, insects resumed their hum, and the stream chattered once more, splashing joyfully into the wider pool. In one liquid movement, Kari swept the remaining garment over her head, threw it on the grass, and, in a blur of white and red, plunged into the water.

Aidan moved quietly out of the trees to sit down next to the dog, which lifted its massive head in enquiring welcome.

"Hallo, Ben," he whispered, gently rubbing the dog's ears.

The wolfhound snuffled gently in response. Maybe a person could get used to an animal, he thought, although it still seemed foolish and unnatural to talk to a dog.

Ben meant a lot to Kari, so he would make the effort. Besides, the dog might have to be returned with her, the woman and the animal seemed well nigh inseparable. At least he should be on good terms with it. The animal seemed obedient from what he had observed. All things considered, he still preferred the option of leaving it behind lest the beast did anything to ruin the return, like he had on Hampstead Heath.

He turned his gaze back to Kari, watching while she dived and wallowed, splashing the cool water over her arms and breasts. He remembered how she had looked in the knot garden, clad in Anne's court gown. He recalled how the stiff bodice was cut low and pushed up the mounds of her breasts so that they swelled deliciously above the embroidered curve over the lacing.

The ruff had accentuated the proud set of her shoulders and the graceful column of her neck, free of the fountain of hair that Anne had piled into a heap on her head. The exaggeratedly wide skirt had swung around her from the narrow waist, hiding the shapely hips and thighs. Her red hair and creamy skin reminded him of the portraits of Queen Elizabeth that he'd discovered in the archives. She even had similar dark eyes, although they were blue. He was willing to bet that Kari's were ten times more appealing than the imperious stare of the Virgin Queen.

And then there was Anne's absurd, childish game of the mock wedding. What did the girl suspect of his feelings for Kari? Was she just assuming a mutual attraction between a man and a woman, or had she guessed how much Kari affected him? This had to come to an end.

At last Kari had her fill and surfaced. Her head shone wet and smooth like a water animal. She reminded him of the playful seals and otters in the SeaWorld hologram. Shedding water, she waded swiftly from the pool, stooping to scoop up her petticoat from the ground. Wrapping it around her like a sarong, she smoothed the droplets of water from her face and pushed her hair back out of her eyes. He sat still, waiting.

She gathered the shift in a bunch between her breasts, then glanced up and caught sight of him under the tree. A jolt of fear crossed her face. She couldn't see him clearly. It hadn't been hard to figure out that her distance vision was poor. But that left her vulnerable. He couldn't do that to her. Quickly, he waved and stood up.

"What the hell do you think you're doing here?" She stood poised, ready for flight.

He had to say something before he messed up again. "No, stay." He kept his voice low.

She froze, took a cautious step backward, then looked around wildly and pulled the thin petticoat closer around her. It barely covered her from breast to hip.

"It's me, Aidan."

"And who else have you brought with you for the show this time?"

His heart went out to her for the bravado. She never gave in. "I'm alone. I thought maybe you didn't recognize me."

"What are you doing here?"

"You're a lovely sight without your clothes. As beautiful as in Anne's gown. So beautiful that I have to forgive you."

"You have to what?" Her head snapped up, eyes flashing. "What a bloody outrageous statement!" She looked entrancing in that silly piece of cloth. He stepped forward. She took a small step back. The water lapped around her ankles.

Of course what he said would offend her. What was the matter with him? He wasn't thinking straight. "Sorry," he said. "That was a poor choice of words. I meant you didn't give me much chance to defend myself yesterday evening on our walk. I hadn't planned that, it was all Malcolm's idea. Unsavory creature."

She nodded. He knew she had to agree. He'd been warned by his first mistake and would only utter positives from now on. He had to make her feel comfortable. He dared another step.

"You know I'm not like him." One more small step. "Vicious, petty."

Kari's skittish glance watched his advancing feet. He kept his voice soothing, mesmerizing.

"Do you trust me after all?" He ventured closer. He'd succeeded in closing the distance until he could see the water droplets falling one by one from her hair to her shoulders.

"As much as I dare trust anyone."

"That's not much, is it?"

"No."

"It will have to do for now." His gaze lingered on her. "I'm tempted to join you," he said. "Such a perfect day, such a pretty setting." His gesture took in the surrounding woods.

He longed to tell her the truth, to stop living a lie. Not for the first time, it was on the tip of his tongue to say, "Kari, you won't believe this, but I'm the reason you're here. My return to the future went wrong and—"

All his training fought against his instincts. All was not yet lost, he just needed more time to steel himself. He took two more steps toward her, unlacing his jerkin.

He hoped she wouldn't take fright. There was more at stake here than winning her confidence. He certainly needed to get her to trust him so he could take her back, but now he wanted more. It was suddenly important that she accept him for himself. He wanted that more than he'd wanted anything for a long time. He hated the idea of deceiving her now, of carrying out his plan to beam her and leave her. What did this woman mean to him? She believed him to be a sixteenth-century farm laborer. That was what she was supposed to think. What good would it do either of them if he told her the truth? But he ached to tell her about himself, about his mission, explain why he had deceived her...

He waited patiently for her response. She seemed to take an eternity to decide. At last she smiled at him. "Turn your back," she said playfully.

With a burst of pure happiness that took him by surprise, he obeyed. From behind him, the water splashed gently. He imagined her slipping out of the cloth covering and back into the pool until only her head and shoulders could be seen. He moistened his lips. His heart was beating fast, as fast as when he had just snatched one of his paintings. What he intended to do was dangerous, a journey into unknown territory. Sure, he had known sexual arousal—there had been great partners in the past. But this was different. He cared about Kari. He wanted to know her thoughts, her hopes, and her desires. He wanted to please her, see her smile at him, and win her approval. Dared he even think it? He wanted to make the Contract with her…

Kari waited a moment before giving him the signal to turn around. She crouched shoulder-deep in the water, looking at his back. There he was, as if conjured up by her fantasy. Her earlier thoughts flooded back, filling her with warmth again. Something stronger than common sense and convention battled to rule her mind. This was a crazy situation, nothing was real, nothing was usual. She came from the twentieth century, an independent woman. Mixed bathing was the norm, skinny-dipping certainly not unheard of. She liked him. Her instincts told her to trust him. Why not?

"You can turn around now," she called from deep in the pool.

He turned to her and pulled the shirt over his head. Their eyes locked and for a long moment her gaze lingered on him. He loosened the fastenings on his hose, ready to slip them down his legs. The muscles of his shoulders rippled as he moved. Fine, dark hairs on his chest led her eye to the edge of his trunk hose and disappeared, only to be revealed again as he pushed down the clinging garments over his hips and thighs. The mystery of his body appeared inch by inch and the pile of rough clothing grew.

He was beautifully put together, sculpted, powerful, perfect! A wave of pure desire washed over her, primitive and wild, scattering all her firm intentions to the four winds. Her gaze was riveted on him, drinking in every taut line, every hard plane. Sunlight played on smooth flesh, gilding the curve of his muscles and turning the shaded hollows to bronze. Kari had seen many a naked male form in her work, but none had ever affected her like this. Her heart pounded in her ears. The tiny ripples undulating through the water teased and touched and brought to tingling life every nerve ending, every secret place in her body.

In a fluid, swift movement he plunged beneath the surface and emerged close to her. The water churned and then calmed.

The eddies swirled, revealing tantalizing glimpses of the dim outline of all the fascinating parts of him, now shrouded from view by the water. She gazed her fill at what she could see. He stood less than an arm's length away and she need only put out a hand to touch him. He did not move, still as a statue of a Greek god.

The space between them vibrated, charged with energy, ready to explode with the slightest movement of their bodies toward each other. The water lapped softly now above her breasts and around his waist. Every detail shone crystal-clear — the weeds floating on the stream's surface, the water beading his chest and shoulders, a strangely shaped tattoo on his upper arms.

One corner of his mouth lifted in a quizzical smile, questioning her, waiting for an answer. Her gaze drank in the line of his lips, the curve of his chin. She smiled back, tentatively. The world did not come to an end.

"Kari," he said. Never had she liked the sound of her name so much.

"Yes?" she whispered, afraid to disturb the fragile balance of the universe.

"Do you want me to come closer?"

She nodded. He strode through the water, making it gurgle and bubble around them again. The tiny wavelets lapped at her shoulders. She put out her hands to welcome him. Lightly, he touched her fingertips, barely making connection, and a tremor raced down her spine. Gently he grasped her hand, slowly drawing her to him. For a long moment, they gazed into each other's eyes, savoring the feel of their hands, tingling with the anticipation of what might come. Even their breathing seemed to be in harmony. A bird trilled from the trees, and the pure notes hung in the air.

As if this were a cue, Aidan released her hand, his eyes still fixed on her face.

"Put your arms around me."

She hesitated for a moment, then raised her arms to rest on his shoulders.

His arms encircled her, holding her fast in sweet possession, and suddenly his mouth was on hers in a long, probing kiss that pierced deep into her soul. His strong lips exerted a gentle pressure, and she gladly opened to him, sighing as he drew her closer. His tongue found hers, gently at first, as if testing her willingness, then stronger, and with a rising passion. Her body responded and her breathing quickened as she met his kiss, and gave in to her need. Her hand caressed his side, her fingertips catching the beating of his heart.

Lost in the sensuous wonders that assailed her, she returned the pressure of his mouth, sliding her hands over him, exploring, smoothing, seeking. The hard muscles of his chest pressed against her breasts.

He moved back and she moaned softly, clutching him more closely to her. He gently pushed her hand away to allow his fingers to mold each breast in turn, gently cupping and tenderly touching the erect nipples.

At last he lifted his mouth, and she lay on his chest struggling to regain her breath while he stroked her wet head. Water droplets clung to her lashes, veiling the scene with myriad points of light. He tipped her chin up with gentle fingers and kissed her again, but slowly and tenderly, barely brushing her open mouth. Her lips throbbed, as if swollen and bruised. A deep ache pulsed inside her and she moved her hips against him, feeling his response. A soft groan came from deep in his throat.

Immediately his hands returned to her breasts and his mouth claimed hers. With a murmur of acquiescence in her throat, she allowed him his way.

When he let her go at last she exhaled a long breath, but she couldn't seem to get enough oxygen. Her legs were weak, her heart pounded.

"I love the beauty of your face." He stroked her cheek. "Soft and pretty as a flower." He touched her lips with his. "Tender, tempting mouth."

She stared at him, her power of thought and reason seemingly gone. What was happening?

He looked at her as if he would never look away. And she loved it. She wanted the moment to go on forever.

Wanted the feel of his flesh. She wanted the full length of his nakedness against hers.

She wanted to feel his sleek muscles rubbing against her softness. She wanted his hot mouth to suckle at her breasts until she melted in his arms.

A cold breeze fluttered across the water, and she shivered. A cloud passed across the sun, cutting the warmth and light. The bird called again, a note of warning this time, and the branches of the trees thrashed in response to a sudden gust of wind.

Suddenly, dark shadows lay over them and the spell broke, shattering the idyllic scene. Kari looked at the now silent, dark trees and the sullen water, and in her mind she saw modern London superimposed on this pleasant spot.

A road should run close by. There should be the smell of diesel fumes and the throb of traffic. A half-mile away people should be bustling through the streets, waiting for a lumbering double-decker bus, queuing for fish and chips. Children should be playing outside the solid houses, built many years after this pond ran dry. Her head swam with the conflicting images. Which were real? What was she doing, making love with this man? She did not belong here. An icy hand clutched her heart, overwhelming her with the pain of desperation. Her energy must go to finding out how to leave this place, certainly not to encouraging a useless, pointless passion. She stepped back, releasing herself from his arms, pushing on his shoulders.

"This is impossible," she gasped.

"Your body says that's not true." He smoothed back the wet hair from her face. His fingers were tender and strong, and she wanted them to be there forever so that she could cling to him and trust him with her dreadful secret.

"You don't know, Aidan. You don't know anything about me, about who I am." Suddenly, the feeling of hopelessness and despair washed over her again. Tears pricked behind her eyes and she blinked, but not before she caught the flicker of pain that passed across his face.

The expressive features became a mask. "Can you bring yourself to trust me?" he said.

She gazed at him seriously. "Where are you from? Who are you? Why should I trust you? Are you cut off from everything you know like I am?"

He took her hand. "Meet me tonight Kari, at the gate. Maybe we can find out about each other. I can help you."

She glanced at him sharply. "Why do you think I need your help?"

He smiled. "Come, Kari. We all know the story of how you were found, and how everyone decided you were demented. You need help."

His eyes were expressionless now. A shutter had come down between them. It was as if the passionate man of a few minutes before had never existed. She longed to bring that man back but dared not even try.

She shivered. "I'm cold. Turn your back again while I get dressed."

He opened his mouth to protest, but then shrugged and turned his back while Kari waded to shore, dried herself and slipped on her dress.

As they prepared to leave, Kari saw the bushes sway close by the path. Aidan had insisted he'd come alone, and she believed him. He was not the same caliber as Malcolm. At the thought of Malcolm watching them, she shivered again. But the movement among the leaves was most likely the wind that was blowing stronger and colder now.

Chapter Eleven

જી

Kari strode back to the Godwin farm, her pulse still racing. She was learning something new about herself every day. Never would she have believed that she would respond so wantonly to a man's sexual appeal. She, Kari Lunne, whose only amorous encounter had been with a fumbling medical student, whose name she could barely recall and whose features had faded entirely from her memory. They had both had more of a callow interest in the basic physical experience than in exploring their emotions. Both had exited from the relationship with relief, a little more knowledgeable, but otherwise untouched.

Since then, there had been no time and little inclination. Sure, several young doctors had been willing to bestow their favors like the god-like creatures most of them imagined themselves to be. She had been grabbed and fumbled by her share of patients, but had built up an icy veneer that soon discouraged any further advances.

The voyage through time had unsettled her in every way possible. She must remember that she was first and foremost a doctor. She was committed to relieving suffering and there was blatant suffering right before her eyes. The situation here demanded action. That was a problem she was confident she could handle.

The afternoon shadows reached all across the small garden, darkening the main door of the house. It stood ajar as usual, allowing the last of the light to fall across the smooth stones of the entry. As she passed under the lintel, Kari hesitated, trying to distinguish the sound that had drawn her attention, even through her distraction. There! She had it, a soft female voice came keening from the sitting room. A man answered, speaking low and haltingly. Anne and Jonathan?

Kari paused, one hand on the newel post of the stairs. Something in the tone of the voices set her instincts on alert. Before she could decide whether to proceed or to go back to the sitting room, Martha appeared through the doorway that led to the kitchens. Her cap sat awry on her hair, a loose covering was flung over her gown and she bore a goblet in her hands. Something was amiss.

"Kari," whispered Martha, scarcely pausing on her way to the sitting room door, "it's Anne. It may be her time. She has the pains."

Kari swung down from the staircase and followed Martha into the room. Anne lay on the wooden settle, propped up with cushions and clinging to Jonathan's hand.

"Now come," said Martha as she bustled in. "Jonathan must leave and we must get you to a bed."

Anne clung all the more strongly to her husband. Jonathan stared wild-eyed at the preparations around him. Kari recognized the expectant father look. She stepped forward.

"Just let me look." She pushed past Jonathan and bent her ear toward the girl's swollen belly. No stethoscope, no medications, no fetal monitor.

"Remember what I told you, Anne," she said gently. "Breathe slow and deep. Don't tense up." She gently detached Anne's hand from Jonathan's arm and pushed him away the distance of a couple of paces.

"Let me see what's happening," she said with what she hoped was a reassuring smile.

The check was fast.

"Well," she said in a cheery voice. She straightened up and pulled the coverlet back into place. "I think you're going to have to wait a little longer. The waters haven't broken and there are no more contractions, although the head is nice and low. I'll need to scrub my hands and get you upstairs before I can examine you properly..." Her voice trailed off as she became conscious of three pairs of eyes staring at her in astonishment. "I—I have some knowledge," she said weakly.

Martha nodded. "I know not who you are," she whispered, "but my girl trusts you, and so do I. More than the sot of a midwife from the village." Briskly she turned to the young couple. "Jonathan, help your wife to your chamber. Kari, there is water on the fire. Tell Joan to give you what you need."

They had soon settled Anne and reassured her with their presence and their comforting words. Kari spent some time explaining what to expect and coaching her for what would inevitably be a natural childbirth.

Anne lay back on her pillows, still pale. She grasped Kari's fingers and clung to her.

"Kari," she whispered, "don't leave me."

Kari smoothed back the fair hair with her free hand. "Don't worry, Anne. You need some rest, I won't be far away."

"No!" Anne's blue eyes were fixed on Kari's face. She moistened her lips. "I mean, stay with us until my time comes. I do not know who you are, Kari. I do not know how you came here. But I know that you can help me." A tear slowly made its way down her cheek, and Kari gently brushed it away.

"Many die in childbirth," Anne continued in a whisper. "I love Jonathan." She swallowed. "And he loves me." She looked fondly at her husband, and Jonathan gave her hand an answering squeeze. "I want more time together," she continued. "I do not wish to leave him without a wife and the babe without a mother." She struggled to sit up. "And I want my baby to live. Don't go—wherever you must go—before my time has come. I know that you strain to leave here, Kari. I know that this is not your world. Say that you will stay to help me."

Anne had no idea how momentous this promise was, or how much she was asking of her friend. Kari hesitated. Martha's eyes were fixed on her, waiting for her answer. Anne needed her both physically and emotionally. How could she refuse the mute appeal in Jonathan's gaze? Kari pushed her gently back against the pillows. "I'll stay," she said. "Don't worry. I'll do my best for you and the baby."

She set a complaining Margaret to scrubbing out the bedchamber and made sure of an ample supply of clean linen. She would do what she could to offset the dangers of infection.

When all was done, she turned her thoughts to her earlier decision. Thomas had returned and sat taking his ease in the sitting room before supper. Kari had no wish to delay. She smoothed her hair, fixed her cap more securely, took a deep breath and knocked on the door. He looked up in surprise as she entered without waiting for his bidding.

* * * * *

As a favor to Joan the cook, Aidan had offered to move wood, stacking it near the kitchen door so that the fires could be stoked and kept in, and hot water would be on hand for Anne, according to Kari's instructions.

The mechanical movement, lifting, carrying, adding to the pile, left his mind free to grapple with the problem of Kari. The situation grew more complicated by the day. It had seemed a straightforward proposition—beam in, isolate her, take the dog if he had to, punch in the coordinates, beam out. She would be deposited back in her own time, he would beam on to his world, and Tanice would fudge the records, so Howard would never find out. Kari would have had no time to leave a mark on history. But now he barely clung to the tatters of his careful objectivity.

He'd always taken refuge in his research, his studies, accounting to no one for his actions. He'd been the rebel, tolerated because he usually brought off his stunts and had never publicly embarrassed his superiors. It was starting to look as if things might change.

What this woman thought and felt mattered to him more than anything else had mattered since the news about the death of his parents. Her smooth skin and thick hair of that wonderful color haunted his thoughts. He could easily lose himself in the pools of her eyes, and the memory of her slim body set his heart to pounding. He recalled the dark mole above her left breast, and the way he had rested his lips on it before they traveled down to the nipple.

Maybe part of his feelings came from the waning anti-pheromones in his system, but that meant he was functioning like a normal male for once. The dry, paternalistic, programmed world that waited for him eight hundred years away loomed like a threat. Most of the pleasure of his trips through time had come from the knowledge that he was beating the system. Now thoughts of this woman had staked a place in his brain, usurping the important concerns in his life that should be commanding his attention.

Instead of acting decisively to solve the problem she had caused and get her out of his life, he sought her out, he watched over her, he worried about her. He knew the spite that Malcolm harbored, he sensed the lascivious intentions of Thomas, and he overheard the thoughtless gossip of the servants.

There was also Reed Flynn. His old adversary was probably not interested in causing mischief to Kari. Aidan himself was the likely target. Flynn would like nothing better than to strand him here. If that happened, all those wonderful paintings that he had plotted and dared to collect would be unprotected, ripe for hijacking by Flynn.

His head told him he must remove Kari — but how could he do that without losing her for all time? His heart no longer accepted the idea of dropping her back into the twentieth century like a mislaid package. He thumped a large piece of wood down on the pile. He would tell her who he was and be damned to Tanice's orders. He would enlist her cooperation and they would plan together, if she wanted him as much as he wanted her.

He bent again to his task. How much damned wood did they need anyway? He'd thought Kari's world primitive, but this place was unbelievable. He'd have something to tell Monika — if he ever got back home!

He grasped another bundle of sticks in his arms. He knew nothing about Kari's life. Exactly what awaited Kari in late twentieth-century London? Was she married, did she have a lover? She wore no rings, but that was no proof. He stopped his work and straightened his back. He had to believe that there was no man in her life — her response to him in the pool had been spontaneous and free. Another man would be easy to fight; it was the twin enemies of time and space that daunted him.

The sound of raised voices from the open window of the sitting room broke into his train of thought. He drew closer to listen. It had to be Kari and Thomas. What was she doing? Didn't she have enough sense to lie low?

"The children," Kari was saying, "think at least of the children!"

"The whelps are no concern of mine," thundered Thomas.

"But children are the future. Look, if the next generation is healthy and productive, then all of society — "

"Arrant nonsense! My concern is for *my* child and her children. Better the ailing spawn of ne'er-do-wells should die young and free us from the burden of the poorhouse. God knows, I give my share to that institution."

Aidan could imagine Thomas standing with one hand arrogantly on his hip. His small cloak would be thrust back over his jutting elbow, and his foot would be tapping in anger. His jaw would be thrust forward pugnaciously, and his color would be rising. If the situation were not so fraught with danger for Kari, it would be amusing to see the pompous ass get some of his own medicine.

Inside, Kari tried another tack.

"Look, Master Godwin, I know you are a charitable man. Your wife and your daughter love and respect you. For their sake, you should see that those around them are strong and free from disease." Aidan could sense the effort it took her to lower her voice and to speak calmly. Apparently encouraged by Thomas's silence, she continued, "The girl Sarah is badly mistreated —"

Her voice dropped, and Aidan lost a few words. He could guess what she was saying. He shook his head. *Bad move, Kari.*

"If you would permit the house to be repaired and make an allowance for food and clothing —"

"NO!" The roar shook the windowpane. "I'll brook no insults to me, or to a man of the cloth! Out of my sight, demented creature! There's no more of my hard-earned gold for wastrels and spendthrifts. Let Edward Miller take his face out of the ale pot and fend for his own family. They have abused too much of my charity. The pack shall leave my cottage tomorrow." His voice rose and fell as he paced. "I'll hear no more of this talk, or it will be the worse for you! A taste of the almshouse and the ducking stool might not come amiss to halt that impudent tongue. Be gone!"

"But, sir —"

Aidan started at the sound of a stinging blow, followed by a cry of pain. But Kari would still have the last word.

"You may strike me like the bully you are, but I know how Edward Miller was injured. That is what lies on your conscience. Responsibility, compensation, social justice — think of that, Master bloody Godwin!"

Another roar of rage shook the glass again, and moments later Kari ran through the door of the house, one hand clasped to her reddened cheek, her eyes blurred with tears from the sting of the blow. Aidan looked up from where he was bending to place a log. Their eyes met as she swung to face him. Something in his posture as he gazed at her from where he crouched, or the play of the shadows in the late afternoon across his face must have triggered a memory. Kari stopped dead and slowly pointed at him, bewilderment and fear written across her face.

"You," she said, "it was you in the park. You're the one who sent me here!"

Fourth report: DAY FOUR

Operator: Aidan Torrance

Location: Godwin House

Date: July 13, midnight

Report: From bad to worse. Must revise all plans to transport her back from here. Can't believe this, Tan, but I caught sight of a man that bears a remarkable resemblance to Reed Flynn. I inquired later in the village, and sure enough that was his name. Can only think he's up to no good. Has he followed me? Has he cooked up some scheme to maroon me here and pick up my collection? Won't be the first time he's tried. I wish you could transmit back to me! To add to the problem of Flynn, Kari has intervened in events and presented her concept of social justice to Thomas Godwin. She angered him so much that he struck her. Now I fear for her safety. If she is shut away, how will I ever beam her back? She ran out of house, saw me and at last, for some reason, recognized me. Was not to be reasoned with. Fear and anger, of course. She blames me for not telling her who I was. Can't blame her. What went wrong with my plan for in and out in a few hours? Have to search out another location before she gives us both away. Something I saw a short while ago has suggested a plan that is beginning to make sense to me, but need to think it through some more. Did a medieval knight feel this foolish? Bet most knights had a more amenable damsel. Having trouble hanging on. What bothers me? Atmosphere, primitive emotions, open air, simplicity of the life? Am discovering deep instincts. Aidan the caveman! Transmitting all my thoughts now. Just be discreet, Tanice. If we don't make it back, I want someone to know why! Out.

Chapter Twelve

∞

Kari tossed and turned all night. A sense of loathing ate away at her. The soft feathers of the bed were detestable. They clumped together in uncomfortable lumps and the ends of the shafts poked through the ticking like tiny barbs. The smells were nauseating. The unhealthy odors of the barnyard mingled with the cloying fragrances of the flowers. She never expected to long for the hospital's pungent pine smells of chemical disinfectants.

Her head throbbed, her eyes were red and sore from the tears she had shed, every muscle ached with tension. This odious existence had trapped her. This was no fantasy, no dream. How could she exist in this environment? With trembling fingers, she explored the tender bruise forming on her cheek.

During the night, the thin line of cloud became a heavy overcast, and the rain began. It pounded on the cobbles of the yard, poured from the eaves and drove countless small creatures deeper into the thatch. The burrowing noises, the twittering, and the occasional clap of thunder kept her constantly on the verge of sleep, never allowing her to slip into oblivion and rest. All night, the storm rolled around the hills surrounding the Thames Valley. The rest of the house had been strangely quiet the whole evening, as if sitting frozen in the eye of the storm.

Most of all she loathed Aidan Torrance, the liar, the manipulator, the cavalier disposer of other people's lives.

"Liar, liar!" she had shouted yesterday evening when he tried to explain. "Don't talk to me of accidents! Look what you've done to me! Look what you've done to my life! All this time you've known who I am and why I'm here. And you could have done something about it! How dare you!"

She'd sunk down onto the stone wall, sobbing with rage and frustration. All the emotions of the last few days poured out. She was vaguely aware of gentle hands that lifted her, and strong arms that held her as she wept. Voices murmured, and then she smelled the familiar scent of her room. Someone laid her carefully on the bed and smoothed the covers over her. She remembered a deep voice whispering her name, and her furious rejection, telling him to go away, to never come near her again.

The first light of morning found her curled in the hollows of her bed, exhausted from weeping and from lack of sleep, but with a clearer head. Her outburst had been unlike her, rarely did she lose control of her feelings. Only her mother, Elena, did that in her family and those storms provided enough emotional upheaval for them all.

In her mind, she stepped carefully around the revelation that Aidan Torrance was the man in the park. Her thoughts circled the knowledge warily at first, testing it, trying to assimilate it. She had to think logically.

She heard her father's voice. "Take it step by step, Rina," he would say. "Think it through carefully." How he had always striven to counteract the impetuous genes from her mother!

The rain had washed all the warmth from the air and she shivered in the cool morning breeze, pulling the woolen covers more snugly over her.

She forced her thoughts into some semblance of order. If Aidan had sent her here and then come back for her as she thought he'd said, then he must have the ability to take her home. She had wasted a whole night. The stress of finding herself in Elizabethan England, and the raw emotions evoked by Aidan himself, must have contributed to her mental shutdown. She would find him and talk to him. He must have a plan. She would use him to get out of here! They could wait for the baby — the child should come anytime now — and then she and Ben would go back!

But where was he from? Thinking of him as a sixteenth-century peasant had been bad enough. What did "come back" mean? Where had he gone when she was catapulted into the past? What people, what world had the technology to allow time travel? Was he even human?

All the episodes of Star Trek that she had seen during endless night hours on call at the hospital flickered through her mind. The bizarre shapes and faces of the imaginary alien worlds paraded before her eyes against the whitewashed walls of the room.

At least he looked human—devastatingly so, in fact. Look at what had happened at the pool. If that wasn't a human reaction, she didn't know what was. So she had to believe that he was a man, that he shared the feelings and emotions of any human being. Apart from anything else, the alternative was too mind-boggling to contemplate.

So she would assume he was human, since she had pretty good proof of that, and also believe that he had the power to help her. Whatever century he was from. If he was human, he certainly wasn't from her time. He'd murmured something about sending her back as he was going forward in time. So he came from the future. She felt like the Red Queen in *Alice* who made a point of believing at least two impossible things before breakfast.

She smiled despite herself and sighed with satisfaction at having settled that point.

What a relief to have pushed the fear and anger to the back of her mind! Neither emotion would do her any good. She needed to think clearly, to have a plan—plus the special magic that Aidan Torrance possessed that would take her home.

She rose from the bed and straightened her clothes. She would never be the same person, of course. For the rest of her life, she would harbor these secret memories that she could never reveal to a living soul, except to Aidan. Her hand paused in the act of smoothing her hair. He would be the only one who would understand, who would be able to talk to her about this farm and this family. Would she ever see him again? How could they ever meet again if they each returned to their own time?

Suddenly, a pang of loss stabbed so acutely that she sank back down on the bed.

Her heart told her that she could have loved this man. In her mind's eye, she saw his face with its strong planes. She dwelt on his dark hair, felt it again under her fingers, rippling to the nape of his neck, recalled his luminous gray eyes, fringed with dark lashes. She remembered the texture of his skin under her fingers, the strength of his muscles in arms and thighs. She lived again the pressure of his lips, soft and questing at first, and then hungrily seeking. Her pulse quickened, and she closed her eyes for a moment.

The rain was still falling, an unbroken gray curtain blocking the light. She could have been under water in the gently moving shadows with no sound but the heavy drops rustling on the thatch and streaming down the windows.

Suddenly she needed to move, to breathe fresh air. She must hang on to the thought that she could go home! Her work waited for her and she would say goodbye to Aidan Torrance.

She paused at the thought and then shook her head. She could resist the pull of pure sexuality—the feelings between them had been no more than that. She took a deep breath, finished arranging her hair and went to the door.

It was barred from the outside.

She banged against the thick wood panels with her fist.

At first, she called for help, wanting to believe that the closed door was an accident or a mistake. When no one came in response to her cries, tears of rage and frustration pricked her eyes.

"Let me out, you bastards," she yelled. "You can't do this!"

But of course they could.

* * * * *

Malcolm came for her at noon. She leaped to her feet as she heard the scrabbling at the fastenings on the other side of the door, ready to spring through the opening, down the stairs and away. But the boy reacted too fast for her. He caught her roughly in the doorway and held her against him. His pockmarked face pressed against her cheek and he whispered obscenities in a crooning song.

In revulsion, Kari wrenched her arm from his grasp, pushed herself away and dealt him a stinging blow with the flat of her hand. He yelped and put a hand to his face.

"Bitch! Whore! Witch!" he screamed and grabbed her as she started down the stairs, yanking her arm even harder behind her back to march her down, pulling her mercilessly to her feet as she stumbled.

At the door of the sitting room, he paused again. His free hand fluttered over her face and down her neck to her breast. She twisted away, but that only made him laugh.

"Find the witch mark, they will," he whispered. "I know where 'tis. They'll strip you bare to find it." He tittered.

What the hell was he talking about?

He opened the door, gave her a thrust, and she stumbled into the room, catching hold of a high-backed chair to save herself from falling. She looked up to see both Thomas and Josiah waiting for her. They stood side by side in the center of the chamber, looming threateningly with their backs to the light. She looked around the room that she had seen for the first time when Martha had ushered her into her house.

Because of the cold rain, the servants had lit a fire in the hearth, but the flames flickered weakly, barely able to survive the spitting logs. The light struggled through the thick, yellowed glass in the tiny windowpanes. The downpour outside had begun again and the sheets of water provided a soft, incessant beat against the cobbles of the yard.

A movement and a sound from across the room caught her attention, distracting her from the imposing presence of the two men. They had tied Ben with a short, rough piece of rope to the table leg. He whimpered and strained at the cord at the sight of her. The cruel leash bit into his neck as he struggled to break free. Ben was too trusting. He had thought all these people were his friends and allowed them to do this to him.

Thomas saw her start toward the dog.

"Hold, mistress!" he barked. "Do not touch the familiar."

He thrust out his cane to bar her way. It struck her across the chest as she sprang forward and involuntarily she cried out. Thomas could not hide a satisfied smile.

"Be still," he said, "or both you and the cur will taste my stick." He moistened his lips salaciously.

Josiah stepped forward with a sneer on his pale face. "You are allowed no contact with the filthy beast until we have ascertained the truth," he said in his high-pitched singsong.

He and Thomas lowered themselves with dignity onto high-backed chairs. The two men fixed their gaze on her and placed their hands on the carved chair arms. There was no seat for Kari.

She stood before them and met their eyes defiantly. This had the feel of a tribunal. What right did they have to sit in judgment? She had done nothing wrong.

"Information has been laid," began Josiah, clearing his throat importantly, "by a worthy man lately come to this village. Information that makes this good gentleman," he nodded toward Thomas, "fear for the welfare of his family. What have you to say?"

No one but Aidan could know anything about her. He would surely not betray her. "I have no idea what you are talking about."

She lifted her chin rebelliously, despite the uncomfortable thudding of her heart, matching the haughty look with the frosty tone that had served her well in the past with rambunctious patients.

Josiah stroked his long jaw with pale fingers and Thomas shifted impatiently in his chair. With a glance at him, Josiah continued, "Do you deny that you spend much time with this animal?"

He aimed a foot at Ben and the wolfhound shrank back. She would like to see how sure of themselves they would be if Ben were free. Cowards.

"Of course, I don't deny it. He's my dog."

"What purpose does this dog serve?"

She looked at Ben, at his ill-kempt fur, his pleading eyes. The rope pulled taut around his neck. *Sit down, Ben. Don't hurt yourself for me.* Aloud, she said, "He—he's my friend, my pet. Let him go. There is no need to tie him up, he will obey whatever I say."

"Aha!" he exclaimed in triumph. "So you admit an unnatural relationship with the beast!"

"No, that's ridiculous, absurd—"

"I shall say what is absurd, madam. That evidence seems clear."

"Evidence? Evidence of what? He's a normal dog and I'm a—" It had been on the tip of her tongue to say "I'm a doctor" but she faltered, searching for words they would understand. She was not normal in this world.

"Yes! Even you cannot deny your true nature. Now," he cleared his throat importantly once more. "You claim healing powers."

Kari remained silent. A small knot of fear was forming in her chest.

"Answer!" Thomas bellowed, startling her.

The surge of adrenaline brought a wave of anger. She would not let them intimidate her. Kari squared her shoulders. "I have medical knowledge."

"Pshaw! And how did you come by such 'medical knowledge'?"

"I studied, trained…"

"Trained by the devil! I put it to you, mistress," Josiah leaned forward, a flush highlighting his pale cheeks. "I put it to you," he repeated, "that you are in league with Satan, who takes the form of this beast, and that you go about seeking whom you may devour!"

His eyes glittered as his voice rose, and spittle flecked the corners of his mouth. A pointing finger stabbed at Kari as he stood and stepped forward.

Kari refused to retreat. "Nonsense," she said, "it is you who are mad. Mad and evil in the unconscionable things that you do to that poor child…"

The veins stood out on Josiah's neck as he searched for words in his rage. "Witch," he shrieked, "I know of the witch mark and we shall all see it—the spot that will not bleed. Malcolm saw it on your breast when you frolicked wantonly in the water. You seduced an honest worker of this estate. He shall repent and tell us how you bewitched him. Then shall you and your dog both do a merry dance at the end of a rope!"

His hand shot forward, and the grasping fingers seized the bodice of Kari's gown. Instinctively, she recoiled from the twisted mouth and bulging eyes that thrust toward her.

"Gently, my friend," Thomas injected a tone of reason. "We may well have to conduct the examination or swim her, but it must be before witnesses." He put a restraining hand on Josiah's arm. "Let me speak to her. While you compose yourself from your very righteous wrath."

Reluctantly, Josiah released his grip. The fingers slid from her gown and the fabric loosened around her throat. She put a hand to her neck.

Thomas placed a gentle hand on her arm to draw her aside toward the window. "Come," he said softly.

Thankful to move away from the ravening Josiah, she followed him. Thomas had faults, but he had a family and responsibilities. He could be considered an educated man. He could not possibly believe the madness that Josiah was spouting.

In the window embrasure, Thomas lifted a hand to brush the hair from her face and laughed softly when she jerked her head away.

"You will not look so pretty if we do the examination for the witch mark, nor if they decide to swim you, or test you with the fire," he said softly. "Such a pity to spoil that fine skin." He stroked her bare arm. "There may be a remedy."

Kari's skin crawled at his touch. There would be no help from this man. She stared at him stonily.

"Be kind to me, and to Josiah if I will it, and maybe we could fail to find the proof of your witchcraft." He leered at her, his meaning clear, and caressed her shoulder.

She had to try to use anything and everything that might help her. Making Thomas an ally could be important. Although the words nearly stuck in her throat she asked, "How could you do this?"

He relaxed a little, pleased at her answer. "I have a house in London. 'Twould be no burden to give you bed and board for as long as you pleased me." He stroked her cheek with the back of his knuckles.

Kari glanced across the room. Josiah's face was turned toward them. "And Mistress Godwin?"

"Come, come, my pretty one, you know better than that. What Mistress Godwin does not know will not harm her."

He misinterpreted her silence for interest. "If you conduct yourself well, who knows? In time our good priest here might consent to wed you, make an honest woman of you." He chuckled. "Now that the clergy can marry. 'Tis better to marry than to burn, as the good book says."

Kari drew in her breath, ready to spit out her contempt and her determination to tell Martha of her husband's treachery. How could that good, kind woman be married to such a monster?

Before she could let out the words that would enrage Thomas again and would lose her all hope, the hinges of the oaken door creaked softly. All eyes turned as it opened to let in the tall form of Aidan Torrance. Never had he looked more wonderful.

Thomas blustered. "What new impudence is this?"

"Pardon, sir." Aidan swept off his cap. His eyes flickered over Kari standing close to Thomas Godwin. "I see that the woman has caused you trouble. I seek to tell you the truth." He stood in a deferential attitude.

"What can you tell us, poor knave?"

Aidan cast his eyes down, twisting his cap between his hands. "Forgive me, sirs, but I had hoped to be discreet."

"Out with it, man." Josiah had recovered his composure. "We have important business at hand. The welfare of all our souls may be at stake. This is an unwarranted delay."

Kari saw Aidan looking around the room, taking in the dog pulling against the rope, Thomas standing close to her, one hand still on her arm. His lips tightened as he assessed what was going on. He looked strong and sure. Now that he was here, he would support her. She would convince Thomas and Josiah of how wrong they were, and Aidan would back her up. Then she would leave with great dignity and with Ben.

Aidan lifted his head and squared his shoulders. He cleared his throat and looked Thomas in the eye. "I have to tell you that the woman is my wife."

Chapter Thirteen

Josiah and Thomas spluttered their astonishment, both now on their feet. Kari started forward. "That's not—"

"Hush, dear wife." Aidan smiled indulgently and put out a hand to stop her forward rush. "These good people must be told. You cannot hide it from them." He held her by one hand and turned to face the two men. "This woman is indeed wed to me. She is—difficult at times."

He lowered his voice to a confidential tone. "Although well-born, and bred to the court, she has had brain fevers since childhood." He gestured toward Kari. "You may see the resemblance, sirs? The red of the hair, the square shoulders, the fine eyes, the fair skin?" He laid one finger against his nose and winked.

"What the hell are you talking about?" Kari faced him in exasperation and tried to wrench her hand away from his firm grasp.

He sighed and pulled her closer to him. "You see, gentlemen, she has the spirit, the royal arrogance, like her mother."

Thomas gazed first at Kari, then at Aidan. "Her mother? You mean, the queen...?" The last word hung in the air, less than a whisper.

Aidan nodded. "Even to have such knowledge is high treason," he spoke solemnly, quietly. "There are many dead men can attest to that. You can judge how hard it has been to keep a bastard at court with the strong resemblance. I am a younger son, but of a good family. I agreed to marry her, since she is not unpleasing to the eye—hush, woman—and to serve our royal lady. Quiet, woman, keep silence." Aidan took hold of Kari's arm and drew her close to him, pinning her against his side.

He winked openly at Thomas and Josiah. "Such spirit has its compensations in our marriage bed, good sirs." Kari gave a gasp of shock and Aidan clasped his hand firmly over her mouth. "She does always so protest when I come after her. What nonsense has she spun this time? From time to time she escapes the surveillance of her serving women and..." He shrugged eloquently.

Both Thomas and Josiah stared at him, aghast.

"Never had we thought to meddle in court affairs," Thomas said, with a nervous clearing of his throat.

"We are honest men, we seek no danger," Josiah added, nodding furiously in agreement.

I bet you don't, Kari thought. The succession to Queen Elizabeth towards the end of her reign had generated a seething snake pit of conflicting claims.

Aidan took swift advantage of their momentary paralysis. "Come, wife," he said sharply. "I have a healing posset shall settle your fevered brain."

Still holding her firmly imprisoned in his arms, he moved her toward the door. "Good day, gentle sirs. Be sure you will be rewarded for your discretion when it comes to the ears of our sovereign lady."

He grabbed Kari firmly and hustled her, squirming and protesting, from the room and through the front door.

"Be quiet," he muttered in her ear, "and follow me."

For once, she did as he said and followed willingly enough as he led her by the hand out of the garden and into the woods. They went quickly through the downpour, past the pond, and down into a glen, thickly carpeted with ferns. There he used his scanner to open the seal he had placed on the door of a hut and ushered her inside.

He pulled the door closed behind them, shutting out the rain and most of the light, and removed his restraining hands.

Kari ran her hand over her mouth where he could see the faint impression of his fingers and then moved as far away from him as she could. She hadn't spoken since they arrived. He supposed she was thinking of a way to thank him.

* * * * *

Feeling decidedly pleased with himself, Aidan settled back a bit, wriggling his shoulders into a more comfortable position in the straw. Kari was beside him, muttering and complaining about the prickly bales.

"God, this is uncomfortable," she said.

He ignored her ingratitude. "No time to bring anything to sit on," he said. "Piece of luck that I came upon this hut anyway. Looks like something built to shelter a shepherd from the rain and wind in the winter."

The boards fitted poorly and let in the drafts, but at least the gaps also allowed in some fresh air. Without them, the stale smell of rancid wool and of animals would be hard to take. Fortunately, the recent good weather had aired it a little, and the sheep had been taken to graze deeper onto the moorland. No one was likely to use it in the near future.

"It will do very well," he added.

He could barely make out the interior in the dimness, the only light strained through the chinks in the walls. The rain had started again and drummed monotonously on the roof. He could hear it splashing in the puddles outside. Soothing.

Aidan did a quick mental review. On the whole, he decided, things had gone well. He'd done a good job of rescuing Kari. No doubt but that Reed Flynn had had a hand somehow in engineering the fiasco. The whole scenario bore the mark of Flynn's devious manipulation, playing on fears, greed, lust and whatever other baser human motives he could use for his own ends.

There was no way Flynn would get his grubby fingers on the pictures, if that was what he wanted. Reed always had a goal, right from when they were in the Space Academy together. His tricks always aimed at a profit for Reed Flynn. Flynn didn't know that Aidan was on to him and it was essential to keep that advantage.

Aidan had to smile a bit at the memory of Thomas and Josiah's faces. Thomas had aspirations, the servants had gossiped freely about the master ingratiating himself with powerful men. Thomas would be turning the story over in his mind, trying it on again for size. There would be a niggling doubt somewhere, but he would not know how to deal with it.

How could he go to one of his friends and say, "I hear our lady queen had a bastard daughter about thirty years ago. Know anything about it? Met the fellow that claims to be her husband. Pity that she is deranged." Thomas would taste the hospitality of the Tower sooner than he ever would have expected.

No, Thomas would have to be circumspect, find out by hints and bribery if this particular audacious rumor bore any shred of truth. Many such tales had surrounded the Virgin Queen in her younger days. Plenty of people willing to swear to secret birthings and even murder.

Thomas would have to watch himself if he started asking too many questions. It would take a few days—weeks probably—to find out for sure. But Thomas was no fool. He would soon start to reason that an unwanted bastard could disappear with no questions asked. It might take him a day or so to come to the conclusion that he had nothing to lose by ridding his household and the village of this disruptive influence. Aidan figured he could count on maybe two days of safety. Plenty of time. Unless Reed Flynn had his fingers in the pie.

He'd enjoyed making up the story. What a relief to have taken some decisive action at last. At least he and Kari could be open now. She would work with him, understand what he had to do.

He looked over at Kari. It hadn't been an easy job to get her here. He had dragged her out of the house, coughing and spluttering under the hand he clamped over her mouth. Not his usual way of treating a woman, but he dared not allow her the chance to make things worse.

"Don't ever do that again." Kari's voice was quiet, but he saw the way her fingers were clenched at her side. "I won't be manhandled. I'm tired of men here putting their hands on me."

She had settled herself into the straw. She sat there now, still rubbing her wrist where he had held it, watching him watching her. Hell, she had shot all his plans to pieces. He was making it up as he went along. He sighed. He hadn't been prepared to deal with thought patterns that relied entirely on instinct and emotions. Didn't these people use any logic, didn't they input into probability calculations that would be second nature to any rational person? To tell the truth, he shared part of Thomas Godwin's dilemma. He wasn't really sure of her, either. Better to let her talk. He continued to watch her through lowered lids.

Her hair curled damply around her face, still wet from their mad dash through the fields. She removed her shawl and cap and laid them to dry with her shoes. She wriggled her toes in the hay and held her clinging skirts spread wide away from her legs. Every few seconds she gave them an impatient shake.

"Here." He rummaged behind some bales. "I have a blanket." He pulled out a roughly woven cover of the kind that had lain folded in the corner chest of her room, ready for cooler nights. "Take off those wet things." He interpreted the look she gave him. "I have more blankets."

He stood to loop two more covers from the low wooden beams, making an effective screen. He stepped back, waiting for her to utter some kind of thanks, some expression of appreciation for his preparations. Without a word, she took the offered blanket and ducked behind the hangings. He heard the soft rustling in the straw. For the second time, he waited while she undressed.

At the pool, he had watched as she pulled off the heavy woolen skirts and stood in her shift. The thin, light material would adhere damply now to her body, clinging to the swell of her breasts. Her skin would be chilled and her nipples would pucker and thrust through the linen. Then she would remove the clammy undergarment and stand naked, reaching for the blanket to wrap around her...

Quickly, he stripped off his own wet clothes and cloaked himself in a tattered piece of cloth that betrayed its stable origins.

Kari emerged, cocooned in the blanket, and resumed her place against the bales. She still sat with lips firmly closed. Did she imagine that he knew what she was thinking? Had the latest events proven too much for even her strong spirit? He sat, motionless. She needed time to recover, that was all. In a short while she would smile again, would start to make plans with him...

His arms ached to comfort her, and his thoughts drifted back again to the pool, to the feel of her under his hands. He was acutely conscious of his own nakedness under the rough cover, and of hers. He didn't want to sit here, patiently waiting. He wanted to push her down on the straw, lay the length of his body over her, nuzzle into that soft neck, kiss her, stroke her...

She interrupted his thoughts. "Do you have anything to drink?"

He nodded. He had stashed some basic provisions under the boards. Silently, he passed her a wooden cup of small beer. She sipped, made a face.

"God, I'll be glad to get a decent drink."

"Shouldn't be long now."

She gave him a strange look. He waited for her to ask how, when, to thank him for rescuing her.

She licked her lips. A damp lock of hair fell over her face, and she pushed it back impatiently.

Again, a look he couldn't interpret. She took a deep breath. "I have to ask you this first," she said, the words tumbling out fast. "Where are you from?"

She took another sip. "I mean—this sounds silly, but—are you from Earth?"

"Yes, but from two thousand, four hundred—"

"No, tell me later." She closed her eyes. "I had to be sure."

Now she would thank him, would let him help her.

She opened her wonderful eyes again and looked at him. He began to smile in anticipation of her gratitude. She must be overwhelmed by the thought that he was a traveler in time. He would have to be gentle, give her time to adjust, to trust him enough to cooperate in her own rescue.

"Where's Ben?"

Damn, he had hoped she wouldn't ask about the dog. "Still at the house, I guess."

"You left him!" It was an accusation, not a question. She gathered her blanket to stand up. "I'll get him."

Aidan sprang to his feet, took her arm. "You can't go back!"

She shook her arm free. "Don't touch me," she said. "So—you botched that pretty well."

This he had not expected. "Botched?"

"Made a right mess of it. With that ridiculous story. And Ben's still there."

The ingratitude hurt his feelings, and in reaction he grew haughty in tone. "I considered it an adequate story. I inputted it to the databank. The computer at headquarters assessed it as a high probability. It seems to have worked."

She snorted. There was no prettier word for the sound she made. "Databank! I could have handled them."

He nodded. "Looked as if you were doing pretty well."

She shot him a glare. "You're bloody pleased with yourself."

This wasn't going the way he expected at all. She acted as if he had made things worse instead of rescuing her. "I did enjoy it, if you must know. I'd always thought that no story could be too exaggerated when stakes are high. In fact—"

"So, what will you do?"

"About what?"

"Getting Ben back, of course. To start with."

To start with? "He could stay there." He shrugged. "Isn't one place as good as another to—"

"To what?" Her eyes narrowed dangerously. "To a mere dog?"

"Well," he spread his hands. "I didn't think—"

"That's just it, you didn't think. Ben is my friend, my companion. I look after him and he looks after me. Where I go, he goes, or I make damn sure he's well cared for and safe. He will not be well cared for *or* safe in the Godwin house. If there's any way of getting back home, Ben goes too. Do you understand me?"

She sat clutching the ridiculous blanket, her head thrown back, defiance and determination clear in every tense muscle.

He nodded. Anything to get some movement on this project, rescue mission, whatever it could be called.

"I'll fetch him when it's dark. When our clothes are dry."

"*We* will."

"Forget it. It's too dangerous for you. I go alone."

"No way. Where you go, I go."

He liked the sound of that, despite his misgivings. But she shouldn't go near that house.

"Kari—"

"Don't argue."

She sat up straighter. Straw clung to the damp strands of her hair. She was clutching the covering to her just beneath the swell of her breasts. Her shoulders were bare, her creamy skin contrasting with the dark cloth and the wet locks that hid her ears and clung to her cheek.

"Look, I've had enough of men trying to decide what's good for me all my life. The medical profession has a long way to go. The men here are even worse. And it seems as if it doesn't get any better in the future."

Ouch.

"Whoever you are, wherever you're from, you're my ticket out of here," she continued. "I'm not letting you out of my sight until we leave."

Aidan raised his hands in surrender. "I'll take you later, when it's dark. But I call the shots, and if I say wait, you wait. Agreed?"

She gazed at him for a moment. A large smudge ran down the side of her face and disappeared into the tangle of her hair. The bruise where Thomas had hit her made a dark blue shadow under her eye. She was tired, disheveled…and still fighting. His heart turned over. He wanted nothing more than to take her and shelter her in his arms. To soothe away the turmoil and the fears and to take her back to safety. All she wanted was to return to her old life with her dog. How could he expect her feelings to match his?

At last, she nodded. "If you explain everything to me and I agree with you. If I don't know what you're doing, it's no deal."

"Agreed." At least she was prepared to cooperate. "Let's get some rest. With these clouds, we have about four hours before dusk."

Chapter Fourteen

୫୬

"Rest while you can," Aidan said, and Kari sank back onto the straw. The continuing downpour drummed on the roof.

"How long will it take them to realize they've been had?" she asked.

Aidan guessed at what she meant. "I calc we have two days."

She huddled into the blanket, silent, considering. "Who—what are you?" she said at last.

He grimaced. "I am human," he said. "Name really Aidan Torrance. I travel in time."

"So I understand." She grinned wryly. He was ridiculously pleased to see her mouth turn up into a semblance of a smile. "So do I."

"Yes, well, that was a mistake."

She arched her eyebrows.

"Was beaming back…"

"Do you really say that?"

"Say what?"

"Beam up, back, whatever. Sounds like *Star Trek*." She enlightened him. "A film…TV…about the future. Entertainment."

He nodded, serious. "Beam is correct, although it's not the same process as in your fantasy shows. Sometimes we say 'flip.' You see there is a force field…"

"Never mind." She held up a hand to stop him. "Just give me the bottom line. Tell me what was going on back in the park. I figure that's where it happened?"

He nodded. "Repulsion effect. You stayed too close. One traveler forward, one back. Simple."

"It is when you say it that way. How much time?"

He looked at her, not understanding.

"How far did you travel?"

"Four hundred years back to your time."

She shook her head in bewilderment. "My mind can't take it in," she said. "How long have you been doing this, traveling through the centuries?"

"Not long. Four trips altogether."

"So, you're good at it?"

He frowned.

"I mean, you know what you're doing? You finish up in the right place at the right time?"

"So far."

"So you can get me back?"

"Yes, I can." He fervently hoped it was true, once he had figured out where the new beam-away point would be. And if he could bring himself to separate from her.

Apparently satisfied, she snuggled into the straw and closed her eyes.

"Kari."

"Mmm?"

"Sorry I manhandled you. I had to—"

She opened her eyes. They shone like dark pools in the shadows. "Forget it. But never again. Agreed?" Her lips sketched a mocking smile as she gave him back his own word.

He nodded and sighed. "Agreed."

Aidan stayed awake, watchful. He lay still, mulling over his scheme yet again. He'd probably silenced Thomas and Josiah for the moment. But at some point, as Kari had said, they would begin to grasp the preposterous nature of the story he had told them. Especially if Reed Flynn had a hand in their scheme. Then there would be inquiries, speculation, and the realization that something was amiss. Next they would begin the search. It wouldn't take long to find this hut.

He and Kari would move once she'd rested, and they had the dog. He'd told Kari two days, but he figured they had three days at the most, if they found a good hiding place. More than enough time to recalculate the coordinates if he had to.

Kari slept on the bales of straw, her hair spread around her, her arms flung wide. She breathed deeply, not moving. She'd lain like that for two hours now, obviously needing the rest. At some point, he would have to tell her that when she beamed back she wouldn't remember him. He wondered how she would feel about that.

* * * * *

Kari woke with a start in a strange place, wrapped only in a scratchy blanket that rubbed against her skin. Irritably, she pushed away a piece of straw that tickled her mouth. Opening her eyes did no good. It was pitch-black all around. The adrenaline started to pump, and her heart pounded in her ears. Where was she? Had Thomas…?

She sat up, and the cover fell away. She grabbed it quickly. Memory flooded back.

"Aidan," she whispered. "Are you there?" There was no answer. She strained to hear him breathing. Nothing.

She'd been brought to camp out in this miserable excuse for a hut, but what had happened to Aidan Torrance? Had he gone and left her, despite his promise? For some reason, she didn't believe he would do that.

She had to confess she trusted him, although he was as alien to her as a creature from another world. To all intents and purposes, that was what he was. How did he manage this time traveling stunt? He didn't appear to have any machinery. What kind of life did he lead four hundred years in the future? Did he have a wife, a family, children? Were there still families, or did children grow in laboratories as some people were forecasting?

Her lips curved in a smile. No, she could safely say that the human reproductive urge was still a powerful force. She'd had proof of the strength of Aidan's feelings as he'd caressed and kissed her. She knew that he'd reacted as men had done through the ages to the stimulus of a naked female body... Her mind drifted to the feel of him, to the touch of his hands on her bare skin, to the hunger in his eyes as he looked at her. She pulled the blanket closer around her and hugged her knees to her chest. Just thinking about him made her temples throb and her skin begin to tingle...

A scratching sound made her sit up, all senses alert. A few feet away, a slab of lighter gray appeared in the gloom and slowly widened. Kari made out the edges of the crude door of the hut as it opened stealthily, creaking a little. She tensed and groped around for a piece of wood, a weapon of any kind, but the straw yielded nothing that could serve. A shadow filled the opening as someone slipped into the hut.

"Kari?" The whisper came from a few feet away. "Are you awake?"

A stronger rustling in the straw as the body moved toward her. She breathed out in relief. "Aidan?"

He slid down beside her, his mouth against her ear. "Shh. Keep your voice down. Just checked outside, and it seems all clear. But voices carry."

"What time is it?" she whispered back.

"Nearly midnight. Everything quiet. Heard voices an hour or so ago, but nothing since."

"They'll find us."

"When we have Ben, we'll move deeper into the woods."

The faint glow from the moon and stars through the open door showed the walls of the hut and the crouched shape of Aidan.

"It's quiet," she said. "It must have stopped raining."

"Soon after you went to sleep. Get dressed now."

He put out a hand to pull her to her feet and she clung to the sliding blanket. No touching or peeping, thank you.

"Can you see to get to your clothes?" he said.

She nodded and then realized he couldn't see her in the darkness. "No problem," she whispered and moved behind the blankets that still hung from the rafters. Quickly, she pulled on the dress and petticoat. There was something to be said after all for the lack of modern underwear.

The hem of the still-damp gown clung unpleasantly 'round her ankles. The air had warmed again since the rain stopped, and she had little need of the shawl, but she wrapped it around her head to cover her hair and part of her face. It might help her to pass unrecognized. She had read the commando books and seen the movies, too, about moving around in enemy territory.

"Good. Let's go." Aidan had pulled down the temporary screen and rapidly stowed the covers into a pack. He'd proven to be pretty resourceful. A little twinge of guilt nagged at her for being so ungrateful.

They crept out of the hut into a starry night. The trees still dripped with water after the violence of the rain, and the world smelled freshly washed. She took a deep breath, savoring it after the musty air of the hut. The moon shone bravely amid the tattered remnants of the clouds that scudded off to the east. The wet leaves shimmered, colorless in the cool light.

"Follow close. Don't trip." Aidan strode off across the meadow and up the hill. Kari scurried after him, concentrating on making one shadowy form with his. He moved swiftly, staying low and close to bushes and trees. Quickly, they retraced the flight of earlier that day until they stood at the gate to Godwin House.

Aidan motioned her to stop, and they waited, listening. The lines of the roof showed blacker still against the dark sky. The thickening clouds had massed to hide the moon and the stars. A deep hush lay upon the house and gardens. No candle flickered at the windows to betray a watcher in the dark.

Kari heard a horse shift its weight in the stable and give a soft whinny. What had they done with Ben? A sudden fear struck her. What if they had hurt him? She could see Josiah lashing out in a vindictive rage, targeting any creature unable to defend itself. Thomas could take revenge with arbitrary commands to his servants to dispose of the animal. Ben was big and strong, he would fight off any attack. But he had been tied up. Aidan's whisper broke into her panic.

"Stay here. I'll check the stable."

"No, I want—"

"Dammit, woman, I know the stables. I know how people move around. Don't you realize there could be some kind of a trap? Will you just let me do this!"

She subsided. He was right. A man moving around the stables at night could find a more plausible excuse than she could. But it irked her, nonetheless.

Aidan slid off silently, blending quickly into the shadows. She forced her eyes to follow his shape, but in a few seconds she lost sight of him. Nothing to do but wait. She prayed that Thomas had not had the foresight to use Ben as bait in a trap. If Aidan were captured or wounded…

Gradually she began to pick out the small sounds in the deeper stillness. An animal moved in the underbrush, an owl hooted from the woods. A silent shape swooped over her head, and she ducked, unable to hold back a gasp of alarm. Only a bat on his nightly hunt.

She looked around at the dark shapes of the bushes, the faint lines of the outbuildings. This spot was now in the heart of the city, owls and bats and foraging creatures long gone, together with the blackberry bushes and the honeysuckle, Martha's kitchens and the prized library. Progress had expanded the town as hundreds flocked to it over the ensuing centuries. This idyllic place had been the site of industrial expansion as people built houses and roads to satisfy the ever-increasing demands of trade and commerce.

A sense of awe came over her. She had been privileged to see this place as it once had been. No book could have explained, or movie recaptured, the close-knit life of this community or the hardworking people, dependant on the rich farmland, the lush pastures and the abundant woodlands. She began to understand Aidan's fascination with the past, and the overwhelming temptation to experience it firsthand. How had the place changed until his time, she wondered. What was here eight hundred years from now?

After what seemed an eternity of waiting, Aidan and Ben materialized beside her and they crept silently back to their hiding place.

* * * * *

Safely back in the hut, Aidan answered her unspoken question, "This area is being hologrammed right now," he volunteered. "In my time, I mean. I'm a historian and that's the project I've been working on. My FLIP when I met you wasn't authorized." He shrugged. "That's been the big problem."

Kari stopped scratching Ben's ears to look at Aidan in bewilderment. Her eyes had begun to readjust to the gloom. The sky had cleared again, and shards of moonlight struck through the cracks, showing the heaps of hay and straw. A pitchfork driven into one bale stuck up at a sharp angle.

Aidan lay back in the straw, arms behind his head, gazing up at the earthen clumps that formed the roof. The faint light etched his profile and threw shadows on his face. A mere five days ago she had been unaware of his existence, and now she was confined with him because he was essential to her survival.

She would not be able to live in this time. Her outspokenness, her modern notions of what the world should be, would war constantly with the reality of life in this

Elizabethan culture. She had to leave, and Aidan was by her side to help her.

But at the beginning she had not known who he was and why he was here. At the beginning, she had felt only an inexplicable and unacceptable tug at her heart when he came near. He'd proved to be intelligent, thoughtful, resourceful, not to mention good-looking. She'd basked in the warmth and compassion of those incredible eyes, knowing that he was not cut from the same cloth as the other servants. Her traitorous body had responded instantly with a quiver and a wave of desire when he touched her.

She could have fallen in love with this kind of man. She frowned. Could have? What should she call this feeling? She tingled when he drew close, she feasted her eyes on him at every chance she got. She wanted to be with him, talk to him, share with him. A dreadful, hollow, sinking feeling in the pit of her stomach clutched at her at the thought of never seeing him again.

"Let's face it," she thought, "this is the closest you've been to being in love. This is the only time anyone has had this kind of effect on you. So it's ridiculous to even think of loving someone after four days. One more ridiculous thing in this ridiculous adventure. If this isn't love, it's close." But this man was alien, as different from her as she was from Martha or Anne.

He broke in on her thoughts, frowning in concentration. His mind still dwelt on his explanation of his work.

"We've done back to twenty-one hundred," he went on. "Holograms exist for the streets and buildings as they used to be for every ten year interval, and can be recalled through the Virtual Reality system as you wish. But earlier than that is difficult. Low technology, primitive record keeping all through the twentieth and twenty-first centuries." He glanced at her apologetically. "They assigned me to collect data for the twentieth century." His lips twisted and he sat up.

"Thought I'd be smart, get a first scan and a head start." He smiled. "Figured I would have time to collect details that interest *me* as well as the stuff for the computers. Picked up some pictures, too."

Kari sank back on her heels and pushed back her hair. Ben lay quiet, licking a paw. She stroked him gently and drew back sharply when he whimpered. She had touched a sore spot on his side. The wolfhound turned his head and licked her arm as if apologizing for startling her.

She winced at the thought of the kicks and bruises he had probably suffered before Aidan had found him in a corner of the stable, untied him and led him back to her. She fondled him behind his ears and he sank back on the straw. She pulled her attention back to Aidan. Somehow, she had to get used to thinking in three different time periods at once.

"Why did you come back for me?"

"What?" Aidan seemed surprised by the question.

"How did you know where I was? Why didn't you leave me here?"

He told her about the supposed repulsion effect and his fears for contamination.

"It's the butterfly effect," he said. "It's been said many times. Does the flap of a butterfly's wings in Brazil set off a tornado in Texas?"

"Jurassic Park," Kari said.

"Where's that?" Aidan frowned.

"Not where—what. It's a book and a movie about recreating dinosaurs, very popular."

"I think I heard of it in an Old Literature class. Pretty farfetched. Anyway, I couldn't leave you here and risk you interfering."

"Would that be so terrible?"

"Of course—there are four centuries of history to consider… Our whole project—"

"So, you didn't do it for me? You didn't care what I might feel, what might happen to me?"

"No, no, I didn't—at the time. I have to be honest with you, Kari. But I realized when I found you…"

To give him his due, he looked contrite and uncomfortable enough.

"Aidan," she said, "I have no way of understanding how you thought and why you decided to come back for me. But once you were here, why didn't you just tell me who you were? Why didn't you just take Ben and me back straight away?"

"I gave my word," he said, miserably. "I promised I would take you back without letting you know. I thought it would be easy." His mouth twisted wryly.

"No contamination?"

He nodded. "And if I did it right, the worst that could happen would be that you thought it all was a bad dream. You wouldn't remember clearly."

"This would all be gone? How?"

"I would take you back to the minute after we met. For you, this wouldn't have happened. I also could give you a pill."

"What kind of a pill?"

"It confuses short term memory. If I was in doubt about you, or about arriving back at the right time, I could slip it into your food or drink."

He would be wiped from her mind, cause a total memory loss of what might be the most meaningful episode in her life. She had never considered that.

"But you didn't do it?"

"No. "

"Why not?"

He pushed back a lock of hair that fell over his brow. "It has to be given at the last minute."

Her mouth was dry. She swallowed and moistened her lips. "And the other?"

"Other?"

"The other question. Why didn't you just whisk us back, Ben and me? You can do all these wonderful things, why didn't you just move us around time like—like pawns on a chess board?"

"At the time, I wished I could. You see, time travel is still quite primitive. That's why we have to be so careful. We don't want the technology in the hands of certain people."

He compressed his lips and frowned, but then seemed to change his mind about pursuing the thought. "There are always changes to the equipment and I'm using a prototype," he continued briskly, warming to the subject. "They tell me it's more accurate but I have to send a signal, get in position and wait for the return message after they've recalibrated. That's why I needed you and Ben with me."

He picked up his little black box, ready to expound further.

Kari held up her hands in mock distress. "Okay, okay. Enough." She sighed. "Well, Aidan, all I can say is, I don't think much of—"

"Shh."

Kari tensed, all her senses alert. Something was moving outside.

Chapter Fifteen

ဢ

Aidan's hand grasped hers, pulled her close. In a supple movement, he uncoiled his body and rose to his feet, reaching for the pitchfork with one hand. His arm enfolded her. Surely he must hear her heart beating fast against him. Hopefully, he wouldn't know it wasn't only fear making her pulse race.

The unseen creature moved slowly, brushing against the wooden slats of the hut. It sounded large—maybe more than one. Grass swished faintly as something pushed through the undergrowth. Mysterious sucking and chewing noises filtered through the cracks in the walls.

Kari suppressed a giggle. "It's a cow!" she whispered. "A cow that's separated from the herd." As if to confirm her diagnosis, a low *moo* sounded beside her ear, followed by the unmistakable sounds of the animal moving away across the field.

Aidan's arm remained around her. "Of course," he sighed in relief. "Animals on the loose. I should remember." He looked down at her. "We obviously need each other," he said. "With your knowledge and mine we could make a good team."

She reveled in the temptation of the thought of making a team. The sudden fear had sent a shot of adrenaline through her system. Combined with the effect of Aidan's arms around her, it had made her quite light-headed.

Reluctantly, Kari extricated herself from his embrace. Enough closeness for now. She looked at him critically. The dark hair melted into the shadows and his eyes glittered in the faint light. Together with the medieval clothing, he made a figure straight out of a period painting. She nodded judiciously. "The pitchfork suits you," she grinned.

Aidan laughed and tossed the pitchfork back into the bale. The shaft quivered and then stilled as the prongs held in the straw.

"No animals in the fields in the future?" she asked lightly.

He took her hand and pulled her to sit beside him on a bale. "No animals, no pets roaming free."

She watched the movement of his long, strong fingers, stroking the back of her hand. Her skin tingled under the feathery touch.

"Certain species are protected in game farms," he continued. "The animal population is strictly controlled."

"People, too?" She strove to keep her voice neutral, refusing to betray what feelings he aroused in her.

He gave her a sideways glance. "To some extent. But technology is not so interesting. Tell me about yourself."

She settled back, one hand on Ben's neck. So Aidan wanted to be reticent about the future. She wondered why. If she talked first, maybe he would open up later.

"My mother is an opera singer," she began. "She emotes constantly, both on and off the stage. Fortunately, my father could shut himself away and study his dusty manuscripts and write his scholarly articles. They were complementary opposites and quite happy."

She took strange comfort in talking freely at last, indulging the thoughts that she had had to keep to herself in this alien world.

"And you?" Aidan settled on his side, one arm bent to support him. His hand still lay lightly on Kari's.

"We traveled a lot, wherever Dad had an appointment as a visiting professor or Mother was booked to sing. Sometimes we were all together, sometimes I went just with one of them, my brother with the other. I went to school all over—the States, Canada, Australia, Europe, wherever. I did my homework and then did research for Dad and pandered to Mother until I knew I had to break away." She smiled in memory.

"I caused one of the most memorable dramatic incidents ever, and that's saying something in my family, when I told them I wanted to be a doctor rather than an actress or a teacher! I flung it down like a challenge. Quite a scene!"

"If your conversation with Thomas was a sample, I can believe it! Why medicine?" He stroked her hair back from her cheek.

"It seemed like something that no one else in my family would do. So of course it drew me. Making a statement, I suppose. But soon I was hooked. Both my parents were takers. Oh, they appeared to contribute, and in a way they did. They advanced knowledge in a small way and provided beauty for those that could appreciate it. But what they really wanted was admiration, fame, and recognition. They loved me and my brother, but we came second to their art."

She paused, considering the implications of telling him more, of revealing herself to him. If she was never to see him again, if they didn't survive this journey through time, then she wanted him to understand her. "I loved — love — them too," she said slowly. "I loved what they produced, their dedication." She looked up at him. "But I wanted to control my own life, be of real use in the world. The family seemed to be in a permanent fantasy. I wanted reality. I was probably looking for something to conquer in my own right. I decided I wanted to do something about the misery, the suffering. I wanted to heal."

Suddenly, her eyes filled with tears. She pulled away from Aidan and turned to look squarely at him. "Look, I had it all worked out. I studied, I planned. No men, no parties, no distractions." Aidan's hand tightened on hers at the words. "I did my spell in Obs, Gynie, and Pediatrics. I even read up on tropical medicine and nutrition. Everything worked out on schedule — until this happened." She gripped his fingers. "You can take us back?"

"I'll take you back, Kari. I won't leave you here."

"I feel so bloody helpless. There's nothing I know that can help me. I hate the feeling."

"We'll do it together. A team, remember?"

That sounded good.

"So tell me more about your plans," Aidan urged.

She leant forward, engrossed by the fervor of her feelings.

"So many people need so little. Some extra food, the right vaccinations, someone to care. I was accepted for assignment with a medical humanitarian organization. Just look at the Miller family here..." She brushed a tear from her cheek. "Look at me, weeping for a family that no longer exists in my time or yours. Except," she frowned with the intensity of her emotions, "they will have descendants, and so the misery perpetuates itself."

Aidan made an impatient gesture. "Kari—" he began.

She knew he was going to make some remark about history, about allowing events to take their course. She'd heard it all before. Suddenly, she resented his aloof calmness. Barely suppressed emotions bubbled to the surface and her mood swung. How could he be so cold?

"So you don't understand or care from your lofty distance," she said angrily. "You call it being objective, I call it indifference."

Aidan tried to speak, but she steamrollered on. "Well, I despise your indifference, Aidan Torrance. I despise the way you put me at risk, and the way you were ready to leave Ben in that stable, to be mistreated for the rest of his life."

"No, I—"

"Don't tell me different. You've told me over and over— you don't want to interfere. Well, let me inform you, high and mighty time traveler, that most of this world's wrongs come from the indifference of people that care only for themselves. Look, that family could still save itself with a little help. A few miserable coins would save this generation and those to come."

Aidan broke in abruptly, "You don't know what you're saying. Who knows what changes that would cause..."

"The only change could be for the better."

"It might alter —"

"It *might* do a lot. It *would* ease their miserable lives and get them out of the clutches of Josiah Small and the likes of him."

She ran out of steam at last. How could she convince this man of such elementary facts? "Never mind," she said wearily. "There's nothing we could do anyway. What am I talking about? We have no money, no power. We need all the help we can get ourselves." She slumped wearily back onto the bales.

She heard him sigh. In fairness, it must be difficult for him. As difficult to see the world through her eyes as for her to see it through Martha's. He didn't lack simple humanity and compassion. But his outlook was colored with a different brush. His world had probably solved all these problems long ago, so he saw no reason to be troubled.

As if reading her thoughts, he spoke, "Forgive me, Kari. Difficult for me to understand. I feel your pain for these people. We'll talk again when you're rested, you can tell me more."

He stood with a blanket in his arms. "Make yourself comfortable and get some more sleep."

"But I don't need —"

"Well, *I* do," he interrupted. "We both do. Stop arguing for once. We'll rest tonight, and I'll assess the situation tomorrow. We may have to move before I can reset."

Of course he needed rest. She sank back without protest. His warm hands moved gently around her, tucking in the cover. Did his fingers linger a moment over her hair? Her body shifted as she felt his touch, ready to betray her despite herself, despite the sensible messages from her brain. Her tingling nerve ends responded to the closeness of him even when his hand moved away. She resolutely kept her eyes tight shut and remained still.

She was unused to this roller coaster ride of emotions. How could she be so angry with him, tell him she despised what he stood for, and at the same time long to feel his hands on her, his lips on hers?

"Goodnight, Kari," he whispered.

"Goodnight, Aidan. Thank you for getting Ben back." After all, he had done that for her. She settled closer to the dog's warm body and composed herself for sleep.

* * * * *

Aidan watched her sleep again. Despite what she believed about his indifference, her words troubled him. They echoed and spun in his brain with all the admonitions of his training that forbade interference in the past. He'd seen the Miller family. He'd heard of Edward's crippling fall, knew that with proper care the man could still regain his pride and take care of his family. A woodcarver could earn money if he had tools and materials.

It would take so little to feed those children, repair the miserable hovel they lived in, and buy warm clothing and fuel for the coming winter. Aidan sat for a long time, reflecting, watching Kari.

The words she had flung at him disturbed him in his very soul. He had come into the past as an observer, intending to keep as much physical and emotional distance as possible between himself and the inhabitants of these worlds. It was an experiment. The past was a living laboratory where everything was set, had been decided long since. Moral dilemmas that had long been settled provided interesting discussion but required no resolution. He'd succeeded in maintaining this objectivity, until he met this woman.

He wanted her physically. He wanted to caress and cajole her into a response that would make her pliant and yielding in his arms. He'd not been able to suppress the surge of joy and relief when she told him that she was alone, that there was no lover. He remembered the feel of her wet, lithe body against him. He savored again the sweet surrender of her mouth, the way her arms had wound around his neck, her legs entwined with his.

His breath came faster as he watched her breast rise and fall with the even breathing of deep sleep. One curved leg revealed a glimpse of creamy thigh. The magnificent hair tumbled about her face, one strand draped across her lips. He bent forward to remove it, and she stirred and muttered.

He admitted the truth of much of what she said. She had a strong and compassionate spirit. She would fight for the right and give of herself freely to those in need. What had he done in his life? He had fought too, but only for himself. He'd taken a perverse pleasure in beating the system whenever he could, to the despair of his instructors and mentors.

He would not be here now if he hadn't decided to use the newly developed technology before permission was granted. He had no patience with the mechanics of bureaucracy, and it had been relatively easy to persuade Tanice to help. His mentor since the loss of his parents, she found it difficult to refuse him anything. But he had another motive that he had not admitted to anyone who might betray him. His paintings were accumulating. On every trip, he had gone armed with the knowledge that certain works were due to "disappear", sometimes destroyed, and sometimes stolen. He'd been able to retrieve a fair number to add to his collection. He owned the largest unpublicized private collection of art works in his time. He reveled in the pleasure of knowing that his hobby would be considered illegal and antisocial was it ever discovered. He had never been afraid to take a chance.

But now these paintings might prove his downfall if that was why Reed Flynn was here. No point in speculating how Flynn had contrived to use the FLIP system, he was a past master at calling in favors and using his accumulated wealth to buy what he wanted. Aidan saw Flynn's hand in the information supposedly given to Josiah and Thomas. Of course, it had fit in nicely with their own schemes.

Suddenly, he stood and fumbled in the pack that lay beside him. He extracted a small, leather bag that chinked as he weighed it thoughtfully in his hand. Monika had included the money at the last minute, but he had used only a few small coins at the inn. Only large gold pieces remained and they wouldn't be needed now with their FLIP so imminent. Still, this was a hard decision for him to make—his training versus Kari's humanitarian arguments.

With an impatient sigh, he thrust the pouch quickly into his jerkin and softly stole from the hut. He should also check up on Reed Flynn. He could take care of two problems at once. Ben woofed gently as he left.

Chapter Sixteen

The first fingers of light inching through the ill-fitting walls woke Kari at dawn. She stirred and looked around. Ben lay tucked into her side. He lifted his shaggy head and licked her face in response to her whisper. She sat up, thrusting aside the straw and pushing the hair from her eyes. She and Ben were alone. Aidan had disappeared. Again.

She scrambled to her feet in sudden panic. But wait a minute. Think. The man was human, not an android. He had the same physical needs as she. He must be outside, answering a call of nature. She relaxed at the simple explanation and ran her fingers through her hair, trying to comb it into some sense of order. She tugged impatiently at a twig entangled at the back of her head.

Where was he?

The minutes dragged by. Dammit, she needed to go outside herself. Too bad if he came back and she was gone. Serve him right for leaving her without so much as a word. She pushed open the door, blinking in the light of the sun rising behind the encircling trees. The rain was now only a memory, lingering in the scents rising from the damp earth as the warm rays crept over the ground. No other creature moved in the early morning landscape. Quickly, she slipped behind a bush, keeping a look out. There was no sign of Aidan.

She had asked him, no, *told* him, not to leave her. It was essential she go with him, know what he planned to do. How could he be so thoughtless and unfeeling as to leave her alone? Had her outburst yesterday angered him? Had he abandoned her?

A sick feeling grasped the pit of her stomach. She had been so sure that he would take her away. Could she start over again and figure out her own way back? Of course not. Without Aidan she was doomed to live out her life in Elizabethan England! She would apologize when he returned.

If he returned.

She would agree not to argue about anything, except the one thing that she had to do.

The promise she'd made had niggled at the back of her mind ever since she left the Godwin House, eventually becoming a compulsion. So there was no logic, no rational reason for it in the larger scheme of things, but it had refused to go away, and her subconscious had settled it for her while she slept. But she would tell him gently, not upset him. If she remained calm and persuasive, helpful to him in any way possible, he could not refuse her request. He liked her. He would want to please her.

She could use all the skills she'd acquired in appeasing her mother's emotional demands, be all sweet reason when he came back, not challenge him as to why he had let her awake alone, why he had left her to all these thoughts about what she would do if he really had gone away.

A movement in the bushes at the far side of the grove drew her attention. She narrowed her eyes to focus. Someone or something was there. She made out a shape, a man. She still could not see who. It could be Thomas, Malcolm... Her heart beat faster and she shrank against the rough wood of the siding, willing whoever it was not to see her. The man drew closer, striding quickly through the thicket. In a few paces, he reached her side and grasped her elbow.

"What are you doing out here?" Aidan hissed. "Go inside." With a firm grasp on her arm, he steered her through the opening. Ben managed to slink in before Aidan dragged the ill-fitting door closed behind him.

All her good intentions evaporated once more. How dare he push her, speak to her that way?

"What am *I* doing? What the hell have *you* been doing? I thought you weren't going to leave me? That I was to go wherever you went? Where did you go?"

"*You* decided that I would take you everywhere. Happened that I had business elsewhere."

"What kind of business?"

"Choose not to say."

"*You* choose! What choice do I have, what choice..."

"Dammit, woman, I'm doing my best! You pound me with your ideas, you hound me to know what to do. Well, give me a chance to tell you. But first we must relocate."

Aidan moved quickly and decisively. The gentle, talkative man of a few hours ago had vanished. Had something happened? Where had he been, what had he learned to galvanize him into action? She decided to wait for a better moment to present her latest decision for discussion.

Over a scanty breakfast of water and dry bread, which they shared with a hungry Ben, Kari tackled him again.

"Where were you?" she demanded.

"There's a man in the village..." He paused, choosing the details of what he would tell her. "I know him."

"How?"

"We were at the Space Academy together—" He told her what he knew and what he suspected about Reed Flynn's presence. "That's why we must fade from the immediate area. Ben's disappearance will betray our presence at the farm last night. It's too risky to stay where we are."

Kari gave a small laugh, shaking her head. "Nothing surprises me now," she said. "Can you believe it? Time travelers, witches, space pirates—I feel as if I'm in the middle of an Indiana Jones movie. Lead on!"

They prepared to move at once, packing up the blankets and remaining food, and set off to a more remote hut that Aidan had found.

"How did you know about these places?" Kari asked, stepping carefully 'round a puddle left by the night's rain.

"Scouted at night. Malcolm thought I was out wenching. Gave me all kinds of directions to find my way in the dark."

"Malcolm!" she shivered. "Not a pleasant character. Too much free inbreeding."

"Think so?"

She shrugged. "Obvious. Small village, poor communications, no roads. Everyone in the village is probably related to everyone else, despite the church's best efforts with the laws for legitimate marriage."

She decided to probe for more information. "I suppose in your world you do things better?"

"Maybe not better, but differently." He seemed more inclined to talk than before. Her cooperation in the move had relaxed him. "You need a procreation permit to start with—"

"You can't have children when you want?"

"Only in the Outer Colonies. Earth people must obey the Family Laws and apply for children."

"Is that what you did?" She tested him with the question. She hung on his answer, waiting with bated breath, even though it should mean nothing to her. Of course she did not know if he had children, but suddenly she needed to know what his commitments were in his time.

Aidan shook his head. "Family is very important. Earth has strict rules about couples with children staying together. Cohabitation is fine and no one cares who you're with or for how long—unless there's a child. I guess I never found anyone I felt that strongly about."

Kari let out her breath gently. In so many words he had told her he had no wife, no children, no attachments. Why did she need to know?

Aidan went on. "The couple makes a contract for support of the child and then they can choose the characteristics…"

"Genetic programming?"

"Only if you wish. Most people make some choices. Hair color, sex of course. They screen for physical defects — "

"Only perfect people allowed?"

"Not quite. Some areas are still quite backward, so the technology is not up-to-date. There are still the birth traumas, the rebels, and the misfits, the eccentrics."

"I'm relieved! Not that there are misfits but that Nature still has some power."

"I should have known you would say that."

"Why?"

"Because you want to make everything perfect, but you want it natural and emotional just the same." He shook his head. "I've learned that you can't have it all ways, Kari." They kept silence for the rest of the trek. Kari mulled over what she had learned so far about this future world.

The new hut was similar in construction to the other, but in an open glade. They would see anyone approaching in good time, but they agreed to take turns to watch. Kari took her turn on lookout, her back to Aidan. She had insisted her distance vision was good enough to make out the difference between a cow and any human shape approaching.

"Tell me about the Outer Colonies," Kari said when they had settled in.

"The Outer Colonies are where the techno-research is done. Space stations, explorations, you know."

"What about Earth?" she asked quietly.

"The planet is still revolving, but it's tired. We're replenishing as best we can."

She turned to glance at him quickly. He stooped, bent over his pack, sorting pieces and fitting them together. He did not see her look at him.

"At the end of the twentieth century," he continued, his hands still busy, "a Russian scientist proposed that Earth should become a backwater, a vacation spot, and that everything progressive and meaningful should go on in space. People could come back to Earth to visit the countries and towns of their ancestors, see how they lived. His name was Nicolai Agajanyan, and he first proposed his idea at a news conference at the International Congress of Physiological Sciences in August 1993."

"Sounds impressive. Who was he?"

"Something to do with the Soviet Union space program before the dissolution."

A fascinating thread linked her time to Aidan's world. "I never heard of him. And yet you know all about him."

"Every child learns about Nicolai. He was recently named Father of the Outer Worlds, although he never lived to see his ideas put to work."

"So what happened?"

"At first everyone laughed at his ideas. After all, Earth was the center of the universe in human terms. But gradually governments began to realize he was right. Earth was tired, depleted, and we saw that its interest lay in its past history, much more than in the future. Earth is now mainly a peaceful vacation station where we can offer realistic glimpses into the past through our hologram reconstructions. We take Outers on vacation and do special educational programs."

"A worldwide Disneyland," she whispered.

He recognized the reference. "In a way. But it works. The forests are restocked, the rivers and oceans are clean."

"But people can't have the children they want and animals aren't free."

He shrugged. "Can't have everything. Things are pretty loose in the Outer Colonies. They want population. It works tolerably well. The ones who like it orderly stay on Earth. The adventurous ones find a job on a space station. The older satellites are fairly safe because the conditions are known and controlled. The new ones are riskier." He stopped what he was doing and looked at the object in his hands. "There," he said. "That's done."

Fifth report. DAY SIX

Operator: Aidan Torrance

Location: Hut, two kilometers from Godwin House

Date: July 15, 7.00 a.m.

Report: Sorry for 24 hour blackout. Girl, dog and I all safe. Was a close thing. Had reason to visit a village family in the night and saw Flynn leaving the Godwin House again. If Thomas confides in him, there will be no delay in setting up the hunt for us. Now in second of refuge spots. Am setting up coordinates for beam back. Expect return within twenty-four hours. Will "hop" in twentieth century, leave Kari and animal, and beam on. No hope of her consenting to leave the dog behind. More complicated to set up, but should be possible within time limits. Out.

* * * * *

Aidan moved to stand by Kari at the opening that served as a window. "All quiet?"

She nodded. His shoulder brushed hers. Amazing that she could still feel what she did, knowing now a little more about his vastly different world. Of course his outlook would be different too. He was a historian, totally caught up with his research into the past, intent on making a show for visiting spacemen. It sounded ridiculous. But he'd landed here and so had she. And he said he could take them back.

"What were you doing?" Kari peered at the black box in his hand. It resembled a smaller version of the handheld organizers that were so popular. She'd bought one herself and used it for notes and reminders as well as for reading and storing medical texts.

"Making my report."

"What are you telling them?" Her mind struggled to visualize the faceless, anonymous technicians receiving this transmission eight hundred years in the future. She could see Aidan standing here, warm flesh and pulsating blood, as real as she and yet not real at all. He was not even born in her time and in his she was long dead. She swallowed. Apprehension, awe, and yes, fear, had dried her mouth, leaving a metallic taste. Never had she so appreciated the twin enormities of death and time.

"That we should be back in twenty-four hours."

Damn, she should have told him earlier. She had made her decision this morning when she woke, but hadn't found the right way to bring it up. She shook her head. "Look, you can't do that."

"Of course I can. Bit more difficult maybe from here with three bodies, and we have to 'hop' in your time—" He paused as she shook her head. "What is it?"

She licked her lips nervously. She could have chosen a better place and time to tell him. Supposing he refused to listen? Could he make her go with him anyway? She could hide. He was obsessed with not leaving her here. He would look for her, wait until she came back. It wouldn't be for long. But she needed him to agree, she needed his help.

She drew in a deep breath and looked square into his brilliant gray eyes. "I can't go back yet, Aidan," she said firmly. "I owe Martha something. She helped me. God knows what might have happened to me if she hadn't taken me in. Her life must be miserable enough with that monster of a husband. Anne is helpless, so young. I promised her I would look after her. I must be there to do what I can to make sure she and Martha's grandchild are safe. Don't you see? I can't leave until the baby is born."

Chapter Seventeen

ॐ

Kari saw him flinch, as if she had dealt him a blow. Which in a way was true. She watched for a moment and hardly dared breathe as he fought for control. The eyes that had been so warm and gentle when he was talking to her freely suddenly became flinty and cold. His jaw tightened, the muscles working under the skin. Kari forced herself to hold his gaze. Her eyes remained locked on his, refusing to waver. He must not know how apprehensive she was that he would resist, would compel her to comply with his timetable.

At last he spoke. His voice was low and she could hear the strain. He was struggling to remain calm. "You don't mean that."

"I do." Kari resisted the urge to look away.

"And you say I'm the one who never kept you informed…?" His eyes had grown hard, a steely gray against the olive skin. Every word was sharp and cold.

"I couldn't—" She began again. "I didn't dare tell you…" Her voice trailed away.

"Am I so frightening?"

She forced a smile. "I was afraid you would leave me," she whispered. "This was so hard for me. I want you to take me home—but I promised." She forced herself to look at him again. "Just like you made a promise to Tanice and kept things from me."

He put his hands gently on her shoulders. "You're right," he said. "Now we're even in that game. No more, Kari, no more secrets for either of us. Agreed?"

She nodded. She loved the feel of his hands on her. She was ridiculously pleased to see his face relax and the eyes turn to warm silver again. "Agreed."

But he still hadn't agreed to stay for Anne's baby. She risked the question. "So you'll wait?" She held her breath.

"Look, Kari." He was making a great effort. "Come and sit down." He took her arm and drew her down again onto the same bale of straw. Except that this time, he didn't hold her hand. This was not going to be an easy conversation.

He sighed and ran his hand through his hair. In a way, Kari felt sorry for him. He had planned it all so carefully. Except, he had not discussed everything with her. He was too used to being alone, making his own decisions. And how could he have comprehended the depth of her commitment?

"There are three reasons that we must leave," he began. This was going to be a logical presentation. "One." He grasped his forefinger. "It's too dangerous to you personally to stay here. Two," another finger was added, "my technicians have given me ten days. They are more than half gone. If we overstay, there will be no way to hide this FLIP from the authorities. They would just have to abort. Then we would both be stranded here. And three." The third finger joined the bunch. "My coordinates are set. We have to be in a place that is still open in both our times. That's not so easy. The calculations have to be very precise." He omitted the fourth reason, which she must not know. *We must beam back from here because it is impossible for us to move anywhere else. We no longer have any money.*

Kari put out a hand to cover his. "Aidan," she began as rationally as he had. "Look, I'm not being perverse or following a whim. I've thought about this. I'm sure the baby will come in the next twenty-four hours." She breathed a silent prayer that this was true. "There's a huge risk of infection and heaven only knows what their delivery practices are. I need to be there. As for personal danger—neither Martha nor Anne would betray me. Thomas will not be anywhere near such women's work." Her voice and mouth betrayed her scorn for the man. "We can

159

return here, use your same calculations and still be in your ten day limit."

Silence hung between them as he reflected. She watched his face, noting the frown of concentration, the succeeding waves of thought so visibly revealed on the mobile face.

Aidan pulled his eyes away from Kari. He could not think logically and clearly with those eyes and that mouth in view. He needed an uncluttered mind. Much as he loved to look at her, delighted in touching her, he was troubled by what was happening to him. He was a scholar, and a man of the twenty-fourth century, dammit. He was accustomed to relying on a database, on making decisions from objectively calculated odds. And to have those around him do the same. True, he sometimes ignored the computer's recommendation, but only to plug in data more to his personal liking. His mouth twisted wryly. A taste of his own medicine! He was beginning to understand the frustration of the authorities when he flagrantly flouted the rules—as he had done to make this FLIP. He could not begin to imagine what would happen if it all came to light back in Tanice's aseptic lab.

When Kari dropped the bombshell about waiting for the baby, he'd nearly reacted with pure emotion, bordering on rage. His feelings were dangerously near the surface, as if floating up from the depths where they had been held so long in abeyance. He'd been annoyed with her before when she pushed him too hard, but this was beyond all reason! The woman had no sense of what had to be done, the technical difficulties of taking them back. First she had been impossible to pin down, flitting around the house and village, involved in her good works. Then, when he had engineered an incredibly creative coup to get her away, she had insisted on going back to fetch the dog! Now it was some promise about a baby that wasn't even born. Who knew when the infant might choose to put in an appearance? In this age, such things were totally subject to the whims of chance!

Nevertheless, he had made a big effort for control beneath her unwavering blue stare. He had explained to her the options, or rather, the constraints. She was playing him at his own game, answering with rational possibilities. *What did we have to lose?* she said sweetly. Only twenty-four or, at the most, forty-eight hours. Still within the limits. And what was there to gain? A life, two lives, perhaps.

He weighed the possibilities. Could he steal a few more hours with her? Would it matter so very much if they delayed? She was not thinking of herself, that was clear. He had expected her to be clamoring to leave, anxiously assisting him to set up the FLIP, not begging with him to give her more time. What would be worse? To leave her here? Unthinkable. To force her to go with him? How?

He looked up at last. "If we stay, I'll need to try to arrange a signal with Joan. But no guarantees," he hastened to add. "Forty-eight hours max. I shall reassess every two hours and if I see problems, we leave. Agreed?"

The smile that broke across her face was a reward in itself. He watched it light up her eyes, curve her sweet lips. His heart tightened in his chest. It was going to be hell to part from her. Her hands grasped his arms, her breath fanned against his face.

"Thank you, Aidan," she whispered. And kissed him lightly on the cheek.

It cost Kari a great deal not to follow up on that kiss. She closed her eyes as the warm wave swept through her. Aidan tensed beside her, and his arms rose to enfold her. With an effort of will, she stood up and stepped back, shaking her head. Forty-eight hours together at the most, and she had a job to do.

She hoped fervently that the work that waited for her would take her mind from this man, from the way her body tingled when he was near, from the way he occupied her thoughts when he was away, from the aching need to reach out and touch him... The tension hung between them like a tangible curtain that neither dared lift, knowing it would open a floodgate of passion.

Kari moved back to the window opening, giving herself time to calm her thudding pulse and her racing heart. She stepped with elaborate care to avoid the smallest risk of a touch from clothing or limbs.

The sun was well up, still fighting to show its face between the remains of the rain clouds. A light breeze blew the tattered remnants of the storm across the sky and shook the last drops from the trees. Kari strained to hear human sounds over the patter of falling water and the rustling of the leaves. All was quiet.

"How will you make a signal?" she asked softly.

She heard him shift on the bale as he answered, "Did a few favors for Joan in the kitchens of Godwin House. She liked me."

Kari could easily understand why the elderly housekeeper had responded to his good looks and his charming manners. She had not been alone.

Aidan continued, "She will know only from the gossip that I claimed you for my wife."

Kari kept her eyes fixed on the meadow, she did not turn. The warmth crept into her cheeks at the notion of being Aidan's wife.

Unaware of the effect of his words, he went on. "Thomas will not have spread anything of the fabrication of your birth." He chuckled. "That was a good touch, I must say. Figure I could ask Joan to place or send a signal when Anne's labor pains start. She would also leave a side door unbarred. As you said, the men are not likely to be around, and you would slip in unseen."

Kari nodded. She heard him move and then sensed the warmth of him behind her. "All clear still?"

She nodded again.

"Will have to leave you for a while."

"No."

"Kari—"

Still staring through the opening, she interrupted, "I shall go with you. I want to know what happens."

"Would be better to stay here with Ben—"

She whirled. "And do what if you are delayed—or don't come back? You're our ticket out of here. I'm grateful to you for waiting, but nothing else has changed. I want to see, to hear, to be right there if there's a change of plan. And I want to be consulted!"

Her face was inches from his. Her head swam with the impulse to bring her mouth just a little closer—just enough to brush his lips—and then... He smiled that warm smile that tore at her heart. How was she going to stand this for two more days? They needed a task to occupy their minds and bodies.

"Agreed. I give in. Let's go talk to Joan."

* * * * *

They did not leave immediately. They argued first about whether to take Ben. Kari won and Ben was accorded a place in the excursion. Then Kari wanted to leave their provisions and blankets in the hut, ready for their return. Aidan thought it more prudent to leave no trace behind, and to have some resources with them. He won. So, burdened with bread and cheese wrapped in the covers, and with Ben padding behind, they set off yet again for Godwin House.

They paused to survey the house from the copse. All was quiet, the laborers long gone to the fields to make up for the time lost by the rain. A solitary figure was busy in the yard. Kari's heart sank as she recognized Malcolm.

"Wait outside the gate," muttered Aidan.

Kari was about to acquiesce when Malcolm suddenly threw down the broom he was wielding and strode to the far gate leading to the stables.

"He grooms the horses every morning when he's cleaned the yard," said Aidan softly. "Let's hope that's what he's doing."

Swiftly, they covered the few yards to the kitchen. Aidan stopped her with a hand and paused to listen. Gently, he pushed open the door. Joan was standing at the trestle table pounding dough in a wooden bowl. She had rolled her sleeves above the elbow, and her strong forearms were covered with flour. Perspiration beaded her round face.

The oven glowed, well stoked with wood, ready to receive the loaves. Joan's skirts were kilted high, almost to her knees, in a vain attempt at comfort in the stifling heat. She paused to wipe her forehead with the back of her hand and looked up at the creak of the door.

"Well," she said, brushing pieces of dough from her hands, "if it isn't the happy husband. What brings you here? Tired of your wife already?" She chuckled, not waiting for an answer. "Sit yourself down, man, and tell me your woes."

She turned away to place her bowl in a warm spot near the oven. "I'll wager you have some trials with that minx. There's some as would console you with no problem. Talk of the household you've been—"

As she turned back, she caught sight of Kari, hovering in the doorway. She stopped her tirade and looked from one to the other, questioning. "What is it? You both look like the barn cat that got his face in the cream jug. You've a guilty secret I'll be bound. Out with it!"

Kari and Ben slid into the room. Joan thrust forward two of the rough chairs and sat at the dusty table.

"Joan," Aidan began, leaning forward and speaking in a low voice. "We expected to leave here immediately."

Joan nodded. "'Twould have been best, since—"

Aidan silenced her with a gesture. "My...my wife," he began, glancing sideways at Kari, but she kept her eyes resolutely on the patterns of flour on the table. She picked up a scrap of dough and began to knead it between her fingers.

"My wife," continued Aidan, "has medical knowledge."

Joan sniffed.

"I assure you it is true. She made a promise to Mistress Anne that she would be with her when the baby comes. Is there any news?"

Kari looked up and fixed her eyes on Joan's homely features. Joan shook her head. She was watching Aidan. Before she could speak, Aidan continued, "Kari expects the birth to be soon."

Joan's eyes flicked to Kari, then back to Aidan.

"Within a day," Kari said quietly.

"Joan," Aidan said. "For the sake of Mistress Martha and for Anne, will you help us?"

"To do what?"

"To let us know when the pains start."

"I'll not put my position in danger. This is my home. I'll not find another if I'm dismissed."

"I understand, Joan." Kari bent forward ignoring Aidan's gesture of impatience. "Look, I don't know what you've heard about me, but I love Martha and Anne. They were good to me when I was—lost. And you were kind to me and to Ben."

Joan glanced down at the dog. "'Tis a clever beast."

Aidan took over again. "Will you send us a signal, Joan? At the right time?"

"And how may I do that?" Joan's voice was scornful. "Poor, addlepated knave."

Kari hid a smile at Aidan's expression of discomfiture.

Joan went on. "How shall I find 'ee? Tell me not where 'ee be 'iding. Then no man can say I knew what Master Thomas would dearly like to find."

"Is he looking for us, Joan?"

"Aye, in a way. Says 'e wishes to make amends for accusing 'er o' witchcraft." Joan nodded toward Kari. "But I know Master Thomas. Been in 'is household since I were a lass. Always 'as a reason for 'isself, 'as Master Thomas." She sniffed again. "An' if

165

the pains be at night? There be no souls as will venture out after dark for fear o' spirits."

Kari and Aidan looked at each other. Neither had reckoned with ancient superstitions.

Joan got up ponderously from the table to turn her bowl. She picked up a bone from a pile and tendered it to Ben. "Gettin' thin," she remarked.

Kari nodded. She was thinking furiously. "Joan," she said, "would you keep Ben here? Keep him out of the way? Then send him to find me when the time comes?"

She heard Aidan draw in his breath to protest. "He knows where we are and will obey. We used to play the game all the time. Say 'Find Kari' – that's all."

Joan looked doubtfully at the dog. "And if he's chased away before?"

"He won't go far. And I know you can keep him out of the way." She patted Joan's floury hand. "Look, I'll write a note. No, that's foolish. Here's a piece of my shawl." She ripped at the fringe. "Tie this to his collar. We'll know you've sent him."

Kari and Aidan stood. "Stay, Ben," Kari commanded.

The dog lay down, his massive head on his forepaws, the gnawed bone close by.

"Thank you, Joan." Kari gave the old woman an impulsive hug.

"Yes, well-a-day, I'll make no promises," harrumphed the cook. "But I'll do my best." She hesitated, wiping her hands on her sackcloth apron, seemed to come to a decision. "Another false labor this morning," she said gruffly. "'Twill not be long."

Kari sighed with relief. "Within the day!" she exclaimed.

"Aye, reckon. Now ye had best be gone and let me bake my bread afore the hands come for their dinner. I'll not let anyone see the dog."

Impetuously, Kari embraced her once more before she slid through the doorway and away after Aidan.

The eight hours before Ben came seemed endless. They took turns to watch and to rest. Kari had learned to snatch sleep where she could, but she dozed fitfully for a few minutes, then woke, tense and listening. She had to be right about the imminence of the birth. Had the waters broken yet? Aidan was on watch when Ben broke through the trees.

Chapter Eighteen

ಬಿ

"Kari, here's Ben," Aidan hissed. "He did it!"

Kari rolled off the straw bales and was on her feet at once while Aidan pulled open the door to let in the dog.

Ben went straight to Kari and sat while she detached the piece of yarn from his collar. She ran her fingers under the leather and scratched behind his ears. Ben sniffed gently at her face as she stroked him, making the whuffling noises that he probably thought was speech. His tail thumped gently on the ground.

"Let's go!" she said.

"All of us?"

She looked at him with impatience. "Surely—"

He held up a hand in defeat. "I know. We go together. But in that case, we take everything." He swung the pack onto his back and motioned her to proceed.

Aidan was close behind as she slid through the side door of the Godwin house into a storage room. The smell of drying vegetables and smoked meats assailed their nostrils. The latch to the door into the passage opened smoothly to the touch. Only Joan and Martha had the key to the precious supply of foodstuffs, and Joan had kept her word.

They stole up the stairs in darkness, feeling and groping their way to Anne's bedchamber. Kari stepped into the room and greeted Martha in silence with a kiss and a clasp of their hands. Ben settled watchfully across the threshold, lying close to Aidan.

The room smelled sweetly of lavender sprinkled on fresh linens, and of soap from a recent scrubbing. Thankfully, Kari noted that her instructions for cleaning had been heeded. A pail of water stood ready with a brush for her hands. She peeled off her shawl and rolled her sleeves. Martha stood by with clean linen, but Kari motioned her aside with a smile and waved her hands to air-dry them.

Anne lay on the bed, covered with a thin sheet. A soft film of sweat clung like dew to her forehead and upper lip. Her small face on the white pillow was drawn with strain and fear. She looked more childlike than ever.

Holding her hands away from all contact, Kari bent to brush her lips against the girl's cheek. She was warm, but not feverish.

Anne smiled bravely. "Thank you for coming, Kari," she whispered.

"Didn't I promise I would? Now, let's see how you're doing."

All through the night they hovered around the bed. Anne was young and healthy, but it was near dawn, and still no baby. Kari had listened as best she could to the fetal heart throughout and bent her ear constantly to the swollen abdomen. The beat was growing fainter each time she bent close.

"Come on, Anne," she whispered. "You can do it. Let's have this baby. Come closer," she said to Aidan, who approached the bed with caution.

She doubted if the girl understood the words. The knuckles on Anne's clenched hands shone white as she grasped Martha's wrist on one side and Aidan's on the other.

Kari glanced at Aidan. "Are you up to this?" she said. "You're not going to pass out, are you? I can't deal with any fainting."

His eyes were large in a pale face. Wordlessly, he swallowed and shook his head. He stroked back the hair from Anne's brow and returned the hand to hold the girl's fingers.

"If you feel yourself going," Kari insisted, "just get out of the way quickly."

"I'm fine."

She turned her attention back to the bed. Now she could hear nothing of the baby's heart. Her anxiety grew. Anne pushed and strained, panting between each exertion as Kari had taught her. Her cries, that had been loud at the beginning, had weakened, reduced now to pathetic whimpers.

"Anne, listen to me. You're doing fine. Work with me, Anne."

The girl's tired eyes fixed on Kari's face.

"That's it. Good girl. Now push when I tell you."

Gently, Kari coached Anne through the last stages until she gave a deep groan, her body tensed as if it might break, and suddenly the baby was there, bloody and unnaturally still. The tiny body lay blue and unmoving. A wail arose from Martha and a groan from Aidan.

Quickly, Kari seized the infant and slapped the small buttocks. No response. She turned the frail body over and thrust her small finger covered with a linen cloth into the mouth. Rapidly, she worked to clear mucus from the airways. Still nothing.

Martha rocked silently in grief, her hands fixed on the cross that swung on her bosom. Anne lay inert, watching with huge eyes, her lip caught in her teeth. There was no sound in the room but the soft breathing of the four as they tensed in apprehension.

Kari laid the baby on the end of the bed. It was a boy, beautifully formed. His lashes lay on his rounded cheeks as if in peaceful sleep. His tiny fingers, each with a perfect nail, curled into loose fists.

"Let me take him," said Martha through a sob. "I shall wrap him decently and take him away."

"No!" Kari said sharply. "Not yet. It's not over yet."

She pressed her mouth firmly over the infant's tiny lips and nose and blew gently into the unused lungs. Once, a pause. Listen at the chest. Twice, a pause. Listen. Not too hard. She closed her eyes. Three times. She turned her ear to the chest. "Come on, baby, you can do it. Breathe!"

Was that a flutter? Again, a tiny puff of air. His little fingers twitched, his nose wrinkled up, his mouth opened, ready to expel breath in a cry. It was the sweetest music possible.

Kari heard the joyful exclamation from Martha and Anne. She hugged the bloody, slimy body to her. "Thank you, baby, thank you," she whispered.

Over the child's fluffy head, she caught Aidan's eye.

He smiled tremulously. "Well done," he mouthed.

Tenderly, Kari placed the baby in Anne's outstretched arms, and he nestled contentedly against her breast.

"Nearly finished," Kari said to Aidan over her shoulder. "Then we can leave."

She busied herself with the remaining tasks and did not notice Martha slip from the room.

A few minutes later, she took the baby from Anne and looked for Martha. There was only Aidan. She held out the warm bundle.

"Here, hold him for a moment, while I check his mom one last time."

It was all she could do not to burst into laughter at the expression on Aidan's face. She managed to limit herself to an uncontrollable twitch of the lips as he hesitantly held out his arms.

"There, he won't break. Just bend your arms and hold him naturally."

Gingerly, Aidan let her place the newborn in the crook of his arm. He gazed down at the tiny face and looked back up at Kari.

"A miracle," he whispered.

"Each one is a miracle," she responded softly and turned back to Anne.

When she looked again, she caught Aidan gently stroking the baby's cheek with a careful forefinger. As she watched, he hesitantly shifted the child's weight and brought him up to his shoulder. The infant immediately snuggled his tiny head into the warm nook at the base of Aidan's neck. Unexpected tears pricked at the back of her eyes at the look of surprised delight on Aidan's face. She swallowed and turned away before he realized she was watching. He was warm, sensitive, intelligent and handsome. All they needed was a way to conquer time.

She pulled herself together. "I'll take him now," she said briskly and returned the child to his mother. Aidan stood with arms dangling as if not knowing what to do now the tiny burden was gone.

Kari knew that in a few more minutes there would be nothing more for her to do. Aidan would take her back to the hut, they would prepare to leave, and this fantastic adventure would be over.

She glanced over at Aidan. He was leaning against the wall, watching her work. He was almost overwhelmingly male in this scene, a primitive symbol of virile manhood surveying the tender new life that was the result of the union of a man and a woman.

She had assisted at many births, but never had she been so conscious of this elemental link, so aware of the engendering, physical act of love. She caught Aidan's eye, and the corner of his mouth lifted in a small smile. His eyes were the color of soft pewter in this light, warm and glowing. The tiny curl of desire flickered deep inside. In a few short hours he would complete whatever it was he had to do, and she would be back in her own time and he in his. A stab of pain merged with the quiver of physical longing. She closed her eyes to the sight of him and turned her head away.

It was as she was folding the last of the linen and doing a final check of Anne's quiet breathing that she became conscious of another presence in the room. She sensed Aidan stiffen as he turned toward the door. She whirled, not knowing who or what she might see.

Jonathan stood hesitantly in the doorway, a look of wonder on his handsome young face. His eyes did not leave the sleeping form of his wife and the child, still held in the crook of her arm. Martha followed close behind her son-in-law, the trace of tears still on her cheeks.

"Come in, Jonathan." Kari moved aside. "Come and meet your son."

Softly, Jonathan Howard stepped into the room and put out a hesitant finger. Gently he stroked his wife's cheek and then the baby's hand. The tiny fingers twitched and grasped. Jonathan smiled with delight.

Kari stepped back and touched Aidan behind her. She watched the young father as he gazed in awe at his family.

"A miracle," he breathed. "I thank God. And you, Kari," he said, turning toward her. "Don't say anything. Mistress Godwin has told me what you did. How my son was blue and dead and how you breathed life into him. I shall pray for you every day of my life."

Tears pricked at the back of Kari's eyes at the irony of his words. How could Jonathan pray for someone not yet born?

Jonathan's face became serious. "But I can do more than that. My father-in-law is a hard man, but not a bad one. He loves his family, but has his weaknesses, as do we all. Please, ask me no questions, but do as I say."

He folded Anne's hand into one of his as he gazed at Kari and Aidan. "Your hiding place was discovered, I know not how."

"Flynn." Aidan breathed the word into Kari's ear.

Jonathan did not hear. "Godwin's men are waiting there for you," he continued, "for he does not suspect that you are here. But we tremble to hide you in the house for some of the servants are not to be trusted. I fear Josiah Small plans some mischief and has convinced Thomas it is the right and godly thing to apprehend you. You must leave here and hide where you will be hard to find."

His voice became urgent. "Two horses are saddled and ready in the stable. Take them and make for London."

"London?" said Aidan sharply.

"Aye," Jonathan nodded. "I fear the other roads are too lonely and are watched."

"Why would the London road be clear?"

"Maybe 'tis not, but I have arranged so that you do not travel alone. There is a troupe of traveling players in the village. They would have performed here, but for the events of this night." He smiled down at the child. "I know the leader of the troupe and have made it worth his while to pass you as two of his players. A villain and a boy." His lips curved, despite his serious expression.

"He says the woman must travel as the boy who plays female roles, and the man shall be the specialist in roaring villains, who have little to say but much action. Joan is below with suitable clothing for Kari." He hurried on. "Leave the animals at the stable in Watling Street by Paul's Gate when you have no more need of them. Or keep them if such is your desire. Now go! And Godspeed!"

Kari looked at Aidan, but it was impossible to read his reaction. She had to follow his lead, for he had the means of taking them out of this century. Of course, Jonathan had no way of knowing that. He believed he was providing the best escape possible.

Would this journey never end? Would she gain yet more time with Aidan? Much as she wanted to return to her own time, the temptation to milk every possible moment of Aidan's presence pulled at her senses, creating indecision and conflict in her mind.

She heard Aidan protesting to Jonathan in a low voice. She made out "preposterous" and "London".

"There is no other hiding place," Jonathan whispered back, and Martha's evident terror at last convinced both Kari and Aidan.

Martha was trembling from the emotions of the night. "Please go," she urged Kari, clutching at her sleeve. Her lips quivered. "Thomas is not a bad man, but I fear for you. I cannot tell you what I know… Please go."

Kari felt Aidan's hand on her arm, pulling her to the door. Impatiently she drew her arm away and went to Jonathan. "Thank you," she said simply and leaned forward to kiss his cheek. "You have done a brave and good thing. Look after your wife and your son and make sure he grows to be as good a man as you."

With a final pat to Anne and the child, a silent embrace to Martha who stood at the door, she turned to Aidan, tears brimming in her eyes. "Now I am ready."

Stepping as silently as they could on the creaking steps, Aidan and Kari followed Jonathan's whispered instructions as he bundled them down the stairs and away.

* * * * *

Hand in hand, hearts pounding, every sense on edge, Kari and Aidan crept out of the house to avoid alerting master or servants of their stealthy departure.

Kari moved as if through a surrealistic universe. Her brain was on overload after the strain of the last few hours, and she was barely aware of the darkness and the muffled movements. Her neck, legs and shoulders ached from the hours of standing at Anne's side. Aidan's fingers lay warm in hers, she clutched them as if they alone linked her to reality. Ben padded along beside them, a darker shape slipping silently past the carts waiting in the yard for the bustle of the morning.

Deep shadows cloaked the nooks and corners of the house and outbuildings. Leaves rustled and branches stirred in the freshening breeze. Kari shivered.

The moon was fading as dawn rose in the east. The tattered remnants of clouds fluttered across the band of sky that showed pink and pale lemon yellow above the trees.

Aidan carried the packs. The horses stood waiting at the stable door, snorting softly, sniffing the morning air. They stamped their hooves and shook their shaggy manes, eager to savor an early morning run.

Chapter Nineteen

ಉ

The black gelding stood higher than the groom's shoulder. The young animal, full of energy and willfulness, tossed his proud head impatiently as the servant held firmly to the bridle. The other was a smaller brown mare. Patient and doe-eyed, she stood ready, wearing a leather harness stripped of all metal attachments. Thoughtful Jonathan had removed or muffled all jingling pieces. Both horses wore thick padding over their hooves to deaden the sound of their shoes over the stones of the yard.

Kari saw with relief that the groom holding the horses was not Malcolm, but a young serving man of Jonathan's. Jem nodded to them briefly and touched his forelock. He motioned for them to mount.

Aidan hesitated. Kari turned and saw the comical look on his face. "Can you ride?" she whispered.

He gazed at the towering side of the black. She saw him swallow. "Never been quite this close to a horse before. What do I do?"

"Satan here is willful," muttered the groom. "Needs a strong hand to show who's master."

"I'll take him," Kari said, and swung lightly up in the saddle before Aidan could protest. She settled herself on the saddle and took the reins. It was wonderful to be dressed in the tunic and hose Martha had found, to be free from clinging skirts. Her hair was pinned tight under a loose cap and the cool air felt good on her neck.

The groom proceeded to help Aidan to boost himself onto the mare's back. No beginner mounts a horse with grace for the first time, and Aidan was no exception. Kari averted her face and pretended to adjust a strap so as not to have to watch Aidan's hands clutching for purchase and the ungainly hoisting of his body into the leather saddle.

"Keep your hands light on the reins," instructed Jem. "She'll shy if you be rough. A gentle touch will do." He fondled the soft nose and bent to whisper close to the mare's ear.

"Is she yours?" Kari asked.

Jem nodded, patting the animal's neck. "I call her Diamond," he said shyly, "because she's precious to me."

"We'll take good care of her. Thank you, Jem." Kari held out her hand. Jem grasped it briefly and then led Satan from the yard. Docilely, Diamond followed on, Ben at her heels.

When they reached a safe distance from the house, Kari reined in and allowed Aidan to come alongside. "Why did you agree to this?" she whispered.

She could make out his bulk on the horse, a darker outline against the night sky, and saw the movement of his shoulders as he shrugged in the darkness.

"Not much time to think," he responded softly. "No chance to input to my databank. Just had to react."

So he'd acted out of instinct, done what his wits told him, without checking it out with some damned machine.

"Anyway, maybe I can get some more data for the project," he continued.

She sensed rather than saw the smile. The project! How he loved to rationalize what he did. Always a second reason for his decisions. Did he welcome this extra time together as much as she did? Would he ever admit it if he did?

The actors were already waiting for the new players outside the inn. A motley crew of men, young and old, they had been recruited and whipped into some kind of a troupe by the actor manager, Tom Siddons. Sideways glances greeted the arrival of the handsome man and the pretty boy on two fine horses, but the players knew better than to question their master.

Tom himself was a large, blustering man full of bombast and good humor. He lay about him with a will, cajoling and threatening, to push his unruly band into some semblance of order.

Jonathan had taken time to explain that Tom was a brilliant actor, a loyal friend and an implacable enemy. He lived as he acted—larger than life, and milking every ounce of drama from every event. His hard and uncertain existence had given him a sharp eye for the ridiculous, and a ready wit to satirize human foibles.

Many of the plays he performed were written or adapted by him. No women, of course, were accepted on the stage, and so he was constantly on the lookout for boys with a slight enough frame and delicate features to pass for the female roles. He'd apparently agreed to pass off Kari as his latest find. Aidan would be revealed as the makeweight in the deal—accepted because Tom had such high hopes of the boy companion.

The crew had been hauled out of bed at first light and showed their resentment. They grumbled and cursed freely as they sluiced aching heads at the pump and packed their belongings onto carts drawn by two sorry mules, as ill-tempered as their masters.

Tom sat astride an old horse that looked in good health, despite its age. It stood patiently as Tom cursed and kicked, and manhandled his actors into the carts and onto the other animals standing by. He acknowledged Aidan and Kari with a nod of his head, but drew no further attention to them. They reined their horses aside and waited in silence.

The wolfhound lay in a safe spot, his huge head on his front paws, watching the chaotic scene, eyes and ears alert for any threat to his mistress in this new situation.

Aidan shifted uncomfortably.

"Are you OK?"

"Been more comfortable."

"She's a beauty. You won't have a problem."

"Felt more in control in ultraspace. At least I knew what the robots were supposed to do."

"She'll know what to do. Here." Kari leaned forward and grasped Diamond's leading rein. Quickly, she attached it to her saddle. "Now you just need to concentrate on staying on. She'll follow us."

Aidan grunted. "This is not a natural position."

"Someone once said that if life was logical, men would ride sidesaddle, but that's the way it is."

She ran her eye down the length of his thighs. She swallowed. "You're sitting well," she said. "Just remember not to slump. Keep your weight even. Use your knees and thighs to guide her." She turned away, pretending to check a fitting on her far rein, as the warm blood rose in her face at her words.

"Suppose you've done this before."

"I went through the usual pony craze. Never had my own horse, but my parents indulged me with lessons before I left home."

She broke off as the ragged pack of men and animals began to move off. "Let's go."

Their little procession of two horses and the dog followed the last cart as they started down the rutted track that passed for a road.

The heavy rains had churned the surface into mud in parts, and the cavalcade was brought to a stop more than once as the wheels became mired in the glue. All available hands were needed to push the heavy carts from behind as the mules strained and pulled from the front.

Kari guessed it must have been two or three hours before they stopped at the top of a particularly difficult rise and led the horses under the trees. She dismounted one more time and led Satan to the stream. He'd been obedient enough, but she could feel his impatience at the slow pace and his irritation at the frequent mounting and dismounting. His restlessness was beginning to show.

He shied and snorted in a display of temperament as Ben came to the water to drink. Kari hung on to the black horse's bridle as he danced away and then patted his neck.

"Behave now, Satan," she crooned. "You know Ben. You and I are a great team. You can run later." Gradually she soothed him with her voice and her hands.

Aidan was behind her, his leading rein still attached, looking apprehensive and then relieved as Kari brought the big horse under control. Grimly, he slid down to the ground and stretched his cramped muscles. He pulled a face. "God, I'd rather pitch hay all day than sit on there."

"Not too much longer. Let me untie Diamond so she can drink."

Tom strode up to them, his black beard seeming to crackle with energy. He rolled his massive shoulders and patted his girth.

"Ready for some sustenance?" He held out two chunks of bread and a chicken leg.

"Meat?" said Kari, eyebrows raised.

"Aye, lad. A good actor's worth his keep. Make 'em laugh, show 'em fire and damnation so they fear for their poor miserable souls, and they pay in kind." Chuckling heartily, he thrust a tankard at them.

His mouth full, he rumbled on, "Now you look a likely lad," he said to Kari. "You could play a girl in my next play to deceive the world."

Kari was not sure how much he knew about her situation. Better to play it safe. "What play would that be?"

"I know not yet. My muse shall inspire me." He struck an exaggeratedly comic attitude, one finger to his forehead, miming intense concentration.

Kari smiled. He was a born comedian. "I hear a man called Shakespeare does some good work," she ventured.

Tom awoke from his reverie as if stung. "Shakespeare?" he thundered. "A scrawny, puny, ne'er-do-well of an actor that has managed to curry favor and steals honest men's ideas."

"How so?"

"I had this play in my head—" Before he could continue, a shout from the carts drew his attention. Two men were rolling on the ground, locked in a battle. Spluttering and bellowing, Tom strode off to restore order.

Aidan put out a hand and caressed Kari's shoulder. They stood in silence for a moment. The roofs and spires of Elizabethan London lay before them. The silver thread of the Thames curled between the jumble of buildings packed cheek-by-jowl within the walls of the city. Plumes of smoke rose from the chimney pots and hung lazily in the warm midday air. A bell tolled in the distance, calling the pious to worship.

"This is bizarre," he said.

She nodded.

"I am caught in the sixteenth century, making my way toward an unknown point in London, riding an animal that I have only ever seen from a distance or in paintings, likely to be put on a stage to earn my bread, accompanied by a woman dressed as a boy, and a dog."

She fixed her eyes on his face and nodded again.

He continued to stroke her. "I have learned things unheard of in my history texts, I have watched things I never expected to see. I have struggled with ideas and feelings that I never knew I could entertain."

Still Kari did not respond. She felt the tingle where his hand lay on her arm. His face came closer, his breath whispered on her face. His silver gray eyes gazed intently into her face, as if he was memorizing every detail.

"This is a bizarre moment in a bizarre situation," he repeated. His voice was low. "I never wanted this to happen between us—I fought it for as long as I could. But I know now that I seized every opportunity to prolong our time, although there was always a reason I could give myself." He smiled. "You know that coming to London was unnecessary, it defies all logic. I wouldn't even dare to scan for probability. But I grasped at it again, Kari, because I wanted this extra time with you."

Kari felt the blood coursing faster in her veins at his words, which echoed so closely her own hidden thoughts.

"I shall do my best to take you back home, Kari," he continued, "but we are in the unknown. I must recalc again and reset the coordinates. It could be tonight, it could be tomorrow, we cannot tell how many hours are left to us. So, I want to, I must tell you now."

Kari held her breath.

"You have touched my life, my heart, my soul. No one has meant so much to me before."

They stood alone in the universe, linked only by Aidan's hand on her shoulder, an electric bond holding them together to the exclusion of all others.

The shouts of the quarrel slowly diminished in the distance. Tom's voice rose and fell as he berated his men. The smell of the horses filled her nostrils; she was conscious of their warmth and the small movements as they tossed their heads and shifted their feet next to her. She put one hand on Satan's stirrup leather as if to steady herself.

Aidan's dear face filled her view, his lips came closer. He whispered against her mouth, "I love you, Kari."

His arms enfolded her. She felt the beating of his heart against her breast, his breath fanned her face. Heat radiated from him, infusing her with warmth and joy. His kiss came at last, soft and sweet, and she melted into his arms.

"Yah, devil!" The shout came from behind them and they sprang apart, hearts thumping. Tom stood glaring at them, arms akimbo. "None o' that in my troupe!" He spat on the ground in disgust. "Leave the lad alone, unnatural lecher! For shame." Roughly, he pushed Aidan aside.

"Come, boy," he said. "Ride alongside me. Leave the likes o' him to fend for hisself." Without more ado, he seized Kari's reins and led Satan to the other side of the copse beside his own horse.

* * * * *

He loves me! Aidan's words echoed over and over in her mind, picking up the rhythm of the clopping hooves. He had dared to speak what she had not allowed herself to think. Kari fought to put order into her thoughts. Her body sang with the joy of the knowledge that he harbored the very same emotions that she had hugged to her heart for days.

Since the meeting at the pond, she had known in her deepest being that this man who had sought her out through space and time was her true soul mate. She cast her mind back, savoring every precious moment, reliving the times they had been together, what they had done, what they had said. Her happiness was bittersweet. One more day, two at the most. Then the journey into the unknown, through time.

Would she see him go as she arrived back in her own time? Would he fade away like the Cheshire cat, until nothing was left but his beloved smile and then not even that? Would they say their goodbyes when they beamed back? Or at some time on their way? Or back in the twentieth century? She felt a physical pain around her heart at the thought of leaving him.

Tom broke into her reverie. He jogged beside her on his patient nag, riding naturally and loosely with the horse's movement.

"Can't allow what happened there!"

Kari started to speak.

"Nay, lass. For I know you are a lass," Tom continued. He twinkled at her. "But these knaves must not know." He waved at the troupe now plodding stolidly downhill. "A wench lying in the same inn, sharing the same beds, would fall prey to the best wrestler or the best roller of dice, depending on their mood. And for some, a lad seen doing what you just did would fare no better." He wagged his head, knowingly. "I shall protect thee, lass, as best I can, but ye must do your part."

"Thank you, Master Siddons."

He threw his head back and guffawed with laughter. "What pretty manners it has! Master Siddons! I am Tom to my players, plain Tom."

Satan pranced nervously at the sudden noise beside him and Tom reached out a hand to grasp the bridle. "Whoa, boy. 'Tis a fine spirit he has." He patted the neck of his placid animal. "My brave boy had a fire in his belly just that way. As great an actor as any in Will Shakespeare's troupe," he said proudly.

"Your horse?" Kari showed surprise.

"Aye, lass. I named him Harry for the king and Agincourt, for he has a noble spirit. He plays as many parts as I. He can prance and pick dainty for the lady entering the castle. Betimes he is the fierce warhorse, ready to do battle." Tom's voice rose and fell expressively as he declaimed the virtues of his mount.

"'Tis a fine beast you ride," he continued. "But no mount for a wench. That knave behind takes the docile mare, like a girl."

"No," Kari protested. "I made him take Diamond. He doesn't know how to ride."

Tom's laugh rang out again. "Poor gullible child," he cried. "How can a man not know how to ride? Every churl in the kingdom sits astride a nag. Where did he tell you he was from? The moon?"

He wheeled his horse and trotted back, still chuckling, to check the carts.

Chapter Twenty

ℵ

Kari had told Aidan that she'd ridden as a girl, but she still felt the pull in her calves and thighs as she adjusted to the movements she had once known so well. Aidan was probably suffering more than she.

For the past hour, signs of habitation and commerce had grown more visible along the road. Satan had settled down, but was now beginning to show signs of nervousness again as the noise and movement around him increased. They had met few strangers on the road, although she'd followed Aidan's instructions to keep watch for a hulking, red-haired man. It would grow more difficult to spot Reed Flynn as more people appeared on the high road. Besides, it sounded as if he wouldn't even do his own spying, but would hire watchers from his generous purse. So it would be impossible to know for sure if they were followed.

Church spires grew clearer in the distance, and dust hung in the air. Kari watched, fascinated, as the daily life of Elizabethan London began to unfold in front of her eyes. Peddlers of all kinds hawked pies and ribbons, farm produce and knives. They jostled and shouted their cries at the top of their voices in a chant that melded into a singsong accompaniment.

Children scrambled between the rumbling carts, darting off across the street if they succeeded in stealing an apple, a scrap of lace, a dropped coin. Screams of protest added to the cacophony. The air was pungent with the smells of cooked meats, fruit and flowers, mixed with the earthy odors of horses, dogs and unwashed bodies, together with the occasional whiff of decay from an open midden.

All the time, Kari was conscious of Aidan at her back as he followed with the carts. In all the throng of people, she felt his eyes on her, knew where he was at every moment. Tom had rejoined her at the front of the procession and forced a passage through the crowd. He was known to many and flung out lusty invitations to his performances.

Soon they would have to leave the protection of Tom's troupe of actors and find their own way. They would be together, alone, relying on their wits and Aidan's technology. They must not be separated

A mixture of emotions flooded through her. Her pulses raced at the thought of being close to Aidan now that he had made the wonderful pronouncement. She too would be able to reveal her feelings. They could kiss, could hold each other. On the other hand, her heart sank at the thought of leaving him. Was there any way that they could be together? It seemed hopeless.

In early afternoon, they crossed the river Fleet. Kari peered at it with interest, trying to remember if she knew when it had been covered over, to flow underground beneath the newspaper offices that would gather there for decades. The carts rumbled down Holborn Hill, swung right at the church of St. Andrew, and continued down Shoe Lane.

Tom broke off his advertising long enough to say that Farringdon without Ward laid this side of the Fleet, Farringdon within Ward on the other. The Farringdons had the dubious distinction of housing three prisons between them—the Fleet, Bridewell, and Newgate, as well as the Old Bailey. Tom pointed them out with the pride that came from the fact that he had never been confined in them himself, but knew many that had. For a small city, London was well served with prisons.

Tom thought to enlighten a country bumpkin and in a way he was right, but not for the reason he imagined. Kari gazed around her in amazement at the tiny, crowded houses, huddling as close as possible to the city walls. From the back of the horse, she could reach out and touch the windows of the upper stories, which leaned drunkenly toward each other. The buildings of the Black Friary loomed on their right as they approached the Ludgate and Saint Paul's Cross.

Tom congratulated himself on making good time. These gates, Cripplegate, Moorgate, Bishopsgate, and Aldgate were still in operation. At dusk, they were pulled closed, and no man entered or left until dawn the next day.

Through the Ludgate, Kari caught sight of Saint Paul's Cathedral. The massive stone dome, sitting imposingly on Ludgate Hill had not yet been built. She glimpsed instead a squared building, lacking a spire, dominating all around. The spire had burned a few years since, Tom said, never to be replaced. Kari did not tell him that in little more than a half century the rest would burn down in the Great Fire, and Sir Christopher Wren would undertake the monumental task of rebuilding.

The troupe was making for Southwark, to the new Rose Theater, where they were to perform near the bear-baiting fields. They were anxious to cross the city and leave by London Bridge near Billingsgate before dusk fell and the gates were closed.

If progress had been slow on the rutted roads from Hampstead, it was at a snail's pace in the narrow, obstructed lanes of the city. Kari and Aidan were to leave their horses near Saint Paul's. They halted at last at the alehouse near Paul's Brewhouse, across from the Deanery.

The foaming tankards of ale supplied promptly by the landlord tasted wonderful after the dust of the journey.

Kari pulled Satan out of the way of the throng and sat in a quieter corner of the yard, burying her face in the mug of beer. Ben settled under a table against a piece of jutting wall. She imagined herself as a small leaf, borne along on the eddies of an uncaring and tumultuous current. Her life since she had been transported back in history had been a succession of periods of slow calm and violent activity.

In the sudden peace from questions and voices and the cessation of the jolting ride, she had time to gather her thoughts. Scenes swam through her mind of her first introduction to the Godwin Farm, her anger at the misery of the Miller family, her confrontation with Thomas, the realization of Aidan's identity, the accusations of witchcraft, the escape with Aidan, the birth of Anne's baby.

Through it all hovered the image of Aidan and her feelings for him. She still cringed at the memory of her one past sexual adventure, that had nothing to do with love. Never had she experienced the pull of a man as she had with Aidan. Her hands had ached to touch him, to hold him, to bury herself in his warmth and affection. For she had found his tenderness, his carefully hidden feelings and his wonderfully loving nature. How could she part from him? How could she bear to plan their separation? Yet was there a choice? For the first time, she allowed the niggling thought to enter her mind. Maybe there was a way. Could she live in the future? Could Aidan live in the twentieth century? Would he?

Tom and Aidan were involved in a serious conversation at the end of the table. Kari leaned back against the high wooden back of the seat and watched them. Ben sat up from his place under the table and thrust his head into her lap. She scratched behind his ears and stroked his shaggy head.

The men's dark heads were together, deep in discussion. It was impossible to hear the words. Somehow, Kari didn't mind not knowing what was going on. She hadn't slept properly in two days, and not at all last night. Fatigue reduced her world to the immediate, to Aidan, to thinking about him, about the time that remained to them, about what they would do with each other, what they would decide.

At last, the talk was ended. Tom turned to her. "So, lass," he boomed. "'Tis fare-thee-well, then." He wiped his lips with the back of his hand. Aidan watched from over the rim of his tankard.

"Yon knave has 'suaded me. I must look for another boy."

Kari smiled. "It would be best."

Tom snorted. "I know not for sure who you are—" He raised a hand. "Nor do I wish to know." He crossed himself. "Methinks I might find it not to my liking. But for Jonathan Howard's sake I shall fulfill my bargain. I hear you have no coin."

Kari raised her eyebrows, then frowned. She was sure that Aidan had spoken of the money he had brought with him, perfect reproductions produced by his futuristic technology.

Tom blundered on. "So I shall direct you to a house I know where ye may find shelter." He nodded at Aidan. "He has the name. Tell them Tom Siddons sent you. Robert Hoodless is a coneyman but will do my bidding if he knows what's good for him." With another burst of laughter he rose from the table.

"Coneyman?" Kari asked.

"A trickster," Aidan answered. "He operates in and around the cathedral. Specializes in gulling visitors from the country, so Tom tells me." He smiled apologetically.

"I see. And where does he live?"

"He runs a brothel."

* * * * *

Kari and Aidan left the alehouse together and took the horses from the boy who had taken them to drink at the stone trough in the street. Each holding a rein, they led a weary Satan and Diamond along the narrow lane to the stable tucked behind Watling Street where it joined Ludgate Hill.

The groom took charge of the animals, promising to brush and feed them and then send word to Jonathan.

Then Kari and Aidan walked. The names were familiar to Kari—Holborn, Newgate Street...but everything else was changed. Gone were the towering gray buildings, the weaving black taxis, the lumbering red buses. The sights, sounds and smells experienced from the back of a horse had seemed bewildering. Close to, they were overwhelming.

London was still crowded. The gray business suits and neat clothes of the twentieth century had given way to an assortment of apparel of extremes of riches and rags. Brilliantly dressed men and women in elaborate ruffs and embroidered sleeves brushed shoulders with tattered beggars and sober merchants. Foreign sailors strode in drunken convoy up from the river, swaggering and eyeing the women.

Kari and Aidan shouldered and jostled their way through the crowds, sidestepping litter and garbage that clogged the inadequate runnels that served as drains, making the cobbled stones slippery and treacherous.

From time to time Kari grasped Ben's collar to keep him close to her side and out of the way of the heedless throng.

The modesty of Martha and Anne Godwin had not prepared Kari for the boldness of the city women. Mistress and serving maid alike eyed the well-built man and the slender boy with unabashed interest. Several made no attempt to step aside, but stood their ground in the narrow passageways, obliging Aidan and Kari to brush against them. The murmured apology and demurely lowered lids could not hide the spark of invitation that shone beneath the lashes. Sounds of approbation and soft laughter followed them down the street.

The inn they sought stood with unintentional irony in Love Lane, hard against the Guildhall. The house was tall and narrow, its upper story leaning crazily across the alley to almost touch the building opposite. The ground floor provided a drinking salon, used more as a waiting room for customers who had other business on their mind.

Several girls stood or leaned in the doorway, scrutinizing the passing men. The invitation in their posture and smiles was unmistakable.

Aidan felt Kari hesitate and pull back. "Come," he said. "Need to get inside if I'm to grep the coordinates for tonight. Take no notice."

Kari took a deep breath and turned her eyes from the waiting girls. Some were no more than children. Dear God, could she just walk by?

"Don't look at them. Remember, they are history."

Aidan was right. There was nothing she could do that could alter that fact. Reluctantly, she followed him into the dim interior that stank of stale beer and men's sweat. Ben was still close on her heels.

Sixth Report DAY SEVEN

Operator: Aidan Torrance

Location: London

Date: July 16, 6.00 p.m.

Report: No longer have any desire to explain what is happening. Just the facts. We are safely ensconced in London in a Tudor brothel. Don't even ask! In the past twenty-four hours, I have held a newborn baby and ridden a horse. Also gave away my money in a fit of compassion brought on by my companion. To say you wouldn't know me would be an understatement. Don't think I know myself. From my calcs, our best bet looks like London Bridge. Will be quiet and open in future times. Slight adjustment needed for landing coordinates in twentieth century. Sure you can handle that. Will leave later tonight and attempt beam back under cover of darkness. Out.

* * * * *

Kari sat on the feather cushions piled on the bed and watched him. There was nowhere else to sit in the tiny room. She had moved as far away from him as she could, up into the corner, her back against the wall, so as to leave him space to work. Ben was on the floor, under Aidan's feet. Like a faithful shadow, he had clung to them in their day's journey.

There was no doubt as to the main purpose of the chamber, dominated as it was by the voluminous bed. The decoration of the room, mainly crude graffiti scrawled on the plaster, provided explicit addition to the sounds coming through the paper-thin walls. The drawings and the noises kept all the possible interactions between men and women in the forefront of her mind. It was impossible to ignore what went on night and day in this house.

It would not have been her choice of a place to spend her last few hours with Aidan. She would not have wanted to associate this man with such things, and she'd imagined their time together as clean and perfect.

This man, who would be her lover, who had appeared mysteriously in her life and would just as mysteriously fade away. For she had decided that, if he wished it, she wanted to make love with him, although she knew in her heart that the centuries would roll inevitably between them, cutting them off from each other forever.

Chapter Twenty-One

ဆာ

Kari watched Aidan as he sat on the edge of the bed, concentrating on his tiny responder, tapping out his message. She had drawn up her legs and sat hugging her knees. The room was small, she could feel every movement he made. The air grew warm and musty, but she didn't care. Every reminder of his humanity, his real presence, was welcome.

Resolutely, she tried to turn her mind away from the thoughts of Aidan. She could think about her surroundings instead. She wondered what had replaced this house of ill repute. How long had it remained a brothel? What stories could it tell?

It was no use. Thoughts of Aidan intruded again. Her brain was in a whirl, refusing to let go of the one topic that consumed her, returning against her will to ponder the enigma of the man from the future. He had said he loved her. Could he not feel what she was feeling? How could he be so controlled? If she kept on thinking this way she would not be able to keep her distance from him.

She felt the attraction emanating from him like a vibrating field, the sexual tension thick in the room. He was busy. What he was doing was important for both of them. It was vital he make contact, wasn't it? She wanted him to take her home, didn't she? He expected to return to his own time, didn't he?

A gurgle from her midriff made Aidan glance up. He raised an eyebrow and smiled, then returned to his task.

There was another preoccupation vying for her attention. She wrenched her mind away from the sexual fantasies that fluttered at the edge of her imagination. It had been more than six hours since Tom had offered the chicken leg.

"I bet there's a restaurant here now."

"Now?" Aidan looked up again from his transmitter.

She had his attention. She propped her chin on her knees. "In my time." Damn, it still made her head spin, all these relations between times.

She went on dreamily. "I bet there's a fish and chip shop. They'll be frying about now. The fish is thick and white, dipped in a puffy batter, the oil is bubbling." She had always despised deep-fried foods. "There's vinegar and salt and pepper on the counter. The potatoes—" she broke off. "God, do these folks now even have potatoes?"

"Just about. Drake or Raleigh brought them back from the New World."

"Anyway, the chips are all cut and ready. In cold water." She paused. "Or maybe it's an Indian takeaway with fluffy rice and spicy poppadoms and that thick curry sauce. On the other hand, it could be more upscale—French, or Italian."

She was doing herself no good. Her stomach growled. "It's the bread I've missed the most…"

"Damn."

"Sorry, I should stop."

"Not that. No transmission."

"Why not?" She sat up, food relegated back to third place.

"Not sure. Always been in the open before when I had to send. Maybe too much interference from the buildings." He sat looking at the instrument and sighed.

"This is a prototype," he said. "Not that I'm a technician anyway. I hope there's a technical reason." He was muttering, talking almost to himself. "I kept watch and didn't see Flynn anywhere around. Still, in those crowds… I'll wait and try later."

"Why do we have to wait for dark? I mean, I don't mind having a few more hours with you, but why can't we go now from here?"

"Darkness usually means not many people. Less risk of drawing unwanted attention—or of taking someone else with me. Unless they're walking a dog, of course." He rubbed Ben's head affectionately. "Also have to find a place that's open now and in the future. Hampstead Heath was good. Bridges are usually safe bets. So I picked London Bridge. They moved it slightly in one of the rebuilds, but Tanice can compensate if she has warning."

Tanice. Who was she? He seemed to read her unspoken question.

"Tanice is in charge of the lab. She's also my surrogate."

"What does that mean?" She hardly dared ask.

"Tan took over when my parents were killed. Like a legal guardian. I would have gone completely to pieces without her."

The depth of his affection vibrated through his words. So he had close ties to his world. She'd been selfish not to think of that, not to ask. Despite what her head told her, her heart had toyed with impossible fantasies, her imagination filled with the idea of having him by her side for the rest of their lives.

"It would be hard for you to leave her." It was a statement rather than a question. She was confirming in her mind that he would never find her again.

He nodded. "Of course it would. But Tanice would understand. She worries about me, about me settling down, making the Contract."

Kari wished she could know this woman in the distant future who meant so much to the man she loved.

Aidan had turned his attention back to his responder.

"How does it work?"

He looked up. Her heart skipped a beat. His eyes could turn her insides to jelly.

"Would you show me?" she asked.

He moved to make room beside him and she wriggled forward.

He touched a pad. "This is the screen for messages. I can handwrite or use buttons. But all in code."

"Looks like a shorthand."

"In a way. No vowels, lots of abbreviations. The receiver at the other end decodes."

The "other end" was eight hundred years away. She shivered. He must not know what she felt. For some reason, she wanted the first move to come from him. She needed him to reaffirm what he had told her in the copse.

"Tell me what it says."

He gave her a strange look, hesitated and then began to read from the screen. He paused.

"Go on."

"I also gave away my money…"

She caught her breath. Had he really done that?

Kari looked into his eyes. "When?" Although she knew the answer.

"The last night. When I slipped out."

"And I gave you a hard time for leaving me?"

He nodded. She put out a hand to touch his face. "Was it the Miller family?"

She felt his head move under her fingers, but he did not speak. Instead, he turned his mouth to her hand and quietly kissed her caressing fingers. A quiver went through her, deep inside.

"What shall we do?" She was overwhelmed with love for him. She had not known when they would come together. Just that it would happen.

He knew what she meant. He put his arms around her and she pushed her face into the delicious space between his chin and his shoulder. The rough homespun of his jerkin rubbed her cheek. She breathed in the smell of him that sent her senses reeling. Never had she really believed in chemical attraction until now. Now she knew what it was to feel the pull under hot skin, nerves tingling, heart beating faster just at the sight or sound of him, the knowledge all might well be lost for the love of this man.

"We have to leave," he whispered, stroking her hair. She nodded, miserably, her face still hidden against him.

"We still have some time together."

She lay still against his chest.

"Kari." His voice was low and husky.

She lifted her face. Tears had moistened her cheeks.

"Oh, God, Kari. Don't cry, my love." Gently, he brushed his lips against her wet face, tasting the salt tears with his tongue.

She quivered under his touch and turned her mouth to his. His lips moved slowly to hers and he kissed her so softly at first she barely felt the pressure until his tongue probed gently between her lips. His hands moved on her back and shoulders, pressing her gently to him as if trying to mold her to his shape.

She felt his heart pounding under the thin shirt, his breath wafted warm on her fevered skin and she knew she had no choice. She had to know what it would be like to make love to this man. She had to strip off her clothes and feel his skin against hers. Had to slide her hands over his muscles and feel him thrust into her.

She was still wearing the boy's doublet and leggings. Aidan's hand moved down her thigh to her calf and then began tracing the slow route back up her leg. At the same time, the other hand delved beneath the loose jacket and found the opening of the linen shirt.

"No buttons." She smiled against his lips. He made an inarticulate sound in reply and fastened his mouth again on hers.

The questing fingers had found her breast and now cupped it with tender care. A low moan came from deep in her throat. Unfastening her hands from his shoulders, she started to unlace his jerkin. As if he had been waiting for the signal, Aidan began to pull her clothing from her body, and suddenly they were undressing each other, helping to divest their eager limbs of all covering, until they both sat naked on the edge of the bed. They paused, savoring the moment.

Kari gazed at him. He had the most wonderful body she had seen. Every detail was as perfect as she had remembered from the day at the pond. She drew back a little to feast her eyes. His skin was smooth and pale, gleaming with a pearly sheen in the half-light of the room. Shadows highlighted his cheekbones and well-defined brows. His lips were full and flushed from his arousal.

She caught her breath and tentatively stretched out her fingers. They fluttered down his body until she grasped his upstanding shaft with a cupped hand and heard Aidan suck in his breath. They still sat, poised, unmoving, knowing what would follow, knowing that this might be the only time, forever…

Aidan softly traced the outline of her mouth with the knuckle of one hand. She kissed one finger gently as it fluttered over her lips. He stroked around under her ear and felt for the soft skin at the nape of her neck. His fingers thrust up into her hair and she strained toward him. With one accord, they sank back onto the bed.

Aidan ran his hands down the length of her body, following his fingers with his eyes.

"So beautiful," he whispered. She savored the hunger and delight in his eyes as he drank in the curve of hip and thigh, the valley between her breasts and the curls covering the secret, throbbing place within her.

She felt the wetness between her thighs, felt the irresistible urge to open herself to him. His fingers stroked her leg, finding the silky skin on her inner thigh. With a soft moan, she eased her legs apart, beginning to move with a primal rhythm, allowing him to stroke her quivering flesh. As he felt how ready she was for him, he rose above her and balanced himself on his elbows, holding himself away from her.

"Say it," he whispered hoarsely.

She licked her lips.

"Say it!"

"I—"

He lowered himself a little so that his pulsing erection skimmed her open flesh.

"—love—" she gasped.

The swollen tip pushed against the lips, edging into her. His mouth was close to hers, waiting.

"—you." And he thrust into her, his mouth crushing her lips as he drove in with a throbbing explosion that convulsed them both.

* * * * *

Kari slept, entwined in Aidan's arms. The sleepless night, the horse ride, the lovemaking had combined to send her into a deep, dreamless slumber. They both lay satiated and limp in a tangle of limbs until thumps and groans from outside the door startled them into full awareness. The door shook against its flimsy latch as a heavy weight thudded against it. Ben barked. A curse followed.

Kari sat up. "Thomas!" she whispered.

Aidan signaled her to stay where she was and slipped quietly from the bed. Very gently, he eased the door open a crack. Kari watched the gap widen, her heart thumping. Had they come this far only for Thomas and Josiah to catch up with them again?

Aidan looked out and then closed the door again. He grinned.

"What is it? Who's there?"

Aidan chuckled. "At a guess, a rather heavy client fell down the stairs. They are rather narrow and steep."

Aidan's theory was confirmed by much audible and raucous discussion of how the accident happened and if the man was hurt. Women's shrill voices added to the grumbling complaints of the unhappy client, until the proprietor succeeded in restoring calm.

After that, all was quiet. Even the street noises seemed subdued, reduced to a constant background of iron wheels rumbling over stones and the clop of hooves. Most honest toil was finished for the day in the city. Only cutthroats and purse-snatchers would stay skulking in the alleys toward dusk.

Aidan and Kari lay in each other's arms, listening to the alien noises around them.

"I want you to know that this was the first time for love," he told her.

Kari kissed him. "Mine, too."

He chuckled. "A fine modern pair we are," he said. "Both from an emancipated future and we have to return in time to find love."

Kari ran her hands lightly down his back and kissed him again. She traced the outline of the tattoo on his upper arm with her fingertips.

"What is that?" she whispered.

"My clan totem and my own emblem. A star and an owl. My family are space travelers from way back. The bird still symbolizes knowledge." He went on. "Seeing that Godwin family — and even the Miller family — made me realize how little I had. My parents died in a shuttle accident."

He laid back, one arm over his eyes. Kari remained still. She knew him well enough to realize what it took to make him confide his feelings. This was a man who had lived by his wits, who had suppressed his sensitivities to avoid hurt in the highly civilized, technological culture of his time. She said nothing, but held him close, willing him to feel her love and caring.

"I was fifteen. That was when I decided I would concentrate on events, things, not people. I guess I chose to study history so as not to get involved in the present."

"History is people."

"Don't you think I know that now?" He sat up on one elbow and leaned over her. "Don't you think that I understand that love, and hate, and jealousy, and pride and greed drive every blessed event? That I know that deep inside in a way I never did before?" His face twisted with pain. "I want what you have, Kari. I want to care about people, I want to make a difference in someone's life. I want to be with you."

"Can we? Be together?" She searched his face anxiously.

He shook his head in desperation. "I don't know how, Kari, my love." He turned to sit, his elbows resting on his tented knees. He ran his hands up his face and through his hair.

"I shall send you back to your time, to your family, to your job. And somehow, someway, I'll find you again."

"Don't make me forget you," she whispered. She knelt beside him and cradled him in her arms. "If I have to go back, I want to remember you. I want to cherish every precious moment we have had together. Send me back to a time after we met in the park so that I can think about you. Best of all, stay with me, so I can have you and not some fading memory."

"I want you to remember me as I shall remember you, but only until we meet again, my love." He held her close and kissed the top of her head. "I shall find a way to make it happen, I promise."

He paused, and then took a deep breath. "Will you be my wife?"

Chapter Twenty-Two

ဢ

The suddenness of Aidan's question was like a blow, taking her breath away. As if she wanted anything else! She nodded, her eyes still fixed on his face. Aidan stood and pulled the cover around her shoulders like a cloak. The other blanket he wound around his hips, leaving his chest bare. His sculpted muscles shone in the golden light from the westering sun. Gently, he raised her to her feet. He softly smoothed her hair around her face, placing the longest curls on her shoulders. He stood facing her.

"When the Romans left Ancient Britain," he began, in a solemn, low voice, "they left intact the laws and customs of the islands. At that time, the Celtic chieftain chose his bride to match his own prowess. She was to be as beautiful, as strong, as true as he."

Kari understood he recited from memory, from some ceremony known to him, absorbed through his studies of history and the revival of interest in ancient customs of the Earth. She stood motionless, her hands still in his as he continued with the prelude to the ceremony.

"The Celtic lords lost their power, but the centuries since then have shown the commitment of man to woman is not to be taken lightly, that the nurturing and guiding of children is to be entrusted to those that so commit their lives.

"We stand here together, coerced by no person, committed to no other, to plight our troth." Aidan paused and Kari lightly squeezed his fingers. Reassured, he continued.

"I, Aidan Torrance, do commit myself, my life and my body to you, Karina Lunne. I shall love you with my whole heart through time and eternity. You are my true and only wife." At the last words, his voice sank to a whisper.

Kari passed her tongue over her dry lips. Aidan's eyes held hers, waiting for her to respond.

"I, Karina Lunne," she began firmly, "commit myself, my life and my body to you, Aidan Torrance. I do love you and shall love you with my whole heart through all time and eternity. I take you as my true and only husband."

With one accord, they drew closer together and sealed their bond with a kiss. Kari sank down. She drew him down to her and cradled him on her breast. "Love me again," she whispered.

* * * * *

A while later, hunger pangs could no longer be denied. They had to find something to eat.

"We could sell something," suggested Kari.

"Of course. Prima idea."

Aidan pulled on his clothes and picked up the pack. "Let's see what we have." He tugged out the blankets that were stuffed on top. Kari sat up in the bed and pulled one 'round her bare shoulders.

"Someone might buy these," she said.

"Maybe. But who, at this time of day?"

She hadn't considered that. She sighed in disappointment.

Next to emerge were the shorts and jacket Kari had worn to walk Ben a week ago.

Kari thrust her hand in the pocket. She held up the key. "For my apartment," she said. "We could go there. Except there's no food there either. I had cleaned everything out."

She peered into the bag. "Is there anything I can wear?" she said. "Or do I have to remain as a boy?" She thrust her hand in deeper and tugged on the material stuffed into the bottom.

"Ta ra!" she sang in triumph. Jonathan or Martha had packed a skirt and a shawl for her. She shook out the folds and grabbed too late at the two gold coins that rolled away, bouncing on the wooden floor. Hastily she scooted off the bed and retrieved them before they could disappear down a crack in the boards. God bless Jonathan Howard!

Their spirits rose. It was all so easy. They would eat, leave the brothel before the late dusk of summer and before the Billingsgate was closed.

Kari scrambled into the clothes. Aidan held up the shorts. "Wear these," he said. "Better not to leave them here."

Kari shrugged and pulled them on under the skirt, giggling at the feel of the red nylon under the rough homespun.

Suddenly, they were infused with a sense of euphoria and they exploded with mirth. They were together, they had some time, they were safe, and they were in love. They had to savor every precious moment left to them before Aidan tried to beam them back. But he would come to her, would find her, would be with her for the rest of their lives. He had promised, and she believed him.

Kari kissed him. "I love you, Aidan Torrance," she said seriously. "I love you because you are kind, and good, and brave. And because you love me and you're sexy as hell."

* * * * *

Kari and Aidan set out in search of their wedding breakfast. They found an alehouse tucked into a nearby lane that looked reasonably clean and not too crowded. One empty corner was furnished with high-backed wooden pews and a trestle table dark with age. They pushed aside the empty tankards littering the tabletop to clear a space for themselves, and Ben crept under the table, busy sniffing out dropped crusts and bones.

The tavern keeper's wife was a buxom woman with brawny arms, suited to carrying several full foaming pots of ale. She was proud of her cooking and rattled off a list of dishes she could provide.

They settled for a game pie and plum duff.

Kari sat back as they waited. She tilted the pewter stick holding a plain white candle. It was poorly made and was burning lopsided. "In my time," she said, "it would cost a fortune to eat somewhere like this. Just look at the decor and this location. The Cheshire Cheese off Fleet Street is full of tourists and does 'Olde Englishe' cooking. Atmosphere, authentic food, candlelight and you. What more could I want for my wedding night?"

Aidan's eyes glittered in the soft light. Dusk would not come until nearly ten o'clock at this time of year, but the candles were already needed in the low ceilinged room.

"I meant it, Kari," he said softly. "I will find a way for us. I'll take you home. Wait for me." He grasped her fingers across the table. "We are meant for each other. What is a small matter of four centuries?"

She smiled at him in hope and confidence.

After their meal, they walked out through the Billingsgate onto the waterfront and sat beneath a willow tree. All was quiet. The white stones of the Tower gleamed in the rays of the setting sun. The sounds of the huge black ravens squawking and quarreling as they settled for the night carried on the still air. The last ferryboats deposited their passengers on the shore from south of the river. Boatmen made fast their barges and prepared to bed down and guard them until dawn, when they would set off again to the great houses along the water.

Lights began to gleam in Southwark.

"Tom will be setting up his stage."

Aidan nodded. "Amidst the bear rings and the cockpits."

Kari shuddered. "It looks so peaceful," she said, watching the lights beginning to be reflected in the water. "Hard to believe it hides such cruelty."

"Every age is cruel," Aidan replied. "My age denies true choices and the right to make mistakes, yours allows senseless wars on helpless civilians, this one uses creatures, human and animal, for entertainment."

Kari sighed. Oversimplified, maybe, but basically true, what he said.

"Look." Aidan broke in on her thoughts. He had sent his message and was busy with another task on his responder. He aimed the small device toward London Bridge, which looked very little like the bridge Kari knew. Five spans arched across the river and supported a structure of wood and stone. Small buildings lined every inch of the parapet, and even a minuscule church spire poked its arrow over the jumble of rooftops.

Aidan was still making adjustments. "I'm locking onto the spire," he said. "It's not there in your time or in mine."

"Right."

"Look at this," he repeated. "I want you to know how this works. I want you to hold it. If we get separated, punch in the coordinates for your time."

"Separated?" Her flesh went cold. Once again, the enormity of what they were undertaking overwhelmed her. They would be disembodied in time. There was a risk. Until now, she had thought of Aidan's technology much as she had thought of the new complex hospital machinery—something some technician would understand and fix for her if there was a problem. There was no technical assistance for this. She felt as the first space explorers must have felt.

"Not likely to happen," he said. "But I've never done a double hop before. Look at the controls."

She turned her eyes to the flat, black box. It still looked like a palmtop computer. The tiny screen was flashing. "Coordinates set," it read.

Aidan pointed to two small pads beneath the screen. "These are set to be activated. The top one is for your time, the second for mine. As soon as we are back in the twentieth century, pass me the box and I will activate the second phase." He looked at her. "Can you do this?"

She nodded. "It may be the hardest thing I've ever done, but I can do it."

"Remember, it's not forever."

She would cling to that promise, believe it with every fiber of her being.

When Aidan was sure she could activate the responder, they sat in silence on the riverbank under the rustling trees. The slim branches of the willows curved gracefully down to the water, forming an enclosed bower where they were hidden from view. Aidan slid an arm around her shoulders.

"What is medicine like in your time?" she asked. "Is everything cured?"

"Everything?" he smiled sadly. "Not everything. Space exploration brought new microorganisms, new medical problems. We're pretty good at genetic engineering, at cloning…"

She twisted around in his arms. "I'm not surprised! Dolly the sheep started something. Do you mean there's more than one of everyone?"

"Hardly. Rules against that. As knowledge expands, more laws are needed to keep everything in check. But everyone does have an organ bank."

Was this good news or bad? "You too?"

"Of course. My parents set it up. But I shan't ever use it."

"Why not?"

"Because life would have no meaning if risks could be minimized that way. If I FLIP in time, I need to calc the odds for me, not for some clone bank."

A rat slid across the grass and plopped softly into the water. Ben sat up and Kari drew her feet closer to her.

"Could I function in your time?"

He turned her toward him and kissed her lips. "Darling Kari," he said. "Your love and compassion would shine through wherever you are. I would love you if we stayed here, if we went back to your world or if we emigrated to an Outworld. But my time would not accept you. Would an Elizabethan doctor be able to work in your hospital? Besides, you have no status, no code—no organ bank." He smiled wryly.

She clung to him. "It was a silly question. I just want to be with you," she whispered.

He kissed her again. "You must go back to your family. You have one, don't waste it. They will be frantic with worry."

She nodded guiltily.

"And Ben needs some decent food. What would he do in my time?" He was trying to cheer her, still raining tiny kisses on her face and throat. "I'll find you. I'll fix the archives and grep through time again and come to you."

They waited until darkness had shrouded the Tower and the south bank. Tiny pinpoints of light flickered intermittently as a hardy soul penetrated the blackness or a window was uncovered.

The night watchman called the hours on his round as he passed behind the solid gates of the city, and was echoed by his counterpart in Southwark. The good citizens of London were abed.

At last, Aidan decided it was time.

Chapter Twenty-Three

ॐ

Aidan pulled Kari to her feet and swung the pack onto his back. The responder was ready in his hand. Ben scrambled up and took his station at Kari's heel.

In the darkness, they picked their way carefully over the rough ground that lay between them and the entrance to the bridge. Kari clutched Aidan's hand as he guided her over the rocks and rubbish that littered the path. Unpleasant smells emanated from the river water as the warmth of the day subsided. The dozens of boats rocked at their moorings as water rats, cats and stray dogs hunted in and beside the water, now that the human population was gone.

This river served as highway, sewer and water source for the thousands of people that lived in and around London. It bore disease and contamination in the same water that provided communications and allowed the import of exotic goods from the expanding world across the seas.

London Bridge was an important link in the life of the city. A bridge had existed on roughly this spot since before the Romans had built their wall around the growing settlement. Those walls still stood in this century, pierced by the gates, but the bridge had been rebuilt more than once and would be again. Kari knew one dismantled version would find its way to the United States, while its replacement continued to serve the old city. The words to the children's song echoed in Kari's head. *London Bridge is falling down, my fair lady.*

This one was the stone bridge that divided the waters of the Thames so that one side was a rushing torrent of rapids and the other a calm pool of almost stagnant water. Records of the day spoke of the danger to life and limb of venturing into the turmoil of the frothing water. Pictures showed the calm side in winter when it froze solid enough to hold fairs and light fires on the ice.

The Tudor bridge was lined with houses like any other street of the city and presented the same bewildering maze of alleys and passageways connecting the buildings.

Aidan and Kari trod softly over the cobbles, often proceeding by feel along the enclosing walls. Their hands encountered rough plaster and wooden lathes, interspersed with heavy doors and tiny windows. The overreaching upper floors almost met above their heads, cutting out any remaining light from the moon and forming a dark, echoing tunnel around them.

Kari felt as if she were penetrating into a mysterious labyrinth, leading she knew not where. The last week had been full of alien experiences. The people, the scenes, the beliefs had washed over her in a flowing tide of sensations. In addition, she had come to love a man whose world was as alien to hers as to this one. The brief insights he had given her of his world had underlined the differences. How would a doctor function in that time? Would he or she have any challenge? New diseases, new surgical techniques... Unexpectedly, Aidan stopped, and she bumped gently into him. She saw his hand raised, signaling her to stay where she was. She grasped Ben's collar.

It was impossible to tell exactly where the sound of stealthy footsteps was coming from. The noise was muffled by the walls and yet echoed in the enclosed space. The shuffling and grunting could be located in any street nearby.

Heart pounding, Kari waited, all senses straining. Silence reigned again. Cautiously, Aidan took a step forward, and then another. Almost on tiptoe, Kari followed, and they flitted like shadows to the open space in front of the chapel. It could in no way be called a church square. As if by mutual consent, the encroaching houses had drawn back a little, allowing that the building deserved a little respect from the jostling walls. The space was perhaps the width of two streets, which made it less than a quarter the size of any modern road. The strange footsteps had faded. Whoever had been out prowling the lanes in the dark was gone.

Aidan passed Kari the pack and turned his attention to the responder. All was quiet. Far away, a dog barked, and Ben woofed softly in reply. She grasped his muzzle to quiet him.

In the silence, Kari could clearly make out the slap of tiny waves against the supports of the bridge as the water continued to respond to every breeze. A bell pealed somewhere in the city, presumably summoning the religious to one of the innumerable sessions of prayer. Would it be Lauds at this hour? Kari searched her memory and then smiled at herself. Another trick of the versatile human mind! It threw up such trivia to ease the strain when tensions grew too much. It had happened more than once in the past few days.

She watched Aidan as he checked his settings. What would it feel like to fly through time? Aidan had described the buzz in the head, the tingling in the limbs. She was sure he had downplayed the risks. He was going to do it twice. How could she bear not knowing if he was safe?

Ben heard the assailants first. They must have crept up under cover of the pealing bell, for they were on them before Aidan or Kari could react. Ben sprang to his feet, hackles raised as the first shapeless form rushed toward them.

As if in slow motion, Kari saw the dog leap through the air, glimpsed the flash of the knife as Ben's jaws clamped on an arm, and saw his body go limp as the blade drove into his side.

The dog's weight dragged down the assailant, who was vainly trying to shake off the vise-like teeth, now locked in a death grip on his wrist. Kari screamed and whirled to Aidan, only to see the same scene replayed before her horrified eyes. Another dark shape was already on Aidan's back and a dagger flashed at his throat.

"No!" she shouted and bounded forward to grasp the hand as it drove the weapon home. The impetus of her leap pushed the arm away from Aidan's unprotected neck, and the blade was buried somewhere in his chest. With a soft sigh, Aidan sank to his knees.

At the same moment, a window opened above their heads, and a night-capped head was thrust out.

"God's blood, can an honest man not sleep? Begone you knaves, or I rouse my men!"

The other footpad had freed his arm from Ben's teeth, and he gave a kick to the motionless body as he stood back on his feet. For a moment they both hesitated, weighing their chances, and then took off at full speed, vanishing into the maze of lanes. With a satisfied grunt, the householder closed his window.

The unseen watcher in the shadows drew back, satisfied. No matter if Torrance was dead or just wounded. He would not be returning to his art collection.

Stealthily, Reed Flynn melted into the darkness.

* * * * *

Kari sank down beside Aidan, fumbling blindly in the darkness to feel for his pulse. The tiny flicker was there, barely perceptible in his neck. She put her hand over his heart. She could feel the faint beat, but her hand came away dark and wet with blood. Her thoughts raced frantically. Aidan would surely bleed to death if she went for help. And who would help her? Who would be able to deal with a wound of this gravity? She smothered a sob. *Think, Kari, reason it out. Hold on. Use your mind. Push down the terror, it will take over, stop you from acting. You're Aidan's only chance, just as he was yours only a few days ago.*

Aidan was still clutching the responder in limp fingers. She smoothed his hair back where it had fallen over his forehead. His skin was cold to the touch, a thin film of sweat was forming on his face. Shock. She had no time to waste. She looked around.

Ben's body lay where he had fallen in the vain attempt to protect her one last time. The story had begun and ended with Ben.

213

"Goodbye, Ben," she whispered, "thank you for everything." She blinked back the tears and wiped her face with a dirty sleeve. The dog had faithfully stayed by her side, protecting her, warning her, helping their escape with his strength and his intelligence. She stifled a sob. And one of Ben's legs twitched so slightly that she nearly missed it.

She scrabbled across the cobblestones to the dog's side, heedless of the rubbish and dirt on the roadway.

With trembling fingers she touched the wolfhound's neck — and felt a thin thread of pulse. Ben opened his eyes and his tail thumped weakly twice before he sank back, only the barely perceptible movement of his chest betraying the fact that there was still life in him. Idiot that she was, why hadn't she checked him anyway?

"I'm sorry, Ben," she whispered. "Forgive me, I thought they'd killed you." Strength came from somewhere, and sobbing, she gathered the limp form into her arms, lifting it as gently as she could to set it down beside Aidan.

It was not over. Their love could not end this way. Aidan could live with skilled surgery and careful nursing. Her mind was made up. She gathered Aidan to her and with Ben close to them, held him close in a supporting arm.

"Hold on, my love," she whispered. "Don't die on me. I won't let you go. You promised we would be together, don't let me down."

She took hold of the responder and fitted it snugly into her palm. One last look around.

With Aidan and Ben firmly in her arms, she took a deep breath, pressed the second pad of the responder and beamed them all forward eight hundred years.

* * * * *

The medical robots bothered Kari the most. The tiny ones skittered across the floors, alerted by the merest scrap of lint, sniffing out dirt and dust, spraying disinfectants and sucking up the residue. They popped out of their baseboard housings like little bloodless, non-sentient mice, did their job and popped back to wait, always alert, always ready. They gave her the creeps.

The robots had had a massive job to do when she appeared in the lab, clinging to a half-dead dog and a wounded man. She held them both to her in a vise-like grip, oblivious of the blood and dirt spattered over her.

It had taken gentle strength and persuasion before she let go. The technicians had hidden their surprise at the presence of the dog and followed Tanice's instructions to see to his injuries. Ben was now eating twenty-fourth-century dog food in a specially created kennel.

Larger robots cared for the human patient, connected to him in some way, checking vital signs, adjusting drugs, offering water for parched lips.

No human hand was allowed to intervene in such routine ministrations. There was no aggressiveness in the instructions Kari received, just a bland assumption that she would do as she was told. Without it being said in so many words, she knew her wishes would not even be considered, were she bold enough to offer them. She was obliged to watch from behind the transparent screen, longing to hold Aidan's hand, touch his face, whisper to him. He lay in an enclosed capsule, suspended on a cushion of air, eyes closed in a bloodless face, while machines did what she longed to do.

Tanice had pried her away from Aidan's body as they materialized in the time travel laboratory and then she'd held her, gently restraining her as the robots took their clothes and cleaned the area. Kari could only guess how difficult her insistence on clinging to Aidan had made things for Tanice. The medics had tolerated her presence with supercilious smiles when she told them she was a doctor.

They had given her a whiff of something at last, for she remembered calmly watching the technicians working fast to assess the damage to Aidan's chest and then transporting him through a seamless doorway to God knew where. She had struggled to follow. Tanice's arms had held her.

"Shh," Tanice crooned. "Let him go, goodfriend. They will take care of him."

As the silent stretcher disappeared from sight, Kari felt the strength go from her. She leant weakly against Tanice.

"I couldn't help him," whispered Kari. "I'm a doctor, and I couldn't help him."

"I know, I know." Tears stood in Tanice's eyes.

Kari scanned the older woman's face. She saw the traces of weeping on her cheeks, the signs of strain around her mouth and eyes. Tanice's jaw was clenched as she held back the sobs. Kari was not the only one hurting.

"You love him, too," whispered Kari.

Wordlessly, Tanice nodded her assent, and the two women clung together. Kari thought of the other woman who had held her like a mother, eight hundred years back in time. She resolved that, if ever she went home, she would hug her own mother at the first opportunity.

Tanice was the first to move. "Come, Kari. Let me fetch you something to wear. Then we'll find out what's happening."

The suit Tanice gave her was moss green, soft and comfortable. The Tudor clothing and her red shorts vanished. Ten days ago, she'd longed to be clean and to move freely. Now, the change barely registered on her consciousness. Her mind was totally taken up with imagining what might be happening to Aidan.

She had no way of visualizing what procedures there might be. Was surgery now a risk-free miracle? Could they somehow take the most battered body and put it back together like new? She prayed they could.

The research station was stark and functional in many ways, but care had been taken to provide flowing lines pleasing to the human eye. Space was broken by natural-seeming changes of level and perspective. The design and colors had a calming effect. The air was cool and smelled faintly of pine and lemon, the machines glowed and hummed in a musical cadence soothing to the ear.

Thanks to Tanice, Kari was allowed to watch what they did to Aidan. The surgical procedure was at once as futuristic as she had imagined and as recognizable as in her own time. The surgeons worked from a computer monitor that showed the wound both in real time and in schema. They darted infrequent glances at the body. Laser probes, directed by remote control, hovered over Aidan's ribs and made the incision, while robots mopped the blood and held apart the lips of the wound.

Despite the comfortable temperature of the air, Kari felt cold. The tightness in her chest made it difficult to breathe. She had done the right thing in bringing him here, but could even this technology and level of skill save him? There must be problems that even this civilization could not solve. She narrowed her eyes to bring the distant computer screen into better focus. For the first time in many days, she thought of her contact lenses and glasses back in her apartment.

She felt disconnected. She was in Aidan's world, talking to people who had known him almost all his life. She had only seen him in the stress and turmoil of Tudor England. And yet she knew she loved him, knew they were meant for each other. Her love for him had as much importance as her love of medicine, of healing. If he died, there would be little purpose or meaning left in her life.

Silently she concentrated, willing him to keep fighting. *Please, Aidan, please don't die. Hang on for me, for us. You can't leave me now.*

"Here," Tanice interrupted her concentration. She was holding out three visors, shaped like futuristic ski goggles. "One of these will help with the detail."

Kari tried them and selected the one that brought the scene into proper focus for her. She smiled her thanks at Tanice and turned back to the tense operation.

She leaned as close as possible to the protective screen, her whole body straining to see, to follow the rapid movements of the probes and the robots. The surgeons were riveted on the screens, manipulating the lasers that were now buried deep inside Aidan's chest cavity. No noise penetrated the glass barrier, but Kari could supply the sounds she knew must accompany the procedure—the heavy grunts of the surgeons as they concentrated, the rasp of Aidan's breath as they worked 'round his damaged lung.

Chapter Twenty-Four

ಐ

Kari strained to make out the purpose of each instrument, to see and understand the monitors. She could distinguish the illuminated charts that showed blood pressure and body temperature. The pressure was low and she called out in a panic, tapping frantically on the transparent wall. The doctors continued their work, unaware of her efforts to point out to them that he was losing too much blood, that he was going into shock. The damned doctors didn't know what they were doing! Why didn't they look at the patient for God's sake? *Take your eyes off the bloody screen!*

Then the pressure began to rise, the numbers changed, Aidan's condition was stabilizing. The robots and sensors had known what needed doing and had responded quickly. She relaxed, pulling down her hands from where they were flattened against the screen. She leaned her forehead against the cool window and closed her eyes.

Tanice came to stand behind her again.

"It's going well," she said. "His lung was pierced, but the blade missed his heart. He lost a lot of blood and the FLIP was an added shock to his system. They say he should recover."

The scene before her swam in and out of focus, taking on an air of unreality. She saw the figures sharply outlined as if in a clear photograph, and then the edges blurred so that she could barely see the shapes. Tanice caught her shoulders again.

"Breathe deep," she said. "Take it slow. It's been a shock. He'll be fine."

The surgeons were preparing to leave the operating theater, and at last paused to look directly at their patient. They conferred with each other.

Although she still could not hear a word they said, Kari recognized the positive nod, the squaring of tired shoulders and the uplifted head that signified satisfaction with a job well done. Some things did not change. She felt drained. Wearily, she turned to Tanice.

* * * * *

Tanice looked after her for the next two days. She found her quarters, showed her how to operate the dispensing machines for food and clothing, and talked to her about Aidan. Kari could not get enough. If she could not be with him, the next best thing was hearing about him from another loving friend.

"I received the surrogate assignment when his parents were killed," Tanice told her. They were relaxing over a drink of honeyed lemon.

"Like a guardian?"

Tanice nodded. "Legal and official. Should have been short, until he was of age. But we didn't lose touch. I learned to love him like a son."

"Do you have children?"

The older woman shook her head and a flicker of pain passed over her face. "Never found anyone to make the Contract with. No commitment, no children."

Kari remembered the vows she had exchanged with Aidan. He had been giving her the most precious thing he had—the rest of his life. Kari thought of the turmoil of her own time with single parents, artificial insemination of unmarried women, surrogate mothers. Things must certainly have changed.

"The best that people such as I can hope for is a surrogate contract. Sometimes the child is really young, sometimes a rebellious teener like Aidan." Tanice smiled in reminiscence.

"Was he hard to handle?"

"At times. But soft underneath. He always found it difficult to accept the Social Laws. So he withdrew into history. And followed his own rules."

"Time travel?"

Tanice shook her head. "Not right away. He took advantage at first of the Relaxation months, when the pheromones are increased and sex is possible. That's when some make a Contract and then are allowed to have children. He and Monika—" She stopped abruptly at the look on Kari's face.

"He—" Tanice tried again, looking apologetically at Kari. "I know things are different in your time, not quite sure how—I leave that to the archivists," she said gently. "Aidan did take a companion from here from time to time. It really means nothing unless they both wish it to continue."

Kari fought down the clutch of jealousy. "I understand," she said as casually as she could.

Tanice shook her head. "But Aidan hated the regulation of it and didn't even bother the last couple of times."

Kari found that comforting.

Tanice went on. "Then he found the thrill of time travel and collecting his works of art. He was obsessed. The excuse was the hologramming, but he loved the risk and his paintings were like hunting trophies."

Kari sipped at her drink and listened to Tanice recounting yet another escapade from Aidan's misspent past. He had seen centuries far beyond her ken, even adventuring once into his own future.

"When he came back," Tanice was saying, "he was worried—troubled. I asked him what he had seen and he gave me some details. It was only twenty years into the future, but he never really wanted to talk about it. Of course, it was strictly forbidden to travel that way, and he did it while I was on vacation. All he would say was, 'I couldn't find myself, Tan. I don't think I was there.'"

* * * * *

Kari wandered around the medical facility of the research center like a lost soul. Why had Aidan not found himself in the future? Because he died? Every time she saw Tanice, her heart shrank in dread, but the good reports remained good. Aidan and Ben were both healing fast.

It was impossible to follow what they had done or what they were using—the medical jargon was incomprehensible. According to Tanice, it was working, Aidan's wound was closed and he was regaining strength daily.

At last, they let her in to see him.

He was sitting up, propped by soft pillows. If it were not for the robots skittering around the floor and one still connected to him, he might almost have been in a private room in her own hospital. But where she would have expected to see tubes and wires snaking from the bed into outlets in the wall, there was only one control pad in the head of the bed. A digital display flickered with data in ever-changing readouts.

The room was softly lit, the light gleaming on the rounded corners. Subtle shifts of color washed across the walls, beginning with the pale blue and mauve of a summer sunrise and moving through all the tints of fresh spring leaves and flowers. Kari wondered if Aidan had chosen the colors in memory of the days they had spent in the unspoiled countryside eight hundred years ago.

She thought of the last room they had shared together—the dusty, overcrowded space, hemmed in by thick dark beams and poorly whitewashed plaster, where they had made sweet love and pledged their troth through time and eternity.

She paused in the doorway. At the soft whisper of the panel sliding closed behind her, he looked up from the video book on the rack across the bed and smiled. His silver-gray eyes shone even larger in his pale face above the hollows in his cheeks. The soft, black beard was gone. The firm lines of his jaw and curve of his lips showed clearly now. How close she had come to losing him!

"Hallo," she whispered. Her whole heart was contained in the inadequate greeting.

He held out his hand and fixed his eyes upon her face until she stood beside the bed. She grasped his hand in both of hers and slowly brought it to her lips. His skin felt cool and smooth. The pulse in his wrist beat with amazing life against her fingers. She closed her eyes. She could touch him, hold him. A burst of gratitude swelled in her chest.

Slowly, she sank down beside him, still holding his hand without speaking. His chest moved rhythmically with each breath. It was the most wonderful sight she could imagine. She feasted her eyes on every part of him that was visible to her and clung to his hand as if she would never let go.

"Hallo, my love," he whispered.

She could only smile at him tremulously. Gently, she bent forward and placed her lips on his. His mouth moved hungrily beneath hers as he returned the pressure of her kiss.

"I love you," she said.

"You saved me. Thank you, wife."

A tremor of longing and desire shot through her at his words. His wife! Her husband! She kissed him again.

"My sweet, brave Kari. What you did was incredible."

She touched her fingertips to his lips to silence him and shook her head. How could she have done anything else when it meant life or death for the man she adored?

"It was the only choice. Look, don't talk about me. How do you feel?"

"Better for seeing you, my darling. I'll soon be fit and out of here."

She stroked his arm. She couldn't keep her hands off him. "I love you," she said again. She wished there were a thousand different ways of telling him what he meant to her.

Suddenly, a movement on the floor caught her eye. She lifted her feet. "That tile moved!" she said.

The section of the floor tile in the corner lifted itself from the pattern and slid toward the center of the room. At the same time another tiled scuttled toward an area under the table.

"There! Look! What is it?"

Aidan peered over the side of the bed. "Cleaner tiles," he chuckled. "Just routine. This is a Special Care room. They're the only reason you were allowed in here. The tiles are programmed to detect dirt, dust, spilled liquids, anything brought in that the ventilation system doesn't catch. Don't worry. They'll settle back."

Sure enough, each moving tile found itself an empty space on the floor and fit itself quietly back into the pattern.

Kari laughed. "That's amazing," she said.

Aidan shrugged. "No big deal. They've existed for years."

Such things were as commonplace for him as a telephone was for her.

"This setup's a bit different from making up Martha's herbs in the potting shed," she said.

"You liked that, didn't you?"

Kari nodded. "Oh, I didn't like the dirt, but you could learn a lot from the simple things—"

He pulled her back toward him. "Pay attention to me, wench. I have some things to tell you."

He ran both hands up her arms to her shoulders, then down her back, holding her prisoner beside him. "They say I need another week, then they'll let me go. Tanice will find us a place to stay."

She bent to kiss him again. She let her lips flutter over his face, scattering tiny kisses on his cheeks and lips. The breath of a sigh wafted past her face.

"God, woman, don't do that to me, in my weak state," he said. He shifted his hands from her back and placed his palms on either side of her face. He held her there while he gazed deep into her eyes.

"I love you, Kari," he said softly. "I will love you through time and eternity. You are my wife and the love of my life. In a week's time, I shall be able to hold you as a husband should hold his wife and show you what you mean to me. Imagine what it will be like when we're together." His voice grew throaty with emotion. "I shall be able to touch every part of you, I shall be forever beside you."

Kari drew in a shuddering breath and squeezed his hands.

* * * * *

By the end of the week, they had talked everything through. They'd spoken lovingly of Ben, of all that he'd done for them. Aidan wiped the tears tenderly from her eyes as they spilled over.

"I thought you had left him," he said. "The news was garbled at first. I even thought of going back for him."

"You're not serious!"

He nodded. "I thought that if I calculated it right, I could get him just before the attack. Quick in and out — no problem."

"Where have I heard that before?"

He grinned ruefully. "I must confess I was glad you brought him — and that he's as good as new."

He had considered going back just to rescue her dog! Where was the man who refused to become involved?

As she left the room, she ran into Monika. Ever since Tanice told her that Aidan and Monika had been more than friends in the past, she had preferred not to stay around when the chirpy assistant was present. She made to move past with just a nod and a smile.

To her surprise, Monika laid a hand on her arm, stopping her.

"How is he?" she said.

"Fine."

Monika's hand was still on her arm. "Will they release him soon?"

"I think so."

"Good." Monika smiled and turned to go. Abruptly, she swung back on her heel and stood in front of Kari, blocking her way.

"Kari," she said, "I know what you're thinking. Aidan and I did spend some R and R together…"

Kari closed her eyes. She didn't want to hear this. She didn't want to know how this woman loved Aidan despite what Tanice thought, and was prepared to look after him—

"…but he doesn't love me and I don't love him," Monika finished firmly.

Kari opened her eyes.

"Kari, he's sexy as hell, but he's not Contract material for me. I'm looking for a long-term commitment now and, believe me, Aidan Torrance is not it." She looked at Kari's face. "Oh, hell, forget it. I just thought you should know. Me and my mouth." She turned away.

Kari put out a hand to stop her. "No, wait, Monika. I trust him and I didn't seriously think he would pick up where you two left off…"

Monika chuckled. "Fat chance. We left off three years ago. There hasn't been anyone for Aidan since—not until you." She leaned forward and kissed Kari on the cheek. "Good luck. If there's anything I can do—" With a last broad grin, Monika strode off down the corridor.

* * * * *

One day, Kari visited the hologram site for the twentieth century. The London similar to the one she knew so well was reproduced there in an eerily lifelike form. The traffic sped by, people bustled along the crowded pavements. But when she put out a hand, they were not there at all. The insubstantial shapes could not be touched. How could she be in the midst of this seeming reality that was no reality?

The red pressure pad on the visitor's guide module controlled sound. She amused herself by listening to "Traffic", "Typical speech", "Children playing".

She scrolled through the index until she found the reproduction of St. Mark's Hospital near St Paul's. "Saint Mark's City Hospital" said the heading. Kari ignored the details of its foundation and service over the centuries and activated the hologram.

Suddenly, she was in front of the familiar entrance. She followed the signs to Casualty. Mute doctors and nurses, dressed almost as she had last seen them, tended in silence to uncomplaining patients. They made the same movements, reached for the instruments as she had so often done. Some of the machines she didn't recognize, but knew she could learn to use them. The people looked familiar, they moved like her, they acted as she would.

She called up the sound. She heard the squeak of stretcher wheels, the ringing of a phone, the ubiquitous sound system, paging a doctor. The researchers and technicians had done a good job. Probably Aidan had contributed to this. But there were none of the familiar hospital smells that she remembered. Monika had said that would come later, and maybe Kari could help them in the re-creation.

She had predicated her life on being a part of the medical profession, not on fulfilling a merely passive role. She switched off the program, not wanting to see more.

Chapter Twenty-Five

೫

True to the prognosis, Aidan was to be released, but under a surveillance that was not only medical. The director had been angry when the details of the secret FLIP had been revealed. Aidan was off the time travel program; Monika and Tanice were to be reassigned. An air of gloom hung over the whole laboratory.

Tanice was the most affected. She would take early retirement, she said, do some traveling in the Outworlds, some teaching. She would have liked to finish her career other than under a cloud, but Howard had been generous, all things considered. Aidan had returned, no one outside the Research Station had caught wind of the near disaster, and Aidan had managed to keep the secret when he was away. Bureaucracy was designed to cover up such slips.

"No harm done," they maintained, with determined cheerfulness. Kari wondered who knew about Reed Flynn going back in time, but she didn't know how to pose the questions.

She waited for Aidan to break the news about the decision on an alien woman in the wrong time, with no skills that could be put to any use at all.

* * * * *

Aidan held Kari in his arms in the bed in the quarters Tanice had found for them. He'd eaten lightly and was resting. Apart from a natural lethargy, his recovery had been nothing short of miraculous.

She ran her hands over him, tracing the outline of his mouth with her fingertips. He shivered and raised his head to kiss her. His hand found her breast and slipped gently inside the soft material of the green suit. He moaned gently.

"I didn't know," he murmured.

Kari kissed him. "Know what, my love?"

"That I could love like this, that making love was so sweet."

"Do you want to?" she whispered. "Are you strong enough?"

"Better than new," he said, "or so those doctors tell me."

"Just to be sure," she said softly against his lips, "Lie back and relax."

She pushed him back against the pillows and gently undid the fastenings on his suit. Slowly and tenderly, she slipped the material from his shoulders and down his arms.

She spent time on his upper body, tracing the line of the muscles, touching the hardened nipples, running her fingers through his hair. She put her hands on his shoulders when he tried to sit up.

"No exertion," she commanded. "You may stroke me if you promise not to sit up."

Carefully, she worked further down and slipped the suit from his legs. He lifted his hips to allow her to remove it. He was naked underneath. She smiled wickedly at him when she saw the evidence of the power of his response to her ministrations. Caressing the velvet shaft with one hand, she continued to stroke his chest. He groaned and moved under her.

"No, not yet," she scolded.

He subsided with a moan.

Quickly, she slipped from the bed and removed her own clothing. Naked, she leaned over him again.

"Now, where was I?" she asked.

Aidan raised a hand to her breast, cupping its fullness. She sucked in her breath as his thumb moved back and forth over her nipple. He looked at her through half-closed eyes, a small smile played around his mouth.

"My personal medical attendant," he murmured. "Take good care of me."

She arched over him, every part of her throbbing in anticipation, and slowly lowered herself onto him. He gasped as her softness closed over him, and his arms tightened around her. Her lips sought his hungrily as she gave herself over to the delight of their union.

* * * * *

They slept in each other's arms and woke to a bright, fresh day.

Kari was busy with the breakfast order when she caught the flicker of a message coming through on the mail screen. Aidan retrieved it and cleared the screen without a word. She supposed he would share it later. He was quiet throughout the morning meal and resisted her attempts at conversation.

"What is it, Aidan?" she said at last, in exasperation. "What's happened? Was it the message?"

He pushed away his cup and looked at her at last. His eyes were haunted, his mouth set in a grim line.

"Tell me," she whispered in sudden fear. "Have they decided?"

Still he did not answer.

"For God's sake, tell me what's going on. I can't stand it when you hold back on me."

He smiled, but there was no humor in it. "If I'd told you everything at the start, we wouldn't have had any time together and I wouldn't have learned to love you."

"That may be so, but things are different now."

She knelt beside him and took his hands.

He drew a shuddering breath. "They're going to beam you back, you and Ben," he told her abruptly. "I'm sorry, my love, there's no choice."

Kari sat back on her heels and brought his hand to her mouth. She kissed the fingers. So it had come at last.

"How long have you known?" she whispered.

"Not long. The final decision was on the screen this morning."

"What about you?"

His jaw tightened. "I stay. I'm to be reassigned to an Outworld."

"No—"

He took her in his arms. "They won't keep me. I promised I would find you," he said. "I will."

He hugged her close. "After all we've lived through, this will be nothing. If we can survive Malcolm and Thomas..."

"Josiah and footpads and Flynn..." she finished, forcing a smile.

He nodded.

"How long—before I go and you can come to me?"

"You go tomorrow. Howard himself will supervise to make sure." She shivered in his arms. "Don't worry, my love, you'll be safe."

"I know," she smiled bravely. "'Standard Procedure'," she quoted. "How long must I wait for you?"

He shook his head. "Can't tell. Tanice and Monika will be reassigned in two months. I have to fix it by then and hope for understanding new technicians. I can't risk Tanice and Monika anymore."

It sounded unlikely. He had told her he would need access to the archives to set up an identity, a way to persuade people to help him. But he was used to living this way—relishing the risk, the creative solution to a seemingly impossible problem. She had to believe him—the alternative was too awful to contemplate. Two months, she thought.

"There's more," he said. His eyes were cast down, his mouth set in a grim line. She put her hands either side of his face and raised it to her.

"Look at me, Aidan," she said softly. "Tell me what it is."

He swallowed. "Howard says they must give you the medication—"

Kari frowned. "What— Why?" Understanding dawned. An icy hand gripped her deep inside. "To make me forget," she whispered. "I wouldn't know you. It would be as if we had never met."

Aidan nodded miserably.

"No," she said, standing up. "No, no, no!" She paced in the small room. "I won't let them. I'll go and see Howard, talk to him!"

"Howard isn't Thomas Godwin," he said bitterly. "What Howard wants, he usually gets."

"Don't worry, my love. I'll go back, since I have no choice, but I'll make bloody sure I remember!"

Later that morning, Kari arranged to meet Monika in her quarters.

* * * * *

Kari and Ben materialized on Hampstead Heath very early in the morning. She remembered everything. So Monika had kept her word and given her some innocuous substance rather than the drug that would knock out her short term memory.

Kari glanced down at well-cut pants and a pretty blouse, all made by the archive service. Incredible. She patted her pocket with the recorded account of the last few weeks. It had been her backup in case Howard had won, but it wouldn't be needed now.

It was a beautiful morning, fresh and clean. The dew lay on the grass, sparking in the first rays of the sun. It promised to be a lovely day.

A man came 'round the clump of bushes. He was leading a low-slung dachshund. The little dog burrowed happily under the lowest branches.

"My goodness," the man said, "where did you spring from? I didn't see you coming."

Some people didn't need to worry about surprise encounters. Kari smiled sunnily.

"I woke early. Decided to walk Ben."

The man looked at the huge dog and then at his small creature. "Needs some activity, I'd say. Too much for my old legs. He must keep you busy. Good watchdog, is he?"

"Oh yes," said Kari, rubbing Ben's ears. "He's wonderful. We've had a few adventures together."

The man nodded. "Enjoy your walk." He strode off toward the path, the dachshund's little legs rotating double time to keep up.

Kari looked around. There was the spot where Ben had bumped into Aidan. Over there was the site of the gate to the Godwin estate. Beyond the rise had stood the buttery and the drying sheds. Martha would be about already, supervising her household. Thomas was expected home—

"Come, Ben," she said. "Heel. Let's go home."

From the corner of the street, she saw her brother Mike at the door of her flat and quickened her pace. What did he want? Had something happened to Mother or Dad? She ran the last stretch, Ben loping beside her.

Mike took his thumb from the doorbell as she jogged up to him. His face was set in a scowl.

"Where the hell have you been for the last four days?" he barked. "You scared the hell out of us."

Kari thought furiously. Last four days. Maybe Monika hadn't been as accurate after all.

"I took a few days off—"

"Without a message to anyone? Kari, this is beyond a joke. You take off to parts unknown, worry the parents to death—"

She bit her lip. "I'm sorry Mike. I was—stressed. Just had to get away. The last thing I wanted was to worry you all."

"It's not like you, Kari, to be irresponsible. The police—"

"Police?" she gasped.

"It was a mystery where you'd gone. No trace of you. Dirty dishes in the sink. All your stuff still there in the flat."

She put a hand on his arm. She could feel the tension in his muscles. "I'm sorry," she repeated. "I won't do it again. It was thoughtless of me." She felt him begin to relax.

"Call Mother and Dad in Rome. Tell them you're okay."

She nodded. "Straight away."

"Where were you?" he persisted.

"Just away. I stayed with a—friend. It's rather isolated—I must have got my dates confused."

He looked at her suspiciously. She could see the thoughts scurry through his mind. Secret lover? Memory loss? It was easier to let it go. He sighed.

"You're back, that's the main thing. Now, I'll take the dog. Been here every damned morning to pick him up. Rang every hour."

Mike didn't like surprises. His life was planned to the minute. Even as a kid, he'd needed to know what his birthday presents would be. The last four days must have been hell for him. And her parents must be distraught. She had never thought of them contacting the police.

"It's pretty early still," she said soothingly. "Golf game today?"

He grunted and looked at his watch, relaxing a little. "First booking. I'm playing with a customer. I won't come in. Just give me the dog. Has he been fed?"

She nodded. "Last night." She guessed that was true. "You'll have to get some cans..." She fished in her pocket. Of course there was no money. Her fingers closed around the key to the flat. Another blessing on Monika.

Mike was in too much of a hurry. "Don't worry. Just make sure you let me know when you get back." Of course, she was supposed to be taking a vacation. Mike looked at her more closely.

"You're looking well," he said. "Looks as if you've had some sun wherever you were."

Her brother didn't wait for an answer. He opened the back door of the car to usher Ben inside. Kari dropped to her knees on the dusty pavement and put her arms around the dog. Ben nuzzled her face. He was her link to Aidan. She didn't want to part with him yet. She looked up at Mike.

"I've changed my mind," she said. "Maybe I won't go away after all. The last few days were enough."

Mike rolled his eyes expressively. "For heaven's sake—"

"I'm sorry." She scrambled to her feet and put her hand on his arm. "I'll keep Ben until my assignment and—"

Mike was already walking around the car to the driver's side. "I can't cope with this, Kari. Do what you want. Get some rest. You're sounding a few bricks short for the chimney, if you ask me. Just let me know what you decide in good time. And clean off the knees of your pants," he said. "For once you're wearing something halfway decent."

"Hope you're not late for your game," Kari called out, but the words were lost in the roar of Mike's exhaust.

"Bye, Mike," she said and took out her door key. She had to wash those dishes. She would unpack a few things from the suitcase, go to the bank. Call Rome. Then she would wait. She would gather her strength to fight the black despair that waited like a prowler, ready to slip in when the defenses were down.

Chapter Twenty-Six

໑

In November, Aidan registered for the shuttle to Luna 3, where he had at last located Reed Flynn, official engineer and unofficial collector of artworks, legal or not. Reed was on call in the old sector of satellites, which required frequent service, and he moved around a lot. Of course, the videophone didn't satisfy this fussy customer. Nothing would do but that he examined certified holograms himself before buying, so here Aidan was, waiting for Space Available.

Aidan had assured Kari the paintings would be their salvation. He could sell them to Flynn, raise what he needed to buy his way out. She'd been apprehensive about dealing with Flynn but he'd assured her there was no danger. Reed would not make trouble if he could get his hands on the paintings more or less legitimately. He hoped he was right.

Bribery was still rampant—any well-structured organization tempts the renegades to beat the system. The problem was the time it was taking.

Tanice had reported that Kari's FLIP had gone well. He still got a knot in his stomach if he dwelt too long on what could have gone wrong with Monika tinkering with the settings. He had to believe Kari and Ben were safe wherever they were.

Since she left, he'd been busy. Monika had helped him fix the archives, and Tanice thought she knew someone who would be ready to assist in his last illicit FLIP. Still, it had all taken longer than he'd calculated. He thought again of what the archive search on Kari had revealed. The mere thought of the possibilities gave him the shivers.

The paintings he'd had to take care of himself. It hadn't been easy, but he'd done it. He'd gone over everything in his mind a hundred times.

He closed his eyes and thought of Kari, of her hair and eyes. He remembered the way her skin slid silky smooth under his hands. He pictured the lift of her head as she prepared to argue and do battle. His lips curved in an involuntary smile as he recalled the way she'd stood up to Thomas Godwin, the way she'd insisted on staying for Anne's baby. He relived the tender moments in the unlikely setting of the London brothel, their delight in each other for the brief few hours that had remained when he was recovering and out of danger.

He saw her again on the transportation platform as she waited with Ben behind the screen. She'd kept her eyes fixed on him as he'd gazed helplessly at the technician's preparations. That look had gone through his heart like a sword.

Howard had been there, there had been no chance to circumvent the decision to send her back. She sat, small and still amid the flickering lights and gleaming banks of machinery, Ben tense and watchful at her side. Monika had outfitted her in green slacks and a white blouse. Her hair had been smoothed and brushed, and it lay gleaming on her shoulders in a copper cascade. Her eyes were huge in her pale face. She was tense, afraid. He'd longed to go to her and comfort her, but Tanice had been mercifully quick. One rapid check of the settings, a few words of verification, then Kari gave a last brave smile, a wave of her hand and they were gone. He prayed that her memory of him had survived.

Since then he had brought all his skills to bear on preparing to go back to find her. Reed Flynn would buy the paintings, that would give him enough credits to kit himself, create the ID he needed. There was a week left before Tanice went into retirement. If this shuttle ever arrived, he should just make it. He lay back and dozed.

Tanice intercepted the report when it was flashed around the Earth, including all satellites and space stations. She woke him in his personal cubicle at the Travelers Hostel at the Interspace Terminal to show it to him. He focused blearily on Tanice's face on the inferior quality screen wedged in the corner by the single chair.

"Aidan," she said urgently. "What are you doing now?"

"Trying to sleep."

"Wake up and pay attention. There's an alert out for you. You have to come back."

Tanice vanished and a printed text scrolled across the screen.

"October 30, 2400," he read, "ALL POINT ALERT—for all Earth-based and interstellar units."

A blurred picture of his own face stared back at him. The camera had caught him indoors somewhere, obviously unaware that he was being photographed. He looked older and shifty-eyed as he gazed vacantly into the middle distance. Aidan wondered why they hadn't used one of the clear, official Space Academy shots. They could have enhanced the image to add a few years with no problem. He brought himself back to the notice.

"Wanted for questioning for illegal activities," said the bulletin. Well, that was vague enough. "Apprehend immediately and notify—" He switched off before the ID numbers appeared.

Someone must have leaked the information about his unauthorized trips, damn them. It could be Flynn, hoping to acquire the paintings without laying out a single credit. If so, someone should put the bastard in a space capsule and shoot it off into hyperspace—

The interphone beeped again. It was Tanice.

"Come back, goodfriend," she said. "We've made arrangements. This isn't a secure link, so don't talk. Get on the next shuttle back. Hopefully, they won't be watching for returning ships. I mean it, Aidan. Move now."

The urgency in her voice convinced him. Hastily, he packed his few belongings into the SpacePack. Tanice could only mean she was going to help him FLIP after all. His mouth went dry at the thought of seeing Kari again.

* * * * *

December 2000

The hospital tent stood in a gully between bare hills. The small valley was apparently a riverbed, but no water had run for months—years, probably. The unit would be long gone before there was danger of flooding.

Everything was monochrome—dirty brown, dirty gray or dirty green. The hills stood stark and barren, a few thorn bushes poking from between dun colored rocks. The tops were scoured bare from the desert wind. The olive drab of the tents hardly needed camouflage, marked as they were by the flying sand and the dust.

One of the nurses had sawn off a thorn bush and stuck it in a pail that bore the painted letters UN SUPPLIES. The stem canted at an angle in the sand. A few strands of tinsel draped the spiny branches, and someone had cut a star from cardboard and covered it with silver foil.

There was a party planned for tonight. Christmas Eve with everyone far from home, all determined to be cheerful and hide how homesick they were. *In some ways, an alert for new patients would be a relief*, Kari thought. They could stop the pretense, do what they did best and what they had come here to do.

The last notes were up-to-date and Kari shuffled the papers together, ready to be filed. Although the sun had gone down two hours ago, the heat in the tent hung in the air like a shroud. The temperature would have begun to drop outside and the night air would be cold, chilling the sweat on your body like stepping from a sauna into a cold room.

The sound of a helicopter broke the silence and Kari tensed, listening. No loudspeaker squawking, no banging of doors or pounding of feet. No shouts for medical aid. Probably another journalist hoping for a Pulitzer. She had been here three months, and it felt like forever.

The door of the tent swung open. Gareth Thomas poked in his head. He was as Welsh as his name, small and black-haired and irrepressible. He had a wonderful voice, and he and Kari were supposed to lead the singing tonight.

"Hallo, Kari *fach*," he greeted her. "Still here?"

"As you see, Gareth *bach*."

The Gaelic endearments were part of the verbal sparring that Gareth loved.

"I know, bloody silly question," he said in his singsong. "But it's time to pack it in, love."

"I've nearly finished. Who was that came in?"

Gary shrugged. "Haven't a clue, love. Nobody who needs patching up or we'd have heard about it by now. Come on, they're waiting for us."

"Just give me a few minutes, Gary, okay? Just to collect myself."

"You will come?" He looked at her intently. "You won't skive off like last time?"

She smiled at him. "No, I'll be there."

"You okay, love? Not sickening or anything?"

Damn his observant doctor's eyes. "No, no. I'm fine. Just tired."

She started to close up the files to show she meant it.

Her notes on herbal remedies would lie untouched for yet another day. No matter, she would get to them tomorrow. She picked up the file with the rest.

Gary seemed satisfied. "Ten minutes then, or I'll come back to get you. They're all waiting to hear how we're dreaming of a white Christmas."

When the door slammed behind him, Kari sighed and leaned her head on her hands. She took off her glasses and rubbed her weary eyes. No way she could tolerate contacts in this dusty atmosphere, but the spectacles were a damned nuisance, slipping down her nose as the sweat formed on her face. No matter, she was doing what she had wanted to do. She was making a difference. There was already progress with the mothers and babies in the camp over the hill.

She thought of Anne's baby. Was he thriving? Had Anne remembered to follow her instructions, keeping him clean and letting him move his limbs unrestricted by the traditional enveloping baby clothes? Would he be able to resist the measles and the mumps? What about diphtheria? No tetanus shots if he fell and hurt himself in the manure-covered yard. It was a wonder any babies had survived, but of course they had. Just as the babies in this place were fighting for life against all odds. Her mind was dwelling on babies a lot these days.

She stretched her back against the low ache. She would have to let someone know soon. In a few more weeks, they would guess. She would have to leave in two or three months.

Her thoughts never strayed for long from Aidan. Where was he? Had he tried a FLIP? Had they prevented him? Was he stranded out in—what did he call it? Hyperspace? Was he in another time? Had they exiled him to the Outworlds so he had no access to the time travel lab? Had Reed Flynn won? Was he alive? Her thoughts went 'round and 'round like a squirrel in a cage. If only she knew what had happened.

She reached for the thermos carafe on the desk, poured a glass of water and sipped the lukewarm liquid. It tasted of bleach and the ubiquitous sand. At least at the party there would be some canned drinks. The party! Gareth would be true to his word and come back for her if she didn't turn up soon. Gareth was paying altogether too much attention to her these days. She might have to do something about that.

She slipped out of her white coat and turned to hang it on the rack behind her. A small mirror was tacked to the tent pole and she stretched to her full height to see what she needed to do to her hair. She hummed the old nursery rhyme that buzzed constantly through her head. "London Bridge is falling down…" she sang. Footsteps sounded outside and the door creaked open again.

"I'm coming, Gary," she said impatiently. "Give me a…"

"…my fair lady." A voice deeper than Gareth's pleasant tenor completed her song.

Her voice trailed off as the newcomer appeared in the mirror behind her. Her lips formed his name, but no sound came. She closed her eyes. He was still there when she opened them, smooth dark hair and silver-gray eyes, the features she had committed to memory and treasured in her heart. She dared not move in case he disappeared.

Outside, the desert was quiet. Even the wind had subsided. In the distance she could hear the noise of the party, laughter and shouting. In the breaks of the sound, Bing Crosby started to tell everyone that he was dreaming of a white Christmas. They must have tired of waiting for her.

"Good day, mistress," Aidan said softy. "How goes it with you?"

She turned with a cry and flung herself into his arms, covering his face with kisses, weeping and laughing together. He held her close, his strong arms firmly around her, returning her kisses, murmuring words of love.

* * * * *

Gareth came back for her, but there was no response to his knock. When he opened the door, he saw Dr. Lunne in the arms of the new correspondent who had come in on the chopper. Looked as if they knew each other pretty well. He shrugged philosophically. Looked as if he might be singing solo tonight. They didn't notice when he closed the door.

* * * * *

When they paused for breath, the questions began. Kari led Aidan to the couch in the waiting area and sat down beside him. She couldn't keep her hands from him, touching him and stroking as if she had to convince herself he was real.

He told her how they had set up his cover.

"Although there wasn't much to set up," he said. "Did Tanice ever tell you about my trip to my future?"

Kari frowned, remembering. "Yes," she said, "but I didn't pay much attention—"

"I wasn't there. Scared the hell out of me at the time. We found me in the past."

"How can that be?"

"Aidan Torrance was a journalist—a political correspondent—even looked like me."

"How do you know?"

"TV archives. There are some good shots of him reporting from a medical station in the desert. There's even an interview with a red-haired woman doctor. Looks as if they knew each other pretty well."

"I can't believe it."

The story had come full circle. Her time and Aidan's had meshed. As if it was all preordained in some mysterious way!

Aidan was still talking, telling her how Tanice had warned him in the nick of time, allowing him to escape. Kari breathed yet another prayer of thanks to Tanice, somewhere in the future.

"I did a lot more delving into the archives," he said. "Thought you'd like to know about the Godwins."

"What happened to them?"

"Strangely enough, the records were quite good for the family. Aidan Jonathan Thomas Howard grew to be a wool merchant like his father, married and had three children. His sister, Karina Martha Anne Howard was two years younger and not quite as fruitful—just one child, from her marriage. But one of Aidan Howard's daughters married a Richard Lunne and settled in Ireland."

"Lunne? You mean—?"

Aidan nodded. "The baby was your ancestor, many generations back."

Kari swallowed hard. "What about Martha and Thomas?"

"Seems that Thomas gave up his courtly ambitions and settled down with his wife. He apparently had been doing good works in secret—it came to light he'd been very generous to the poor and afflicted and so had to live by his reputation. There was one particular family that received a purse of gold and blessed his name far and wide." Aidan grinned broadly.

Kari burst out laughing. "Whatever it takes," she said. "Poor Thomas, forced into a life of virtue."

Aidan grew serious again. "I checked further into the future," he said. "As far as May 2001 in fact."

He stroked her face gently and fingered her hair. He folded her into his arms and rested his cheek on her head. "I know about our son."

She closed her eyes as his fingers stroked her back. She tilted her face so he could find her mouth and he kissed her. Softly and tenderly. Her head spun when he released her and she came up for air.

His gaze swept over her face until his eyes lowered to her middle.

"I have no words, Kari," he said breathlessly, one hand touching her through her thin blouse.

"I love you, Aidan Torrance."

"I know it. I plan to spend the rest of my life loving you in return. And looking after you if you'll let me. I promise you there'll never be a day when you wonder if I love you. I'll prove it to you every way I can."

Kari felt the joy bubbling from her heart. "The perfect ending to a long journey. "

The End

Enjoy An Excerpt From:

WALKING ON THE MOON

© Copyright SUSAN SIZEMORE, 2005.

Walking On the Moon

"You mean it's alcoholic?" Morrison asked in shock, and slid under the checkered tablecloth. "Ouzo is liquor?"

They'd been passing the ouzo bottles to slake their thirst for nearly an hour. Hand-loading a cargo hauler was mighty thirsty work.

"Tastes like licorice-flavored tar," Cleary contributed, voice slurred. He held up his half-full bottle. "I like it."

"I've never had real alcohol before," Fox said. "You know, this planet looks funny." He squinted, peering into the distance. The flat-roofed houses, the big pots of red flowers bordering the perimeter of the outdoor cafe where they sat, the boats in the harbor below all wavered hazily in and out of focus.

"Are we drunk?" Toffler questioned.

"Not like a happy pill," Harcort contributed.

Sakretis smiled benignly. "No, it isn't. These ancestors of mine have a good thing here." He poked a fragrant mound on his plate. "This grape leaf stuff is good too. But it's not chili," he added wistfully. "I could really go for a bowl of chili."

"Me too," several voices chimed in.

It took him a couple of tries, but Morrison managed to pull himself out from under the table. "Where's Duchamp? My legs are all funny."

"Took a walk by the water," Fox said. "New Sydney's a water world. He's homesick. I like the desert. Heat." He licked his lips. "Chili."

"I've got an idea," Cleary declared, climbing unsteadily to his feet. "Let's go grocery shopping while everybody's still asleep. Sleepray's a wonderful thing," he added. "While everyone's asleep we can raid the commissary we saw up the street. Take back some real food."

"Duchamp won't like that," Harcort said.

"Don't have to tell him," Fox contributed.

"We got an empty storage chest on the shuttle," Morrison added encouragingly.

"Let's do it," Sakretis assented.

"Yeah," Toffler chimed in, then gulped down the rest of the bottle of ouzo.

They wobbled to their feet and trooped drunkenly a few doors up the street. All was quiet and dark inside the little store. They found baskets and began filling them with anything on the shelves that looked like it might be food. Not that the crew's vision or judgment was any too clear by this time.

They laughed and joked and made two trips to the shuttle, and were back for a third when the door opened behind them. Cans and bags crashed noisily to the floor as three of the drunken crewmen went for their sleeprays while the others began to speak all at once.

"Duchamp!"

"We'll put it back!"

"We'll leave cash for the supplies!"

"That's not Duchamp!" Fox declared.

Long seconds went by as they came to realize there was a startled woman standing in the shaft of sunlight by the open door.

She was a vision.

The answer to a hungry, drunken man's dreams.

Six desperate men suddenly believed there was indeed justice in the universe.

"It's her!"

"Claudia!"

"Chili!"

"Get her!" Cleary shouted.

Three sleeprays fired as one.

"Where have you been?" Denys demanded as he climbed into the shuttle from the storage bay's rear entrance.

He'd looked all over the small village for his shift crew before giving up and heading back to use the ship's recall signal. The last place he'd expected to find the crewmen was where they were supposed to be.

Three of them sat down hastily on a storage chest as he entered.

The other three started guiltily as he came toward them. Cleary gave him an innocent grin. The one he always gave when he was up to something.

Fox began tunelessly whistling. They all smelled of alcohol. *Hmmm.* Denys rubbed his chin as he tried to decide whether or not to find out what they'd just stowed in the chest. *It's food*, he decided. It's what he would have pilfered if his shift officer had left him on his own long enough.

Should he confiscate it? Did they have time? There was a wide-awake woman running around Doros. She'd probably noticed a few sleeping citizens by now. Why hadn't he thought to put her under? It wouldn't have hurt her. He felt a pang of guilt for something he hadn't even done to Claudia Cameron. It would have just put her to sleep — but it would have seemed too much like hurting her, or cheating her. *Never mind Claudia Cameron. Think of duty. It's better to just get out of here,* he decided. Away from Claudia. He'd already had too many thoughts about the woman from the cooking show, even before he met her. Having met her, all he could do was flee the scene before he had an urge to grab her and bring her back to the ship to warm his nights with something more than her spicy cooking.

To keep from thinking about that improper fantasy, he looked sternly at his men. "You better have paid for whatever you took," he told the crew.

Several of them turned various shades of red. There were several nods. Fox's eyes closed and he quietly passed out. The men had either not done the required research about twenty-first century Earth, or they had and had decided to try out some of the available stimulants. Duchamp sighed. Good thing he was the designated driver.

"Let's get these supplies to the HATTON. Strap in."

"Yes, sir!" five voices declared enthusiastically. Fox began gently snoring as Harcort and Sakretis carried him into the passenger compartment. Denys followed after them, thinking how glad he'd be to get this mission over and get back home to the twenty-third century.

Why an electronic book?

We live in the Information Age—an exciting time in the history of human civilization, in which technology rules supreme and continues to progress in leaps and bounds every minute of every day. For a multitude of reasons, more and more avid literary fans are opting to purchase e-books instead of paper books. The question from those not yet initiated into the world of electronic reading is simply: *Why?*

1. *Price.* An electronic title at Ellora's Cave Publishing and Cerridwen Press runs anywhere from 40% to 75% less than the cover price of the exact same title in paperback format. Why? Basic mathematics and cost. It is less expensive to publish an e-book (no paper and printing, no warehousing and shipping) than it is to publish a paperback, so the savings are passed along to the consumer.

2. *Space.* Running out of room in your house for your books? That is one worry you will never have with electronic books. For a low one-time cost, you can purchase a handheld device specifically designed for e-reading. Many e-readers have large, convenient screens for viewing. Better yet, hundreds of titles can be stored within your new library—on a single microchip. There are a variety of e-readers from different manufacturers. You can also read e-books on your PC or laptop computer. (Please note that Ellora's

3. Cave does not endorse any specific brands. You can check our websites at www.ellorascave.com or www.cerridwenpress.com for information we make available to new consumers.)

4. *Mobility.* Because your new e-library consists of only a microchip within a small, easily transportable e-reader, your entire cache of books can be taken with you wherever you go.

5. *Personal Viewing Preferences.* Are the words you are currently reading too small? Too large? Too... ANNOYING? Paperback books cannot be modified according to personal preferences, but e-books can.

6. *Instant Gratification.* Is it the middle of the night and all the bookstores near you are closed? Are you tired of waiting days, sometimes weeks, for bookstores to ship the novels you bought? Ellora's Cave Publishing sells instantaneous downloads twenty-four hours a day, seven days a week, every day of the year. Our webstore is never closed. Our e-book delivery system is 100% automated, meaning your order is filled as soon as you pay for it.

Those are a few of the top reasons why electronic books are replacing paperbacks for many avid readers.

As always, Ellora's Cave and Cerridwen Press welcome your questions and comments. We invite you to email us at Comments@ellorascave.com or write to us directly at Ellora's Cave Publishing Inc., 1056 Home Avenue, Akron, OH 44310-3502.

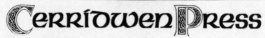